TRUE BLUE
CHRISTMAS

Center Point
Large Print

Also by Susan Page Davis and available from Center Point Large Print:

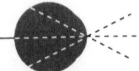

**This Large Print Book carries the
Seal of Approval of N.A.V.H.**

TRUE BLUE MYSTERIES
BOOK FIVE

TRUE BLUE CHRISTMAS

SUSAN PAGE DAVIS

CENTER POINT LARGE PRINT
THORNDIKE, MAINE

Chapter 1

Campbell McBride gulped the rest of her coffee, grabbed her purse, and double-checked to make sure her summons was inside.

" 'Bye, Dad."

"See you later," Bill said. "Have fun."

She laughed and dropped a kiss on his forehead before striding to the garage.

As she backed out, she noticed a car parked on the driveway at the house next door. Nell Calhoun, the real estate agent who'd listed the vacant home, was doing something to the sign out front. Campbell slowed as she drove by and rolled down her passenger window.

"Nell!"

The woman looked up and then straightened. "Hi, Campbell." She walked toward the car smiling.

"You sold the house?" Campbell stared at the SOLD banner now blazing across the FOR SALE sign.

"I sure did. It took a while, but yeah. You'll have new neighbors. We closed yesterday, and they said they plan to move in over Christmas break."

"Wow, terrific." Campbell understood the headaches Nell had dealt with, trying to sell a house where a murder had occurred. "Congrats! I've got to run."

"See you around," Nell called as Campbell pushed the button to raise the window. She wished she'd had more time so she could have asked about the buyers. Maybe there'd be some kids next door. But she couldn't be late for jury duty.

This wasn't exactly what she'd planned on for the first week of December. For some reason, she'd had the idea that the courts wouldn't do much this month. Her father had assured her they'd take Christmas week off, and probably the week after that.

Meanwhile, she had a solid three weeks when she might have to sit in court every day. And then she'd pick it up in January, after the holiday break, possibly for the entire month.

Could have been worse, I guess. Jury duty in summer would be dreadful.

As she drove through town, she noted the Christmas decorations on light poles and in store windows. Several downtown businesses displayed seasonal sale announcements. Campbell smiled to herself. One of these days she had to get her Christmas shopping done—but not today.

Parking was always tricky at the judicial building on Fourth Street. With a hundred or so potential jurors reporting this morning, it was worse than usual. After surveying the clogged parking lot, Campbell pulled in across the street at a funeral home. The owners had given permission for jurors to park in their lot if there was no hearse out front, signifying a funeral that day.

She waited half a minute for a break in traffic and dashed across the street. As she entered the imposing building, she looked at the people standing in line. On Friday, when she'd first reported for orientation, she'd spotted two people she knew—a librarian and a server from the Barn Owl diner. If she played things right, maybe she'd get to sit beside one of them and while away some of the inevitable waiting periods chatting.

"Good morning," said the woman sitting behind the conveyor belt that led to the X-ray machine.

Campbell smiled at her and laid her purse and jacket on the belt. She walked through the metal detector and paused on the mat to give a deputy time to wave his wand up and down over her body, front and back.

"You're good," he said.

"Thanks." She gathered her things and went on to the stairway. Stepping out into the hallway on the second floor, she heard her name and swiveled.

"Campbell! Hey. I thought I saw you in here Friday."

"Yeah, same here. Good to see you."

Hallee Rickman, one of the librarians at the city's public library, beckoned to her, and Campbell walked over.

"Go check in. I'll save you a place," Hallee said.

At least fifty people were lined up against the wall, around the large room. Before the windows on the far side, the city clerk and an assistant were checking off potential jurors. The doors to the courtroom where they would spend their morning were closed.

"Thanks." Campbell got in line and shuffled with the others until she reached the desk and handed over her summons. The assistant read off her number, and the clerk marked her name on a list. When the assistant handed back her paperwork, Campbell turned to find Hallee again.

"Think we'll be picked today?" her friend asked as she slid into line with her.

"I don't know. If they're only selecting a jury for one trial, they've got way more than enough people here."

"Yeah, I figure we have a pretty good chance of not being called," Hallee said.

Campbell had mixed feelings about that. She'd agreed with her father, private investigator Bill McBride, that this would be good experience for her. She'd have to testify in a couple of court cases sometime in the coming year, and this stint might help allay her nervousness.

On the other hand, she was newly certified as a P.I., and she loved working with her dad. She hoped she wouldn't miss too many days of work.

They entered the large courtroom and found seats on the benches at the back.

"How are things going at the library?" Campbell whispered.

"Great. We've got more people coming in than ever since the renovations were finished." Hallee's satisfied smile told Campbell that all of the library employees were tickled the newly expanded building was back in service, bigger and better than ever.

"I love the new computer room and—"

"All rise," the bailiff intoned.

Everyone jumped up as the judge entered through a doorway behind the bench.

After some instruction on the *voir dire* process of selection, the prospective jurors listened carefully as the clerk called out numbers and names. When the juror numbers skipped from nineteen to thirty-four, Hallee exhaled and grinned.

"I'm number twenty. Looks like today's not my day."

Campbell clenched her teeth as the numbers went higher.

"Number 126, Campbell McBride."

She froze for a moment then looked at Hallee and shrugged. "That's me." She got up and made her way to the end of the row then to the front,

9

where those being called were seated before the judge.

Her cell phone was set on silent. As other names were intoned, she took it out and quickly texted to her father, "I'm picked for *voir dire*." Her dad would understand that she might still be excused—or she might be here all day. He and his other employee, Nick Emerson, would plan their day as if she wouldn't be there to help them with the workload.

Soon thirty-two potential jurors had been chosen, and the prosecuting attorney, Mitchell Vaughn, stepped forward to ask them questions. Did any of them know the judge, the prosecutor, the defense attorney, or the defendant personally? A couple of people raised their hands, and the lawyer asked them how they knew the principals. After hearing them out, one was asked to approach the bench, and a few minutes later was dismissed.

Another person was chosen from the pool at the back of the courtroom to fill out their ranks, and the questions continued. Campbell had no inkling that she might be considered a problem until the prosecutor asked if any of them were private investigators.

Her heart pounding, Campbell raised her hand.

"Please approach."

As she made her way to the end of the row and walked forward, Campbell's mind raced. Would they send her home immediately? Someone turned on a "white noise" recording so that no one who wasn't within a few feet of them could hear what they said.

"You're a private investigator?" the judge asked.

"Yes, Your Honor." Campbell's throat was dry, and her voice sounded a little croaky.

The judge looked at the prosecutor.

"Are you licensed in the commonwealth of Kentucky?" Vaughn asked.

"Yes."

"Do you have your license with you?"

She fumbled with the clasp of her purse and drew out her wallet. Two months ago, she'd been so proud to receive the laminated card in the mail from Frankfort. Now it could keep her off the jury.

Did she really want to be on a jury? She'd gone round and round about the pros and cons. It would be an inconvenience, yet it would help her do her job better. Now that the privilege was perhaps about to be snatched away from her, she realized that she wanted badly to be chosen.

She held out the card. The prosecutor took it, scrutinized it, and handed it to the judge, who looked at it and then passed it to the defense attorney, Robert Soule.

"Are you related to Bill McBride?" he asked.

Campbell turned to face the bearded man. It

11

figured that he knew her father. Bill knew every lawyer in town.

"I'm his daughter."

"I don't know McBride well, but I know who he is." The lawyer leaned in and spoke in low tones with the judge and the prosecutor. After a moment, the judge met her gaze.

"Do you know anything about the Abbott case?"

Campbell shook her head.

"One thing about P.I.s, sometimes they think they can solve the case better than the police can."

"Oh, I would never think that, Your Honor," Campbell said.

"You work for your father?"

"Yes."

"What sort of work do you do for him?" Soule asked.

Campbell shrugged. "A lot of background checks, skip traces, that sort of thing mostly."

"Have you ever testified in court?" Vaughn asked.

She hesitated. "Not yet, but I'm told I will in a few months."

"What case?"

"The—the Chase case."

Vaughn's eyebrows shot up. "You'll be a witness?"

"Yes." Her voice shook as she recalled the terrifying evening she'd spent with the defendant in that case.

"How were you involved?" the judge asked.

Briefly, Campbell explained what had happened six months earlier. Now she was certain they would dismiss her.

The prosecutor gazed at her keenly. "Do you think that experience will impact your ability to be impartial in this case?"

"I don't."

The two lawyers huddled with the judge for a moment, and then the prosecutor said, "We'll allow it for now, unless you wish to be excused."

"I—I'd like to serve," Campbell said.

Vaughn looked at Soule, who nodded.

"All right," said the judge. "Please be seated."

Campbell could hardly believe it. As she returned to her place, she wondered why they hadn't questioned her individually when they asked if the prospective jurors knew any local police officers. She knew several, in fact, but she hadn't elaborated on her relationship with Detective Keith Fuller. If they learned she was dating a local officer, they'd boot her off in the blink of an eye.

Should she tell them now? She didn't want them to think she was hiding it, but they hadn't seemed to be concerned when she'd said she'd met several officers through her job. Now she felt guilty. But at the time, she had figured it didn't matter. Keith wasn't involved in this case. Or was he?

One officer was in the courtroom, sitting at the prosecutor's table. Vaughn had introduced him earlier as the arresting officer in the Abbott case, and Campbell had assumed Keith had nothing to do with it. Maybe she ought to ask him.

To her surprise, a few minutes later the clerk read off the names of the twelve jurors and two alternates for the trial. Her pulse galloped as names were called out.

"And number 126, Campbell McBride."

She exhaled slowly. They'd chosen her. Why? Maybe one of the lawyers liked the fact that she was involved in investigation.

All of the people at the back of the courtroom were dismissed. When that part of the room had emptied, the clerk announced, "We will now take a one-hour break for lunch. Be back in this room by 12:15 p.m."

Campbell grabbed her purse and jacket and stood. She surveyed the back of the big room, but Hallee was long gone, and she'd never gotten close enough to the diner's server to speak to her. She wondered if she should dash home for lunch but decided to grab a sandwich at a coffee shop a couple of blocks away instead. When she had her lunch in front of her, she called Keith.

"They picked you?" His voice rose in amazement.

"Yes. They asked a lot of questions about my P.I. work, but they didn't go into details about the police officers I told them I knew. I think they got sidetracked on that one by a woman whose son is an officer."

"Wow. I honestly didn't think they'd put you on a jury."

"You didn't tell me that," Campbell said.

"I know. I didn't want to influence your feelings about it."

"Oh." She thought for a moment and decided he'd done the right thing. "Listen, I can't talk to you about the case, but, uh, if you were involved in it, maybe I should let them know. They did pick two alternates."

"As far as I know, I'm not involved in any cases coming to trial this month."

"Okay."

"But you're right. We shouldn't talk about it."

Something inside Campbell wanted to rebel. Was she going to have to censor everything she said to Keith for the next couple of months? And her dad and Nick too?

"Do they think it will be a long trial?" he asked.

"They haven't said, but judging by the questions they asked, I suppose it could be. I mean, I don't think it's a simple drug possession or something like that, but we haven't been told the charges yet. We go back in after lunch, and I think that's when things will get under way."

"Listen carefully to the opening statements," he said.

"I will. But I wish we could discuss it later."
She sighed. "Maybe we shouldn't see each other
while this trial's in session."

"Too tempting?"

"Maybe." Campbell wasn't one to chatter aimlessly or gossip, but she didn't like being isolated
either.

"I'll call you tonight. You'll know more then."

"Thank you." It was the best they could do
at the moment. She signed off and checked the
time. After forcing down half her sandwich, she
called home.

"Hi, Dad. Looks like I'm on this one. I probably
won't be home until suppertime."

"Okay, Soup. Focus on that, and we'll handle
things here. See you later."

"Love you, Dad."

"Back atcha."

She closed the connection and finished her
scanty meal. Her stomach was a little unsettled,
and she wished she hadn't ordered coffee. She
tossed the remaining half a cup and went to the
counter for a bottle of water.

Fifteen minutes later, she was back in her seat
with the other eleven jurors and two alternates.

The charges were read against Leila Abbott,
the defendant. Her main offense seemed to be
possession of stolen property.

When the prosecutor began his opening statement, Campbell was hooked.

Vaughn, a man of at least fifty with a mustache and nearly silver hair, stood before them in his charcoal gray suit and red power tie.

". . . and we will prove that Ms. Abbott knowingly possessed and tried to sell stolen property, to wit, a valuable painting that she found in the home of her late grandmother."

Campbell studied the defendant curiously. The young woman looked to be in her early twenties. Her face was blotchy, as though she'd done a lot of crying recently. She wore a green-and-white print top with smocking on the yoke—a department store find, Campbell decided—and wire-framed glasses. Her shoulder-length blonde hair was rumpled, and her coral lipstick had been chewed off her bottom lip.

Poor girl. Campbell checked herself. She mustn't form an opinion yet, based solely on appearances. But selling stolen property? Could this young woman possibly be guilty? She settled back to listen as the defense attorney stepped forward. This trial might turn out to be more interesting than she'd anticipated.

Chapter 2

The first witness in Leila Abbott's trial was the police officer who arrested her, Detective John Smalley. Campbell frowned when he was introduced. Murray had only a handful of detectives, and she knew two of them. She had also met the detective sergeant, but only at a press conference she'd attended at the police station. She'd never heard of Smalley.

Her unspoken questions were answered when the prosecutor explained to the jury that Smalley had moved in July to the Lexington Police Department but had returned to Murray for the trial.

"Our unit was called in by an antique dealer in town, Michael Harder," the detective said in answer to a question from Vaughn. "He said a young woman had brought in a painting, wanting to sell it. He examined it and realized it was genuine and old. After looking up prices on works by the artist, he offered her five thousand dollars for it."

Vaughn frowned and turned so both the jury and the defendant could see his face. "And if he bought the painting, why did he call the police about it?"

"He didn't buy it. She refused his offer and left with the picture."

"I see. So after she turned down his offer, he called the police?"

"Not immediately," Smalley said. "He said he thought it over for a while and realized later the painting must be stolen."

The defense attorney called out, "Hearsay."

"Sustained," said the judge.

Vaughn was ready to move on. Campbell figured he'd call the dealer to the stand later to tell his own story.

"How much time went by before Mr. Harder called the police?" Vaughn asked.

"About three days," Smalley said. "Apparently he was bothered by the customer's demeanor and did some online research—"

"Hearsay!"

"Sustained."

Vaughn quickly came out with a different question. "Detective, in the course of your investigation, were you able to determine that the painting was authentic?"

"Yes. Once we had possession of it, we took it to an expert in Louisville, and he confirmed it."

Vaughn turned to the judge. "Your Honor, the expert's letter of authentication is Commonwealth's exhibit number three."

The judge nodded.

"What else did you learn about the painting?" Vaughn asked the detective.

"That it was stolen about twenty years ago, from a resident of Calloway County."

"And where did you find the painting?"

"In the defendant's house, here in Murray."

Campbell frowned. The defendant wasn't old enough to have stolen the painting twenty years ago. But then, Leila Abbott wasn't charged with stealing it, only possessing it and attempting to sell it. Why hadn't she accepted the offer of five thousand dollars? She must have known somehow that the artwork was worth more than that. Very interesting.

Bill McBride dropped by the police station after lunch. He glanced through the log that was open to news reporters and other interested citizens like him. It never hurt to see what was recorded there, although Bill usually heard about any arrests or other important happenings through his friends on the force.

When he was satisfied that he hadn't missed out on anything of note, he moseyed into the detectives' office. Keith was at his desk, and he glanced up from his computer screen as Bill approached.

"Hi, how's it going?"

"Not bad," Bill said. "A little slow, but that's okay. Campbell's in court today, and Nick and I are tying up loose ends."

"No big cases right now?"

"Nope. Just the usual."

"Did you know there's a new P.I. in town?"

Bill blinked. "No, I did not." He sat down on the corner of Keith's desk. "What's the scoop on him?"

Keith smiled. "*She* is newly licensed and moved here from Elizabethtown. She's setting up shop on Chestnut Street."

"You got the jump on me with that one."

"Well, you're all required to let us know when you open for business in our jurisdiction."

"That's true. Does she have a name?"

"Chilton," Keith said. "Marissa Chilton. Her firm is Chilton Investigations."

Bill eyed him sharply. "She's setting up solo, then?"

"That's my understanding—much as you did six or seven years ago."

"Where did she train?"

"She worked with a P.I. in E-town for several years."

"But she wasn't a police officer before that?"

"No, you have the advantage of her there."

Bill scowled.

"What are you thinking?" Keith asked.

"That maybe this is why business is so slow lately."

"Oh, I doubt it. She's only just hung her shingle this week. I believe she opened for business yesterday." Keith punched a few computer keys and stood. "Coffee?"

"You got the good stuff?"

"Always, in this room." Keith led him to the detectives' refreshment station and poured a mug for Bill then another for himself. "You know your regulars won't jump ship on you."

Bill shrugged. It was true the local attorneys and businessmen he worked with frequently seemed very pleased with the work True Blue Investigations did.

"I guess we'll see if this town's big enough for another agency."

Keith nodded and sipped his coffee. "This case Campbell's on—the trial—"

"I don't know what it is," Bill said. "She called me at noon, but only for a minute, to say she'd been picked. Didn't tell me what it was about."

"She called me too. Same status—but I think I know what case it is."

Bill lifted an eyebrow. "There's no law against the two of us discussing it."

"No, there's not. I took a look at today's court calendar. They've blocked out the entire week for a case from last year."

"Something that happened before Campbell came home?"

"Yes. A stolen painting."

"I remember that. It had something to do with an old lady dying, and her kid—no, her granddaughter—tried to sell off her things, and some of them turned out to be stolen goods."

"One thing," Keith corrected him as they walked back to his desk. "At least, as far as I know, it was only one. A painting that the grand-daughter claims was in with a bunch of junk in the attic. The defendant says she'd never seen it before. The grandmother was dead, so she couldn't ask her about it. She was going to hold a garage sale to get rid of stuff, but she thought that one item might be worth more than she'd get at a yard sale."

"Oh, yeah. It was interesting, but I didn't have anything to do with it." Bill pulled over an extra chair and settled into it, across the desk from Keith. "I haven't heard any more about it for months. Forgot all about it."

"Well, it's still active, and the trial begins today."

Bill chuckled. "Campbell should find it inter-esting. Nick was regaling her last night with a list of all the ho-hum cases she'd probably have to hear. Drugs, shoplifting, domestics."

"You can't talk to her about it." Keith's pointed gaze brought Bill out of his reverie.

"Right. Understood. But when it's over, she can tell me all about it. Of course, there might be something in the newspaper while it's under way."

"Don't let her read about it, if there is."

"I won't. Do you think the woman's guilty?"

"I have no idea," Keith said. "When it happened,

I was in the middle of a big drug case. I kept on with that, and I think Matt Jackson was working a fraud, or maybe an embezzlement. Anyway, John Smalley picked it up, but we all figured the painting thing wasn't going anywhere."

"But here we are. And Smalley left the Murray P.D. a while ago, didn't he?"

"Yeah, last summer, but since he was the arresting officer, they called him to come testify."

"I get you." Bill eyed him curiously. "So, if you're not in on that, what are you working on?"

"Oh, somebody stole a bunch of equipment from Murray State's theater department. Camera, microphones, that kind of stuff."

"Huh." It sounded boring. Bill stood. "I'd better get home and get to work, or that new P.I. will start poaching all my clients. What'd you say her name was? Hilton?"

"Chilton. My opinion? She won't last. Not unless she has someone working with her."

"Well, don't look at me. I don't have room for another employee right now."

Keith grinned. "If she asks me, I'll tell her you said that."

When Campbell left the judicial building at five o'clock, her head was full of details. The jurors were allowed to take notes, and she'd filled several pages in the small notebook she carried in her purse.

She found her sympathies lay mostly with the defendant. From what the jury had heard so far, it seemed Leila Abbott had never intended to commit a crime.

The young woman had been her grandmother's main caretaker for the past couple of years, since she lived closer to her than any other family members. Her grandmother, Teresa Abbott, had lived alone in a small house she'd rented with her husband for decades. When he died, Teresa stayed in the same home, and the accumulation of her adult life filled the attic and closets.

Toward the end, Teresa had gone into a nursing home. Leila had hoped her grandmother would recover enough to return home, but that hadn't happened. On her death, the landlord had been civil, but he'd let Leila and her mom know that he'd like the rental cleaned out by the end of the last month Teresa had paid for. They had only about three weeks to remove all of Mrs. Abbott's belongings.

Campbell wished she could sit down with Leila and hear the story from her. Maybe she would take the stand after the other witnesses were done. That seemed like a good idea to Campbell. Let her explain how she found the painting and why she thought she had a right to sell it. She wanted to hear Leila swear she knew nothing about the painting or its origins before her grandmother's death.

Tomorrow. Surely tomorrow would tell the jury what they needed to know to make their decision.

"So, how's it going?" her father asked when she went to the door of his private office. "In general, of course."

"Not bad. But it's a little boring. We aren't getting—" Campbell broke off, unsure of how much she should reveal the day's happenings.

Bill grunted. "I hope tomorrow's better. Want to go out for supper?"

"Not really. Is there anything in the fridge?"

"Let's go see." Bill rose and accompanied her to the kitchen, where they found an assortment of leftovers and sandwich makings.

Over a plate of leftover lasagna, tossed salad, and a corn muffin, Campbell found other topics to discuss with her dad.

"Oh, and the latest from Vera Hill," Bill said with a hefty ham sandwich suspended halfway to his mouth. "Her daughter has a new love interest."

Campbell quickly swallowed. "What? Dorothy's dating someone new?"

"That's right. Apparently she's getting over her unfortunate relationship from last fall."

After a moment's consideration, Campbell said, "I hope it goes well for her. But also that she doesn't jump into anything too fast."

"That's what I said, or at least, what I felt. I didn't exactly say it out loud." Bill took a big bite and set down the sandwich.

Poor Dad. Campbell knew he'd had hopes for himself when an old friend of her mother's moved into town. But the circumstances that brought Jackie Fleming to Calloway County were too messy. Bill liked things tied up neatly, as with all of his investigations. Jackie still attended their church, and the McBrides remained on friendly terms with her, but Bill hadn't asked her out again since helping put her ex in jail.

"Have you heard any more about the people who bought the Tatton house?" she asked.

Bill shook his head as he reached for his glass of root beer. "I saw a car out front this morning, but I was on my way downtown. Nick may have seen something."

"Where *is* Nick?" He wasn't in evidence when she got back from court, but she hadn't thought much about it.

"He's out chasing an errant husband."

Campbell made a face. "Ew. A divorce case?"

"Maybe. Right now, it's a potential fraud case."

"Not one of those." Jackie's tale of woe with her short-term husband was too fresh in all their minds.

"Well, we'll see what happens. I agreed to do two days' work on it. If we can't turn up anything solid, that's it."

"And what are you working on?" Campbell asked.

"An insurance case. Oh, and get this. Keith

27

told me today that a new P.I. has set up shop in Murray."

"What?" She stared at him. "We have competition, eh?"

"So it seems. She's from E-town. Trained with someone over there, but she's going solo now."

"Why did she pick our town?"

"Who knows."

"Interesting. I suppose you've done a little background?"

"You know me too well." Bill took another bite of his sandwich.

Campbell chuckled. "All right, Dad. Spill it."

After he swallowed, he rocked his head back and forth. "She worked for two years with an investigator over there."

"Elizabethtown."

"Right."

"Do you know him?"

"I've met him. Ran into him once at a conference and another time when I had to testify in Frankfort, in a case the state was prosecuting."

"And?"

"His name's Tucker, and he's a straight-up guy."

"Then why did his trainee leave him after she qualified?"

"I don't have an answer to that."

"Yet," she said.

Her father cracked a smile. "I'd say you know

me too well, but I just said it. I may give him a call if I think it will be helpful."

She waited, her eyebrows arched.

"I just don't see a need to know unless I cross paths with her."

"Sure, Dad."

"What's that supposed to mean?"

"You always want to know everything, and I've never heard you apply the need-to-know rule to yourself."

"There's a first time for everything," he said mildly.

"Huh. Well, let me know if you do run across her. I'll be interested to hear more about her. Uh, what's her name?"

Bill frowned as if trying to remember, but he didn't fool Campbell for one second.

"Chilton, I think."

"Oh, you think."

"Marissa Chilton, that's it."

She made a mental note. Her dad wasn't the only one who could unearth a person's past.

Chapter 3

Keith hesitated before calling Campbell that evening. Maybe he should keep his distance while she was serving on the jury.

No way. That case could drag on for weeks. After a quick supper at home and a change into casual clothes, he drove to the McBride house.

"Hi!" Campbell had come downstairs to admit him. "Dad's upstairs watching TV, if you want to see him."

"What do you think?"

She laughed and accepted a quick kiss. Keith and Bill were friends, but she had no illusions as to the purpose of this visit.

"So, how's it going?" he asked.

"Can't talk about it."

"Oh, I know. I just meant . . . your life . . . in general."

"Fine." Her smile faded. "I admit this c—this thing I'm involved in—has me a little down."

"Why is that?" Keith asked. He wished he could tell her he'd read Detective Smalley's case file, but even that would probably be revealing too much. It would be hard to hold back the fact that he'd found a few rough spots in the investigation—or at least what he considered gaps in the file. Missing bits of information.

Things that should have been spelled out but weren't.

"Can't talk about it."

"Right. Well, let's think of something you *can* talk about."

"Sounds good." She led him into the large office she shared with Nick most days. It was the home's former owner's living room, and she took Keith to the comfortable seating area in front of the fireplace. They settled in together on the couch. "Dad says there's a new investigator in town."

"Yeah, that's right. We were notified that she's open for business."

"On Chestnut Street."

"Yup." They gazed into each other's eyes.

"That's a much busier area than here," Campbell noted.

Keith nodded. Chestnut Street held the city's post office, a movie theater, some restaurants and garages, among other points of interest. On the far side of Twelfth Street, it wended its way to the Murray State University campus.

"But True Blue's been here—what—six years?"

"Seven, I think."

"Bill has a lot of clients who trust him and bring him their repeat business," Keith said.

That was true. Campbell had worked on some of those repeat requests for background checks, locating witnesses and missing family members, and surveillance of lawsuit participants. The attorneys and insurance brokers of Murray trusted Bill McBride.

"Still, there's only so much of this type of work in a town this size. What if she starts advertising and enticing people to her agency? Dad likes to keep a low profile—you know, discreet and efficient."

"Don't worry," Keith said. "Most people who want to hire a P.I. want that too."

Campbell tried unsuccessfully to quell her misgivings.

"What have *you* been doing today?" she asked.

"Oh, trying to chase down some stolen equipment from MSU."

"Dad mentioned that at supper. Cameras and stuff?"

"Yeah." Keith shrugged. "Not much to go on yet. So, I hear you have new neighbors," he said brightly.

"So I'm told. I haven't seen them yet."

"Well, I can tell you that your new neighbor is a middle-aged woman who will have an adult son living with her."

"How do you know that? Wait!" Campbell pulled back and stared at him. "Don't tell me he's a sex offender and had to register with the P.D."

Keith chuckled. "No, I'm happy to say it's not that. We would definitely warn you if it was. No,

I just happened to run into Nell Calhoun this afternoon, and she told me."

"Wow. She's allowed to tell people about her clients?"

"Well, I *am* a police officer. I don't think she'd tell just anyone. And you'll find out soon enough, anyhow."

"Yeah, Dad's probably done a deep background on both of them by now. That is, if he hasn't been too busy compiling a file on Marissa Chilton."

Keith smiled but didn't comment. She had her father pegged, all right.

"Hey, do you want some coffee or something? I think there's pie in the fridge."

"That sounds like a great idea." He stood and offered his hand to pull her up off the sofa.

Nick came in the next morning before she left for the judicial building.

"Yo, Professor." He slung his backpack off his shoulder onto his desk. "Heading for court?"

"Yep. Probably every day this week."

"Oh, it's a complicated case?"

"Yeah, sort of. Wish I could discuss it, but I can't."

He nodded. "Hey, I met the new guy next door. He was outside when I drove in just now."

"Really?" She took a step toward the window.

"He's gone now," Nick said.

Disappointed she wouldn't get a look, Campbell sighed. "What's he like?"

"He's about my age. Or your age."

"We're in the same generation, Nick."

He shrugged. "Okay, early to mid-twenties then. Blond hair, five-ten, looks fit."

"*Hmm.*" Campbell wiggled her eyebrows. "How interested should I be?"

"Up to you, but I'm gonna tell Keith you said that."

"Don't you dare. I was joking, and you know it."

Nick chuckled as he sat down and unzipped his backpack. "His name's Greg, and he's a student at MSU."

"Oh?" Maybe he wasn't in her age bracket after all.

"Said his mother moved here from Louisville to be closer to him."

"Okay. What do you know about her?"

"Zilch."

"Not even a last name?"

"Nope. Greg and I just said hi. I told him my name was Nick, and I work here. He said, 'I'm Greg. I'll probably see ya around.' Oh, and he did tell me what I said about his mother moving here."

"Huh. Keith told Dad he'd be living with her. I wonder if he's been living on campus till now."

"I don't know. A lot of college guys wouldn't

34

be too happy to move out of the dorm or the frat house to move in with Mom."

"Agreed. Hey, what do you want for Christmas?"

Nick stared at her. "You're getting me a Christmas present?"

"Sure." She hesitated. "I mean, we work together every day and . . . Doesn't Dad give you a present?"

"A modest bonus usually."

"Oh." She curled her lip. "I wish I knew what to get Dad."

"Bill's easy. He'll like whatever you give him."

She supposed that was true. Her father always accepted gifts graciously. "But I'd like to get him something really special."

"I don't know about that," Nick said. "He's been alone so long, if he really wants something, I think he just buys it."

That was the sad truth.

"What did you get him last year?" Nick asked.

"A shirt and a book."

"Safe gifts."

"I suppose." The designation didn't sit well with her. Was she a safe-gift giver? She wanted to give the men in her life something they'd really love. That included Nick, as well as her dad and Keith.

Well, I'd better step on it. Can't be late for court." She grabbed her purse. "If you want, you can text me your Christmas list."

"Oh, like a letter to Santa?"

"Kind of. Just don't expect the elves to get everything on the list."

He laughed as she headed toward the garage.

As she backed out the driveway, a young man was coming out of the brick house next door, walking toward a black pickup truck in the drive. Campbell recalled Nick's description of the new neighbor, and he fit it to a *T*. This had to be Greg—if he'd left earlier, apparently he'd come back. He glanced her way, and she lifted a hand. Immediately, she transferred her attention back to her side-view mirror, but she was sure he'd waved back.

When she reached her destination, Campbell had to park in the lower lot, as the upper one was full and a hearse sat in front of the funeral home. She hurried up to the entrance, hoping her few minutes of conversation with Nick hadn't made her late.

Once she reached the courtroom, she slid into the seat next to a bearded man about her dad's age.

"Did I miss anything?"

He smiled. "Nope. Cutting it fine, though."

"I know." She determined to leave home earlier the next day. If she arrived after the judge was seated, she wasn't sure what would happen.

"All rise."

She jumped up with the other jurors, scarcely having time to note that the attorneys and their staff, as well as the defendant and court clerk, were in place. The judge came in and took his place at the bench.

The estate attorney took the stand first. Mrs. Abbott had made a will after her husband's death, about ten years previously. In it, she bequeathed her estate to her three children, Randall, Marcella, and Jacob. Jacob was still alive, but the other two children were now deceased.

The attorney explained that in a case such as that of Leila Abbott, as her grandmother's executor, Leila was responsible for distributing the testator's assets.

Since Randall Abbott and his sister, Marcella Smith, had died, their shares would now go to their children, who were Mrs. Abbott's grand-children, and Leila, her sister, and cousins. One third of the estate would go to Leila's uncle, Jacob Abbott, and the other two thirds was to be equally divided among the five children of Randall and Marcella.

At this point, the prosecutor asked the lawyer if this had gone as instructed.

"There was some disagreement at first," she said. "Jacob Abbott, the testator's only remaining child, thought he should be the one to represent the estate."

"And how was this addressed?" Vaughn asked.

"I told him that the law is clear. Mrs. Abbott had named her granddaughter as executrix, at a time when all three of her children were living. Clearly, it was her wish that Leila be the one to serve."

"And was the estate distributed?"

"The cash and income from some other assets were," the lawyer said. "However, there were some items that Leila felt should be evaluated before being sold."

"Such as the Banitier painting?"

"I don't know." The lawyer darted a glance at the defendant. "She didn't give me a list. She only said there were a few things that should be sold, and that she wanted to make sure they got a fair price for them."

Campbell listened avidly and took notes, drawing a crude family tree in her notebook. Would Leila Abbott take the stand? She was eager to know what other items Leila had held back from the estate.

To her surprise, the next witness was Leila's cousin Anna Irwin, one of the other heirs.

"Did you receive money from your cousin as part of the estate distribution?" Vaughn asked her.

"Yes," Anna replied. "We held an estate sale, where we sold most of Grandma's things, and later we held another, smaller yard sale. The things that were left from that, we donated to a charity store."

"And did you understand that more funds would be coming to you from items that were to be sold individually?"

Anna hesitated. "Leila had said something about Grandma's engagement ring. There were some dishes she sold and gave us money from. I didn't know about the painting at the time."

"Were there other things?"

"If there were, she didn't tell me about them."

"Think carefully, Mrs. Irwin. Did your grandmother have any other things that you felt were somewhat valuable and that were not sold at either of the two sales your family held?"

"No. We sold her furniture and silverware and all her knickknacks. Didn't get much for anything."

"And did you and your siblings and cousins receive any items that had belonged to Mrs. Abbott?"

"We each got to choose one thing, before the estate sale."

"Did you choose something?"

"Yes. I got a flow blue plate she used to display in her dining room."

"Did your cousin Leila get something?"

Anna frowned. "I believe she chose a small lap desk. I know my brother Blaine got Grandma's television, and Corey got something too—I can't remember what. And I'm not sure about Danielle."

"The defendant's sister?"

"Yes. I don't know what she got."

"And your uncle, Jacob Abbott?"

"I don't know."

"No further questions."

The defense attorney rose to cross-examine Anna.

"Did Leila ever give you any more money connected to your grandmother's estate?"

"No."

Soule's eyebrows shot up. "What about the engagement ring? Did she ever sell it?"

"Not that I'm aware of. She did tell me she'd taken it to a jeweler, and he said it wasn't worth a whole lot. Maybe six hundred."

"But you never received your share of that?"

"No. I assumed she hadn't actually sold it yet, and that when she did, a third would go to Uncle Jacob and the rest would be split five ways to us cousins. But it wouldn't be much—probably less than a hundred apiece."

"I see. And as far as you knew, that was the only asset from which funds had not yet been distributed?"

"That's correct."

"And those items each of you chose from among your grandmother's things—none of them was worth significantly more than the others?"

"No. I think if they were, Leila would have said they needed to be valued, like the ring."

Soule faced the bench. "No further questions, Your Honor."

Court was recessed for an hour's lunch, and the jury was taken into a conference room. Sandwiches, soft drinks, and desserts were waiting for them there, and each member was allowed to go to the restroom, accompanied by a court officer. Campbell assumed it was so that no one would approach the jury members to try to influence them.

Keith closed the computer file and gazed down at the folder on his desk. Unless the reports were incomplete, he could see several ways that case should have been investigated further. Not that Smalley's conclusions weren't reasonable, but there were loose ends. Had the detective stopped following up on tangential leads when he'd found the obvious answers?

With a sigh, he turned back to the cases he was currently investigating. He'd wasted enough time on an old case. It wasn't a cold case, either, but one that was being actively prosecuted in the courts. Not his job to pursue it.

He spent several hours delving into a case of drug dealing and ended up with a suspect in custody. He'd barely sat down to complete the intake paperwork when his desk phone rang.

Detective Sergeant Vickers asked him to come to his office. Keith went, expecting to discuss the drug bust.

As soon as he walked through the door, Vickers

looked up at him and said, "Have you been looking at the Abbott case?"

"The . . . oh, yes. I glanced at the files this morning."

"Well, someone noticed that you'd opened the electronic files and told the chief."

Keith swallowed hard. "Why?"

"I'm not sure, but what I do know is, the chief says leave it alone. It's out of our hands now."

"Yes, it is. And he doesn't want us reading up on the case?"

"Apparently not."

"I just wanted to inform myself about it."

"And now you have," Vickers said. "So let that be the end of it."

But those loose ends . . .

Keith caught a hard glint in the sergeant's gaze. "Yes, sir."

"When the trial is over, maybe we can talk about it then."

"I'd like to." But that might be too late to change anything. Keith rose and returned to his paperwork.

An hour later, he sat in Bill McBride's office.

"I suppose that technically I shouldn't even be talking to you about it."

Bill frowned. "It does seem odd. First of all, that anyone took note of your reading material, and secondly, that the chief stepped in and told you to stop."

"And Vickers and I usually get along quite well," Keith noted. "I was surprised, I'll tell you. I felt like I couldn't say anything at all."

"You have misgivings about the way the case was handled."

"It's a strange case. Under most circumstances, it wouldn't have even come to our attention."

"Why did it?"

"The antique dealer. He thought something was fishy when the girl brought the painting to him, and he reported it. But not right away. He waited several days. Said he'd been mulling it over and decided it was worth advising the police about it."

"Tell me about these loose ends you mentioned. I take it there were other witnesses Smalley should have talked to and didn't."

"If he did, he didn't leave a record of it in the file. It seems incomplete—or slipshod. But, Bill, if we talk about this in detail, you have to keep mum about it. Campbell can't know."

"Absolutely." A tight smile crossed Bill's face. "If the court found out her father was looking at the case, there could be fireworks."

Keith nodded soberly. "This is all unofficial. Between two friends."

Chapter 4

The most interesting witness that afternoon, in Campbell's opinion, was the owner of an antique shop in Murray. Campbell had previously visited the store and had found the prices a little high. Though located in a small city in a rural community, it held a wide array of goods not as varied as those in the group shops nearby, but somewhat more sophisticated.

The dealer, Michael Harder, testified about the day Leila Abbott had brought the painting in question to his shop. As Detective Smalley had stated the previous day, Harder said he'd examined the painting.

"I recognized the artist's name. I thought the piece had some value."

"How much?"

"I offered her five thousand dollars."

"Is that in the range of what this artist's work usually sells for?" Vaughn asked.

"They generally go higher."

"How high?"

Harder paused then said, "I did some searching online after she left. I found records of recent sales ranging from twenty to fifty thousand."

"Why did you offer so little?"

The witness cleared his throat. "You have

to understand, at the time she showed me the painting, I hadn't done any research. Yes, I knew who the painter was, but I would need more time to do a thorough evaluation—and I told her that."

"But you offered her five grand."

"Well, yes. She didn't seem to want to wait or to leave the painting with me while I researched it."

"Were you certain the painting was genuine?"

"I . . . was pretty sure."

"What if you'd bought it, and it turned out to be a fake?"

"Then I'd have been out five thousand dollars."

"Did Ms. Abbott say that wasn't enough?"

"No. As I recall, she said she'd like to get a second opinion. She took the painting and left my store."

"Did you ever hear from her again?"

"No."

The next witness was a dealer from Paducah, a larger city an hour to the northwest. Monique Kaplan stated that she owned an art gallery. Her graying hair was caught back in a bun, and she wore a flowing caftan in a geometric print.

"You're an expert in local art?" the prosecutor asked.

"I suppose I am, to some extent."

"And when did you first meet Ms. Abbott?"

"She came to me on August nineteenth."

"The day after she visited Mr. Harding in Murray."

"I wouldn't know."

"And did she show you a painting?"

"Yes, a landscape by an Ohio Valley artist from the mid-twentieth century, Elroy Banitier."

"Had you seen this artist's work before?"

"Oh, yes. I've seen it in museums and auctions, and I actually had one of his paintings in my shop about twelve years ago."

"Did you have it long?"

"Only about a month. There was a lot of interest in it."

"How much did that painting sell for?"

"I believe it was twenty-two thousand."

"Do you think it would fetch that much today?"

"More, I'm certain. The market for Banitier's art has gone up over the last decade."

Court was recessed at four thirty that afternoon. Still the jury didn't have all the facts. Campbell wondered why they hadn't continued until five. Maybe the judge knew the next session of questioning would be lengthy. Did that mean Leila Abbott would be on the stand tomorrow?

Her father didn't say a word about the trial that evening, other than a benign, "How's it going?"

She gave him a generic answer.

"Mart called today," Bill said over the supper table.

Campbell smiled, glad that her dad and his old friend kept up their contact. "Oh? How are things in Bowling Green?"

"Good. He wondered if we wanted to go over there on Christmas Day."

"What do you think?" She knew they'd both enjoy the gathering. Mart and his daughters, with their families, would welcome them and provide a full day of warmth and entertainment, she was sure. On the other hand, it could mean traveling in iffy weather and doing more shopping. They couldn't arrive on Christmas without gifts for everyone.

"Let's think about it," Bill said.

Campbell nodded and tried to read his face. "It'll be our first Christmas in our new home."

"I got out the box of decorations if you want a little glitz."

She grinned at that. "It would be fun to sparkle up this old house. Oh, and don't forget we found a box of ornaments in the storage unit too."

"Yeah. Guess we'd better plan on getting a tree in a week or so."

She could picture it on the other end of the office from the fireplace. "Let's do it."

"All right."

He looked satisfied, and that made her happy. Her dad was regaining some bits of personality he'd seemed to lose after Mom died. Maybe one day he'd feel a real joy again. Wanting to decorate for Christmas was a good start.

When Keith phoned her that evening, they had a leisurely chat of twenty minutes or so. Nothing about court. Campbell thought that was a little odd, but far be it from her to bring it up. If Keith and her dad were trying to help her follow the rules and be a good juror, so be it.

Instead, they talked about Keith's parents and the upcoming holidays. His sister and brother-in-law planned to arrive a few days before Christmas and stay about a week.

"Your mom must be thrilled," Campbell said.

"Yeah, we haven't seen them since last summer. It will be good to catch up. And I want you to meet Nicole and Todd, of course."

"I'd like that."

"Great, because Nic is really eager to see what you're like."

Campbell laughed. "I want to get to know her too. But I have a picture of her in my head already—a younger version of Angela."

"Well, I dunno. You have to mix in some of Dad's humor too."

"Good. I think I'm going to love Nicole."

Arriving at the judicial building on Wednesday morning, Campbell went straight up to the courtroom. She mentally patted herself on the back for being ten minutes early.

When the judge entered, the prosecutor and defense attorney immediately approached the bench and leaned in to speak to him. Campbell looked around. She couldn't see behind the jury area, as a chest-high wall separated it from the rest of the courtroom. Were there any spectators? She hadn't noticed particularly as she hurried in, but she had a vague impression of a sprinkling of people sitting in the back.

The bailiff appeared suddenly at the end of her row. He threw her a quick look then frowned at a paper in his hand.

"Number 126, Ms. McBride?"

Campbell's heart lurched. "Yes?"

"Would you please approach the bench."

It wasn't a question. She rose hesitantly and grabbed her purse. Her cheeks heated as she walked forward and faced the judge. The two lawyers flanked her, and she drew in a deep breath.

"Ms. McBride, you stated yesterday that you will be a witness in the trial of Bella Chase." The judge's face was somber, and her pulse quickened.

"That's correct, Your Honor. And probably her son's trial as well."

He nodded gravely. "I spoke to the police chief about it and learned you also have a personal relationship with a sworn officer?"

She gulped. Her face was on fire. "I—yes, Your Honor. Detective Keith Fuller. But he's not involved in this case."

"Nevertheless, on further reflection, we've decided to remove you from this jury."

"Y-yes, sir." She hesitated. "Should I check in—"

"Thank you for your willingness to serve, but you are no longer considered eligible for jury duty. Consider your service ended."

"I—yes, Your Honor. Thank you."

Everyone was staring at her. She could tell, even though she kept her eyes on the carpet. Her exit from the courtroom felt like a lengthy walk of shame. She hadn't done anything wrong, had she? She supposed she should have gone into more detail when they asked if any of them knew any local police officers. She'd said she knew several, but they hadn't asked her to elaborate.

She pushed open one of the double doors and stepped into the hallway. Even outside the courtroom, she could barely breathe. She entered the stairway and strode quickly down to the ground floor. As she left the building, a cool breeze smacked her in the face, helping to calm her. Slowing her steps, she took her time getting down to the lower parking lot and her car. She opened the driver's door and sat down. With both hands on the wheel, she stared straight ahead for a full minute.

Going home and having to explain loomed over her, a dark cloud of dread. Oh, she'd have to lay it all out for Dad eventually, but she decided to delay that moment for a short time and drove to the library on Main Street.

Usually when she entered the remodeled library, Campbell felt happy, but today her mood was all gloom. She wandered aimlessly from section to section until she spotted Hallee in the stacks, reshelving books from a cart.

"Hey!" Hallee's face lit up, and she laid the book she was holding back on the pile of returns. "You're not in court today? Is the trial finished?"

Campbell grimaced. "They dismissed me."

"Oh, what happened?"

She shrugged. "I thought they were okay with me, but I guess I ought to have given them a better picture of my relationship with Keith. I think maybe the police chief said something. And they weren't real happy with me being a potential witness in an upcoming trial."

"You told them about Keith in *voir dire*, right?"

"Yes. Well, I said I knew several officers. But they kind of skipped over that and focused on that woman who's an officer's mom."

"Oh, yeah. I remember."

"They never came back to me, so I assumed I was okay. And they didn't dismiss that mom, either."

"Was she on the jury?" Hallee asked.

"Well, no. She wasn't in the final ones they picked, but they didn't boot her off after they talked to her up front about her son." Campbell sighed. "It is what it is."

"I know you wanted to serve. Me, I'm just as

glad they haven't chosen me for anything yet. Of course, that could change next week."

"They told me not to come back."

"Wow." Hallee pulled her in for a quick hug. "Sorry. They don't know what they're giving up. You'd be terrific. In fact, I'd have bet on you to be the foreperson."

Campbell gave her a wry smile. She'd imagined herself being the lead juror too. Maybe this was the Lord's way of cutting her pride down to size. "I guess I should go home and report to Dad for work."

"Hey, we got in a new James Scott Bell novel."

"Really? I love his books."

"If nobody's snatched it, you can be the first patron to read it. Or you can get the audio." Hallee guided her cheerfully toward the front desk.

"Remember, not a word about this to Campbell," Bill said as he turned onto Willow Street.

"Got it," Nick replied.

"Better get back on the Riley case."

Nick went into the house with him for just a few minutes and gathered his things for a bout of surveillance.

"You don't need to come back today unless something breaks," Bill said.

"Right. How long should I stay on her?"

"If she's at home when you get there, stay until

at least three. I hope our little jaunt this morning didn't mess things up."

Nick shrugged. "If she's out now, we can't help it."

"Yeah. I just hope she's not out playing tennis or something."

"You want me to go back later?"

"Maybe hit her place around five. You said her husband doesn't usually get home until six or so. Stay through dinner and make sure she's not going out this evening. If she's still there by eight, call it a night."

"Okay. And if she goes out, she'd better be wearing that cervical collar."

Bill waited until Nick had left in his own vehicle before calling Keith.

"Hey, just wanted you to know, Nick and I talked to another art dealer—not the one who's involved in the Abbott case. That painting's worth a bundle if it's genuine."

"I figured," Keith replied. "I can't really talk now, but I'll call you later."

"Okay," Bill said. "But listen, I also initiated contact with a cousin of—" He stopped, wondering if he should say it aloud. He'd called Keith's cell phone, not his desk phone, but still.

"That could be risky," Keith said, as though Bill didn't need to finish the sentence.

"You think?"

"Let's talk about it later."

"Okay, buddy." Bill hung up and sat frowning at his monitor for a few seconds then opened a computer file.

When Campbell arrived home with the book under her arm, it was after eleven o'clock, and the big office was empty. She'd seen her father's car in the garage, so she went to his door and tapped on it.

"Come in." His eyes widened when he saw her. "You're out early."

"I'm out permanently." She flopped down on a chair he kept for visitors. "Apparently the judge chatted with the police chief and was told that I was close to Keith. I guess the judge felt I should have made that clear earlier."

"Huh. Imagine that."

"I know. And imagine the police chief knowing who Keith's dating."

"Mind-boggling." Bill reached for his ubiquitous mug of coffee.

"They also mentioned my upcoming role as a witness in Bella and J.J. Chase's trials, but we'd addressed that on Monday. I'm pretty sure it's my connection to Keith that made them change their minds."

"I'm sorry." He sipped his coffee and made a face. Must be cold.

She shrugged. "I just hope Keith doesn't get in trouble over it."

"Oh, I don't think he will." Still, her dad didn't look happy. Would this give him a black mark in the police chief's books? She hoped not. Private investigators needed the goodwill of the local police. "So, what do you want to do today? Do you need the afternoon off to settle yourself?"

"I can work. In fact, I'd like to work. Let's get some lunch, and then I'll dive in."

Three hours later, Campbell was immersed in research for one of the firm's legal cases when Nick sauntered in. He laid a package on her desk and turned away.

Campbell glanced at the padded envelope. "Oh, thanks. I think that's our ink that I ordered online."

Nick swung back to retrieve the package and took it over to their printer stand.

"Court get out early?" he asked.

"No, but I did. I'm done."

"Whoa. What happened?"

"They decided they don't like me. What about you? I thought you were surveilling somebody."

"Yeah, I was. Taking a break, but I'm going back at dinnertime to see what happens when hubby comes home."

"Ah," she said absently, scrolling through a report on her screen.

Nick was soon tapping away at his keyboard,

and they both worked in silence. At ten past four, Bill strode into the room.

"Listen up, you two. The jury just voted Leila Abbott's not guilty."

"What?" Campbell jerk her head up and stared at him. "Already? They just tossed me this morning."

"Apparently they went into deliberations just before noon and emerged about twenty minutes ago."

"How do you know this?" Campbell asked.

"I have a source." Bill shrugged as if it was nothing.

"At the courthouse?" Her voice rose in protest. "You didn't tell me."

"It's kind of hush-hush, but I trust this source. Leila Abbott is walking."

"Wow." Campbell leaned back in her chair and tried to absorb the news.

"From what little I know, that was the right decision," Nick said. "It didn't sound like they had enough evidence to convict her. I mean, the painting was stolen before she was born, right?"

"Not quite that long ago," Bill said. "The prosecutor was trying to prove she stole it from the estate, not from the original owner. They still have no idea who stole it first."

"But the jury says she wasn't stealing it?" Campbell asked.

"Right. She claims she was just trying to get it

fairly evaluated so she could sell it and split the money with the other heirs."

Nick frowned. "But they don't know she would have actually shared it."

"They don't know she wouldn't have either," Campbell said.

"That's right." Her father walked over to the coffeemaker. "This case should never have gone to court. They were prosecuting her for a potential crime, not one she'd committed."

Campbell considered that. "But they thought she was hiding it from the heirs—her sister and her cousins and her uncle. Vaughn said in his opening statement that they'd show she was defrauding the heirs."

"And he failed to prove it," Bill said.

"So it's over?" Nick eyed his boss sharply.

"Maybe not. The other heirs could file a civil suit, I suppose."

"And now they can't sell the painting, so I'd think that would be an expensive waste of time." Campbell shook her head, wondering if anything would come of all this fuss, and if the original owner would get his art back.

"Cheer up," Bill told her. "Keith's coming over after supper. We'll have a confab and see what we can come up with."

"Is Keith working on it officially now?" she asked.

"Yes, because Detective Smalley isn't with the

Murray P.D. anymore. He'll be contacting the people the painting was stolen from years ago, to see if they can return it to them."

"What about us?"

"We're free to nose around and find out everything we can about Leila Abbott and Anna Irwin's grandparents."

Nick shoved his chair back. "I'd better get going, but count me in on that. It sounds interesting, and I think I'll wrap this case up soon."

When he'd left, Bill smiled at Campbell. "After supper, we can hash this out with Keith. I want to be sure we're not duplicating anything he's doing, but I doubt they've had time to do much on it yet. Of course, he won't give us anything sensitive. We don't want to step on any toes at the police station."

"Right." Campbell remembered the awful feeling in her chest when she'd been excused from court that morning. She didn't want to go through it again with the police department. But she did want to know the whole story on that painting.

Chapter 5

Two days later, Campbell collected the mail that had been slipped through the slot in the front door and took it to the breakfast table. Friday was often a light day for the agency, and she expected to spend it writing reports and wrapping up a couple of background checks for a local business. She handed three envelopes to her father and sat down with the fourth one.

"Is Nick coming in this morning?" she asked, as she peeled open the flap on the stiff envelope.

"I told him to come in at noon, since he worked into the evening yesterday. What have you got?" her dad asked.

"It's from Uncle Rick, for both of us. I think it's a Christmas card."

"Already?"

"It's only three weeks away, Dad."

"*Hmm.* I suppose so. Do you send Christmas cards?"

"A few. How about you?"

"I haven't sent any since your mother died. I suppose I should—to clients, anyway."

"Yes, it's good business. And apparently your relatives still love you, so you should reciprocate to them." She looked up from the card. "Uncle Rick says he hopes he can come see us after the holiday. How long has it been since you saw your brother?"

Bill sighed. "Eight or nine months, I suppose. We met up last spring in Louisville. I had to go over there on business, and Richard decided to go to Churchill Downs."

"Did you go to the races?"

"No, I didn't, but we had dinner together. He paid for it with his track winnings."

Campbell laughed. "I didn't know he was a gambler."

"I don't think he's much of one, but he enjoys a trip to the races once a year or so."

"What's that?" She nodded to the item in his hand, which was obviously another Christmas card.

"Oh, let's see." He opened it and frowned. "Hoping you have a merry Christmas and a happy New Year."

Campbell squinted at the glittery snowman on the front. "Who's it from?"

"It's not signed."

"What?" She picked up the envelope he'd discarded. "No return address either, but it's post-marked here in town."

"There is a handwritten message, though." Bill's eyebrows drew together as he stared at it. "I think this is some sort of code or something."

"What? Let me see."

Campbell took it and surveyed the block letters

written in black ink below the printed greeting he'd read. While they were separated into what could be eight words, the letters seemed like a random jumble. "*Hmm.* It makes no sense." She looked over at him. "Why would anyone sign their card in code?"

"I don't know. My brother and I used to send each other coded messages when we were kids, but we haven't mentioned it in years."

"And you just got a card from him in plain English today," she pointed out.

"Yeah. And he lives in Virginia."

She examined the message again. The first four letter groups had four characters each, but the last four were of varying lengths—three letters, nine, two, and five. She picked up the envelope. "The address is in the same block letters as the weird signature—or whatever that is inside the card."

"Maybe it's a simple substitution code," her father mused.

"Aren't there computer programs to solve things like that?"

"Probably."

"Anyway, after I finish up the backgrounds, what do you want me to do today?"

He set the card aside and picked up the rest of the mail. "Looks like I'll need to pay a few bills first thing. Why don't you do a little research on the Abbott family?"

"I thought we gave up on that. Keith said they were going to talk to the original painting's owner."

"He's long dead. His wife too."

"Oh."

"I'll send you what I have so far."

"So far?" Campbell stared at him. "You've already started digging on them?"

"It seemed like the thing to do. Keith has another big case—you heard about the credit union robbery?"

"Yeah."

"I don't think he's got much time for the painting thing, and it's lower priority, since the theft was so long ago. But we might be able to find something that would help him."

When they'd finished eating, Campbell went right to work on her assignments. She wanted to skip to the more interesting Abbott file, but she felt an obligation to close out the background checks first, both for the agency's reputation and her dad's satisfaction.

At last she finished and sent them to Bill for approval. She fixed herself a fresh cup of coffee and opened the file he'd started. The amount of information her father and Nick had collected in a couple of days amazed her. Until the court case came up, she had never heard of the artist whose painting was at the center of the controversy. Elroy Banitier had gained some fame and prestige during his lifetime but had died in 2001. His paintings definitely had a market, especially in the Ohio Valley.

Nick had logged a condensed article about the artist, and her dad had found results of auctions where a couple of Banitier's paintings had been sold.

Campbell also noted that the two had consulted a gallery owner in Paducah, who stated that a genuine Banitier at auction today would probably bring at least twenty thousand dollars and perhaps as much as fifty thousand, depending on the composition, size, and condition. In a gallery sale, the dealer said she would expect it to be priced at forty thousand or more.

Campbell sat back and thought about that. From what little she knew about Leila Abbott, fifty thousand dollars could be life-changing. Her attorney had told the jury she worked as a clerk in a gift shop, and Campbell imagined that she drew minimum wage or close to it. Leila was single and lived in a small apartment. A large influx of cash could help her upgrade her housing, if nothing else.

Nick came in, rummaged through his desk, talked to Bill for a few minutes, and left again. Campbell started work on a family tree to give her a better idea of who was affected by the elderly Mrs. Abbott's will.

About ten thirty, her dad ambled into the room.

"Hey, kiddo, Leila Abbott's attorney just called me. They'd like to meet with us."

Campbell blinked up at him. "You mean, she wants to hire us?"

"It's possible."

"Do you think the other heirs want to go after Leila, maybe sue her?"

He hesitated. "I didn't get that impression. I think she's really anxious to know how the painting got there. See, the court made them turn it over as evidence, and the police are probably going to give it back to the family of the person it was stolen from."

"I'm not sure I like that."

"Why not?"

"Do we have proof it was ever stolen?"

Bill smiled. "I love the way your mind works. There's plenty of proof that it was reported stolen at the time. Beyond that, you got me."

"The owners could have sold it to Mr. Abbott and filed the theft claim, hoping to get insurance money." True Blue Investigations handled several cases of that nature each year.

"That's always a possibility, but I'm not sure why Leila Abbott would care."

"To protect her grandfather's reputation?"

"Maybe. Let's listen to her and see what she's thinking."

Campbell nodded slowly.

"Good! Because she'll be here in ten minutes."

"What?" She jumped up and glanced around the room. No time to vacuum, or even to straighten up things. Actually, Rita did a pretty thorough job of keeping the office area clean. "Rita made cookies yesterday. Should I fix us some refreshments?"

"We always offer coffee and iced tea."

"Okay. Yeah."

The situation still felt a little bizarre. Campbell closed the computer file she'd had open and shoved the notebook she'd carried to the court-house into her desk drawer. Her hair. She hurried to the bathroom and brushed it. When she came out, she dashed toward the kitchen but heard the front door open at the end of the hallway behind her.

She turned as a young woman entered. It was Leila, all right.

"Hello," Campbell said.

"Hi. The sign said to walk in."

"That's right."

"I'm here to see Bill McBride. I'm Leila Abbott."

Campbell stepped forward, extending her hand. "I'm Campbell, Bill's daughter."

Leila grasped her fingers and appraised her. "My lawyer said you were on the jury. I'm sorry, but I don't remember you."

"I was there."

"And they kicked you off because you were a private investigator."

Startled, Campbell drew back. "No, actually it was because I'm friends with a police officer in town."

Leila frowned. "That's not what my lawyer told me."

Campbell froze for a moment, looking her over. Leila had an air of openness about her—and besides, why would she say something like that if it wasn't true? Brushing back a lock of hair, she said, "Well, my father's expecting you. Is Mr. Soule coming?"

"Yes, he'll be right along. We drove separately."

"May I bring you some coffee or iced tea?"

"Sweet tea would be great."

At that moment, her dad appeared in his doorway.

"Ms. Abbott? I guess you've met my daughter, Campbell."

Leila nodded.

"Do you mind if we meet out here?" Bill asked, waving toward the larger office, across the hall from his. "I'd like Campbell to sit in, if that's all right with you."

Leila shot a glance at Campbell then said, "Okay."

"I'll get the refreshments," Campbell said.

In the kitchen, she quickly fixed a tray with a plate of home-baked cookies, a glass of sweet iced tea and one sugar-free, and a mug of coffee for her dad. The two tumblers of iced tea were from a set that had different game birds on them. "I'm the pheasant," she muttered as she placed them carefully on the tray.

Carrying the tray warily down the hall, she heard a male voice that wasn't her dad's. At the office doorway, she paused as Bill led Leila's defense attorney across the room to the seating area. Campbell managed to reach the coffee table without spilling anything. Ignoring the twinges of anxiety she felt at meeting the defense attorney again, she straightened and faced him.

"Hello, Mr. Soule. May I get you some coffee or iced tea?"

"No, I'm good, Ms. McBride." His smile relieved her faint unease.

Leila was seated in one of the armchairs near the fireplace, and Bill had taken a place on the end of the sofa nearest her. Soule took the second armchair. Campbell handed the mallard glass to Leila.

"Here you go."

"Thanks."

Realizing she'd want to take notes, Campbell excused herself and strode to her desk for a notebook and pen. When she returned, she sat down with a smile.

"Did I miss anything?"

"No," Bill said. "We were just settling in."

Soule cleared his throat. "I called you because Leila feels strongly about the Banitier painting.

Since this agency has a good reputation among the local legal community, and since I knew Ms. McBride was familiar with the case, it seemed like a good fit."

"We appreciate it," Bill said.

Campbell glanced at him then spoke up. "So, there's no problem with my involvement?"

"None at all, since the case was closed," the lawyer said.

Leila leaned forward. "Mr. Soule thought you'd do a thorough job on this, and he apparently got some good recommendations."

"Oh?" Bill looked expectantly at Soule.

"It's nothing, really. A certain detective is a friend of one of my colleagues. He assured me that True Blue is the best in the area. And we should probably say no more about that."

Campbell's pulse picked up. This man was a friend of Keith? Keith hadn't said anything to her about it. Maybe he was a friend of a friend. Or maybe Soule meant Detective Smalley. And as for being the best in the area, it was true—they were. On the other hand, until this week, they'd been the only private investigation agency in Murray.

"Well, then," Bill said, "Ms. Abbott, why don't you tell us about your concerns—the painting, your family—all the things that combined to bring you here."

Leila sighed and then straightened her shoulders. "I wasn't trying to cheat anyone, honest.

I'll admit, when I first found the painting, I did consider keeping the whole thing a secret. But I don't do that sort of thing. Mostly, I didn't want everyone to get excited until I knew if that picture was really worth anything. See, my Uncle Jake—" She threw a look at Soule.

"It's all right," the lawyer said gently. "I'm sure the McBrides are discreet."

Leila nodded. "There were some dishes. Uncle Jake tried to take them first thing. He said Grandma wanted him to have them. Well, Grandma didn't say anything about that to me, and she didn't have it in her will. My mom was there when he said it, and she stood up to him. After he left, she said I'd better get those dishes appraised."

"And did you?" Bill asked.

"Yeah. There's a big group shop up in Paducah, and Ma knew about a place there with lots of old dishes. We took them up there. The lady told us what she'd give for them if we were selling them wholesale—because she'd have to resell them, you know—and also what she thought they'd bring retail."

"Did you sell them?"

Leila nodded. "I called my cousins and my sister, and they all wanted to sell. So then I called Uncle Jake. He was furious."

Bill said to Robert Soule, "Did you handle Mrs. Abbott's estate?"

"No, I do mostly criminal work. Ms. Abbott—Leila—hired me to defend her when charges were brought against her for stealing the painting."

"I see," Bill said.

Leila gave him the name of the attorney who'd drawn up her grandmother's will, and Campbell remembered the woman's testimony.

"I asked her about it before I even took the dishes to Paducah," Leila said. "She told me it was totally my decision, and I didn't have to ask the others. But I did it anyway. That seemed fair. But Uncle Jake made such a stink that when I found the painting, I decided not to announce it until I knew if it was valuable."

"Makes sense to me," Bill said with an easy smile.

"Thanks. But that's what got me in trouble, I guess. Not telling anyone else I'd found it and was going to have it valued."

"But you did sell the dishes?" Campbell asked.

"Yes. The dealer who appraised them knew about an auction that was coming up. She said that if we put them in the auction, we might get more than she'd told me. So I told the others I wanted to do that. Uncle Jake wasn't happy, but the others agreed. We got a little over two thousand dollars for the whole batch of dishes, which was more than she'd quoted me for the wholesale price."

"How much of that did your uncle receive?" Bill asked.

"A third of the total, after the auctioneer's fee. And I split the rest five ways for my three cousins, my sister, and me. It wasn't a lot for each of us, but hey, it was a couple hundred bucks apiece that we didn't have before."

"Was this before you found the painting?"

"I found the painting a few days after the first blowup with Uncle Jake. I got all shaky just thinking about what he'd do, so I kept quiet about the painting. I just wanted to find out more about it and not give him a chance to get mad at me." Leila took a gulp of her iced tea.

Bill sighed. "Sounds as if you were feeling some pressure."

"I was. Pressure to do things his way and let him take charge. But I didn't. My mom stood by me on that, and Grandma's lawyer—well, she didn't really want to get into it, but she did tell me twice that disposal of those things was my decision, so long as all the heirs got their share of the proceeds."

Chapter 6

Campbell mulled over what Leila had told them so far. She'd never seen the uncle, and she didn't think she wanted to. She sipped her tea, still thinking about it as her father went on with the questions.

"Tell me about the day you found the painting," Bill said.

"Okay." Leila set down her glass. "I went over to Grandma's house with some empty boxes and trash bags. Uncle Jake's truck was parked in the driveway, and when I went inside, he was there."

"Did he have a key?" Bill asked.

"Yeah. I think Grandma gave him one a long time ago. Either that, or he had one made at some point."

"Did he help with her care?"

"Not really. It was mostly me, but my cousin Anna helped quite a bit, and my mom, too, now and then. We all loved Grandma."

"I'm sure you did. So, what did Jacob do when you went into the house?"

"I asked what he was doing there, and he said he came over to see if any repairs needed to be done before we gave the keys back to the landlord. He said if there was damage, we wouldn't get

Grandma's deposit back." Leila glanced at the attorney.

Soule said, "Since Ms. Abbott hired me, I've examined the lease. Apparently there was a deposit of five hundred dollars when the Abbotts first moved in."

Bill nodded, and Campbell wrote it down. It was a fairly small amount, and she was surprised Jacob Abbott was willing to invest in repairs in order to recover it.

"Uncle Jacob said he didn't find anything that needed fixing, and he left." Leila sat still for a moment, her lips pressed together. "Then . . . then I found the door to the attic stairway was open a little bit."

"And that was unusual?" Bill said.

"Yes. I'd only ever been up there a couple of times, once when Grandma wanted something that was stored in the attic, and once when she had me carry up a box of canning jars. She said she probably would never use them again, but she wasn't ready to get rid of them, so I put them up there for her."

Everyone fell silent, and after a few seconds, Campbell said softly, "Do you think your uncle went up there to look for damages to repair?"

Leila looked over at her bleakly. "Not really. At first I wondered, but when I went up to look, I saw that an old trunk and some boxes had been opened. I think he was looking for valuable stuff he could take without me knowing about it."

"Were you suspicious of your uncle before that?" Bill asked.

"Kind of. One time about a year ago, Grandma started fretting about Grandpa's old stamp collection. She said it wasn't worth a lot, but she wanted to look at it, and she couldn't find it. I asked my cousins about it, and they had no clue. So I asked Uncle Jake. He denied knowing anything about it, but he said something like, 'Oh, she probably stuck it up in the attic and forgot about it.' Well, I wasn't convinced, but Grandma's health started failing seriously, and I let it go."

"Did you ever find the stamp collection?"

Leila shook her head.

"Not even when you cleaned out the house after she died?"

"No. And I wouldn't be surprised if other things were missing. I'm only twenty-three, and I'm sure there was stuff in that house I either didn't know about or didn't remember. But I was uneasy that day—the day I found the door ajar, so I went up to the attic and rummaged around. That's when I found the painting. It was wrapped in an old sheet, back behind a bunch of boxes and other stuff."

"Had you ever seen it before?"

"Never. I don't even know now if Grandma knew it was there. If she did, she never mentioned it to me."

"But how could it be there without her knowing?" Campbell asked.

Leila heaved a big sigh and slumped in her chair. "I don't know. Maybe she did. Or maybe it was in the house when they rented it."

"Surely the owner wouldn't leave something that valuable in the rental," Bill said.

"Maybe not, unless he thought it was worthless. Anyway, I know Grandma hardly ever went up there, at least in the last ten years. If she didn't put it there, I guess the only other option is that Grandpa did. But I wouldn't have thought he'd put something like that up there without telling Grandma."

Bill nodded slowly. "Do you remember your grandfather?"

"Barely. I was about five when he died. He used to smoke. I remember him sitting in their living room and lighting up. Grandma would scold him and tell him he shouldn't smoke when we kids were there."

Campbell's mind raced. "You said you were suspicious of your uncle. Was he suspicious of you?"

"I didn't think so at the time, but now I wonder. He may have thought I wanted to take things without telling the rest of them. He was still mad about the dishes. He probably wanted to make sure I didn't find something else valuable and dispose of it without his consent—or without him even knowing it existed."

"But he didn't find the painting," Bill pointed out.

"True. I think he was up there when I drove in and heard my car arrive, so he came downstairs to meet me without finishing his look around. But once the painting's existence became common knowledge, he seemed to think I was hiding it from him and my cousins. I know it was one of my cousins who called the police, but Uncle Jake may have stirred them up and planted the idea in their minds."

"Why would he do that?" Campbell asked. "Why not make the complaint himself?"

"I figure it was to keep his nose clean. He didn't want to look like the bad guy, but he sure did want to stick it to me. Several times he insinuated that I was hiding other stuff."

"From the estate, you mean?" Bill asked.

"Yes. Grandma wasn't rich. We all knew that. And yet, she had those beautiful old dishes, and here's this super valuable painting in her attic. Maybe there were other things he'd taken over the years, and he didn't want anyone looking at him too closely."

Campbell frowned. "From what I heard in the courtroom, I thought your cousins didn't know anything about the painting until you were arrested."

"That's right. I called my mom. I asked her not to tell my sister Danielle."

"Danielle's in college in Louisville," Mr. Soule put in.

"That's right," Leila said. "I didn't want to upset her, and she couldn't help me in that situation. So, Ma said she'd come down to the police station and get me. But before she left, Anna called her to ask about the cleaning session we'd planned that day, and Ma told her the police took me away."

"So your mother bailed you out?" Bill asked.

"Yeah. She came over to the police station and did some paperwork. They told her how to arrange it. The bail wasn't that high, and she agreed to pay it, with the understanding that I'd pay her back."

"And did you pay her back?"

Leila nodded, holding his gaze. "It was five hundred dollars. Not much, like I said. I mean . . . it's like a week's pay, but I did have that much. I was totally embarrassed, and I didn't want anyone else to know, but she'd already told Anna. By the time we got home, the whole family knew."

"So, by the time the police came into it, you'd already taken the painting to two dealers," Bill said.

She nodded. "I was shocked when I first found that painting. I didn't dare believe it was valuable. But after the second dealer told me it was probably worth quite a bit, I was going to tell the others. I still wasn't ready to tell Uncle Jake, though. I thought I'd start with my mom and Anna. I knew Anna would tell her husband and her two brothers. But I wasn't sure how to handle Uncle Jake. I sort of wanted to have the sale arranged before I told him."

Bill sat back in his chair. "As I understand it, you would like us to find out the circumstances surrounding the painting's theft a couple of decades ago and how it got into your grand-parents' attic. Is that right?"

"Yeah. I always assumed they owned that house until a couple of years ago, when Grandma's health started going downhill and I started helping her pay bills. She told me that she knew she couldn't stay there forever. But I thought we should help her keep her home as long as we could."

"How much care did you do for your grand-mother?"

"I went over nearly every day, after I got off work. Anna went at least once a week. She'd do a little cooking and some laundry. Mom ran errands and brought meals to Grandma now and then. Between us, we took Grandma to her appoint-ments."

"What did you do?"

"Everything else. Shopping, cleaning, all of that. I made sure the rent got paid, and the other bills. I think that's why Grandma made me the executrix. I knew her situation and her finances and everything. But I also spent a lot of quiet time with her. We used to play cards in the evening, and when her eyes got bad she liked me to read to her. I set up an audiobook account for her, too, so she could listen to books when I wasn't there."

"You managed to keep her in her home until she died. That's quite an accomplishment," Bill said.

"Thanks. She was only in the hospital for a few days, then a nursing home for a couple of weeks. We thought she'd pull through, so I paid her rent for the next month. But then Grandma died." Her mouth skewed, and her eyes crinkled.

Campbell hopped up and brought her a box of tissues.

"Thank you." Leila took one and wiped her eyes. "When she went, there was almost a month left that was paid for. The landlord asked us to clean the place out by then."

"At least you had a few weeks." Campbell patted her shoulder and resumed her seat.

"I guess you know everything now." Leila sighed. "We decided to wait until after the funeral to clean up. The service was on a Saturday, and I had to work the next week. Anna did, too, but her hours are more flexible than mine. Anyway, we decided to wait until the next Saturday. Mom agreed to come, too, and Anna's husband, Pete, said he'd come with his pickup to haul stuff, once we decided where to take it."

Leila sniffed and was silent for a moment.

"So, you all got together on Saturday?" Campbell prodded.

"Yeah. But a few days before that, I had the creepy run-in with Uncle Jake and found the painting. Mom and Anna and I finally got the house cleaned out, and we didn't find anything else worth having evaluated. We held a big sale and donated what was left over." She let out a big sigh. "Then the whole thing broke, with the police coming to my house about that stupid painting."

Bill said, "I can see that it's important to you to get to the bottom of this."

Leila nodded. "Because I really need to know how that painting got in Grandma's attic, and who stole it in the first place. To speak plainly, Mr. McBride, I want to know if my grandfather was a thief."

"The police still have the painting in evidence?" Campbell asked.

"Yes. I doubt we'll ever get it back."

Campbell sighed. She'd really like to see it. It wasn't displayed in court the days she was there. Had the rest of the jury seen it after she left?

"There's no way they'll let you take possession of it and sell it now," Bill said. "The official view is that it never belonged to you."

"But can you find out who it does rightfully belong to?" Tears pooled in Leila's eyes. "Mostly I want to know how we got it and—and about Grandpa. How much will it cost me, Mr. McBride?"

Bill told her their daily and hourly rates and gave her an estimate. "It all depends on how many hours we have to put in. What do you say we take this on for three days' worth of work? If we haven't resolved it by then, we can talk about whether or not you want us to continue. Of course, if we find any answers before then, we'll give them to you right away."

She sniffled and nodded. "Thank you. I set aside what money I did get from the estate, and I think I could handle three days. And—and my mom might help if it takes longer."

Leila signed a contract making the hire official, and Soule had promised to email Bill everything he had on the case. Campbell followed them as her father escorted them to the door.

Soule hung back a moment and said to Bill, "Thanks for doing this, Mr. McBride. I told Leila I'd come with her gratis this morning because I want to see this tied up—and I wanted to make sure she was in good hands."

"You can depend on us." Bill shook the attorney's hand.

"Oh, that reminds me." Soule smiled. "A woman came to my office yesterday and left her business card. Chilton, I think was her name. Do you know her?"

Bill frowned. "New investigator in town. So, she's trying to drum up business?"

"Apparently. But I'm sure you have far more experience than her, and an established reputation. I don't think you need to worry too much."

"Thanks." Bill closed the door behind them. He turned to face his daughter. "Well, Soup, what do you think?"

"About Marissa Chilton going around to lawyers and trying to scrape up business?"

"No, I meant about Leila Abbott's case."

"Hard to say. Do you think everything she said was the truth?"

He considered for a moment. "Probably. At least, she thinks it is."

"What if she really did intend to sell it and keep the money herself?"

"I don't know. Maybe we'll find out more when we've talked to the people involved."

"Where do we start?" It all seemed like a huge jumble to Campbell.

"Teresa Abbott's landlord, I think. His address should be in the files Soule's sending me. Type up your notes, and I'll open a case file. I want to go over it all once more, then we'll begin."

Half an hour later, Bill received the electronic files and integrated them with his own. Campbell fixed a quick lunch, and they set off in her father's

82

car. The owner of the house Teresa Abbott had occupied for many years, Brad Standish, lived within the city limits, and they soon parked in front of his house.

"New construction," Campbell murmured as they left the car and walked up the driveway.

"Within the last ten years, I'd say." Bill surveyed the dwelling and the yard.

Campbell knew her dad was taking in every detail, and she wondered what he saw that she hadn't yet noticed. The trees had lost their foliage for the winter, but she thought she spotted a redbud and an oak. The attached garage had only one wide door. Overall, the house seemed well maintained.

Her father rang the doorbell, and they stood waiting for someone to open it.

"I thought you called him," Campbell said after a moment.

"I did. He's expecting us." Bill pressed the bell again.

"Maybe he's in the backyard," Campbell suggested when no one came to the door.

"In December?" Bill knocked firmly on the door, though they'd both heard the muffled bell when he rang it. "Brad Standish? It's Bill McBride, Mr. Standish."

The porch wrapped around the right side of the house, and Campbell strolled to the corner. No one was out there, and she couldn't see anyone beyond it, in the visible portion of the backyard. She glanced back at her dad. He was tapping his cell phone. When he put it to his ear, she waited.

Bill frowned. "Not answering."

Campbell walked along the side porch to a window and leaned close. She could see between the drapes into a bright living room with what appeared to be a fairly new sofa and armchairs set, Shaker style end tables and coffee table, and built-in shelves that housed books, vases, and framed photos.

"I can't see anybody inside," she called. She was about to walk onward to the end of the porch, so she could look over the railing and see more of the backyard, when she heard tires on the driveway. She hastened to her father's side, and they were both standing by the front door smiling when a middle-aged woman got out of the car and approached.

"Hi," Bill said. "I'm here to see Brad Standish."

"I'm his wife, Colleen," she replied. "Brad should be inside."

"Well, I've rung and knocked, but he hasn't answered." Bill turned on the charm. "Maybe you can tell him we're here. I'm Bill McBride, and this is my daughter."

"Of course." Mrs. Standish reached for the doorknob, but it didn't turn for her. "*Hmm.* That's odd. Maybe he's in the shower, but he did know you were coming. He told me that when I got back from downtown, you'd probably be here." As she talked, she took a keyring from her purse and sorted for the house key. She inserted it into the keyhole, turned it, and flung the door open. "There we go."

Bill and Campbell followed her inside.

"You have a lovely home," Campbell said, looking around in appreciation at the tasteful decorations.

"Thank you. We moved over here two years ago." Mrs. Standish stepped into the living room. "Sit down, won't you? I'll see if I can track down Brad for you."

She strode from the room with her jacket over her arm and breezed up the stairs. "Brad?" she called softly. Five seconds later, she shrieked.

Chapter 7

Bill McBride charged out of the room and up the stairs. Startled, Campbell followed, her heart racing. When she reached the upstairs landing, Mrs. Standish was standing in a doorway, a hand to her mouth. Bill wasn't in sight. Campbell slowed her steps and approached the woman.

"Mrs. Standish? Is something wrong?"

The woman stared at her, wordless, her mouth hanging open, and pointed into the nearest room.

Campbell stepped gingerly over the threshold into a cozy study. Her father was kneeling on the floor near an oak rolltop desk beside the sprawled form of a man. Cautiously, Campbell went to his side.

"Dad?"

Bill glanced up. "Call an ambulance. But it may be too late." He had been holding the man's wrist, trying to find a pulse. Now he shifted his fingers to Standish's neck.

Campbell pulled her cell from her pocket and hit 911.

"We need an ambulance quickly," she told the dispatcher. Briefly, she described Standish's position on the floor.

"I'm not getting a pulse," Bill said.

"And we don't think he has a pulse," Campbell added into the phone.

"Now call Keith," Bill said.

Campbell muted her phone. "She wants me to stay on with her."

Bill shifted and handed her his own cell. "Give me yours. Take mine and go outside and call Keith. Watch for the ambulance."

She traded phones with him. As she headed for the door, Bill unmuted hers and explained to the dispatcher who he was.

When she reached the doorway, Mrs. Standish grabbed Campbell's sleeve. "Is he—"

"I don't know." Campbell swallowed hard. "I'm going down to guide the EMTs up here when they arrive."

"Thank you." The woman let her go and stood helplessly looking in at Bill and her inert husband.

Campbell jogged down the stairs and through the entry. Outside, she hurried down the driveway and positioned herself beside the Standishes' mailbox. She couldn't hear a siren yet. Bringing up her father's frequent contacts, she found Keith near the top, right below herself and Nick. She tapped the little phone icon by Keith's name and listened as it rang.

"Keith Fuller. That you, Bill?"

"No, It's Campbell. Keith, we've got an emergency."

"Your dad?"

"No, he's fine. It's the landlord in the Abbott case—he owns the house Teresa Abbott lived in.

We came to interview him, and he's lying on the floor unconscious. I've called an ambulance, and Dad's with him now. But, Keith, he may already be dead."

"You say he's in his own home?"

"Yes." She gave him the address. "His wife let us in. He knew we were coming, but he didn't answer the door. She'd been out, and she came home while we were wondering what to do."

"Okay, I'm on my way. You and Bill stay there."

Campbell caught a wailing. "I think the ambulance is almost here."

"I'll see you soon," Keith assured her.

The ambulance approached, and Campbell stepped into the street and waved her arms. The driver cut the siren and slowed. She moved out of the way, and he drove in. She followed them up the drive until they stopped.

A woman of about thirty-five got out on the passenger side. With relief, Campbell recognized Kate Maxey from another brush with EMTs.

"Kate! Thanks for coming so fast. He's inside."

Kate and her partner hauled out their gear, peppering Campbell with questions.

"Last I knew, Dad couldn't get a pulse."

She swung the front door open, and they hustled inside. Campbell led them upstairs. Colleen was still in the upper hallway, wringing her hands.

"This is Mrs. Standish," Campbell said. "He's in there." She pointed to the study doorway and let the EMTs go in then walked slowly over to Colleen. "I'm so sorry you're going through this. Is there anything I can do for you?"

"You're already helping. I just—" Her voice faded.

"Maybe you should sit down." Campbell touched her shoulder lightly. "Would you like to come downstairs?"

Colleen looked nervously toward the study. "I can't. Not until I know about Brad. Your father—"

Her dad came out of the room and stopped in front of Colleen. "I'm sorry, Mrs. Standish."

She blinked at him. "Are they going to put him in the ambulance? I should get over to the hospital."

"No," Bill said gently. "I'm afraid they can't take him. He's gone."

With a gasp, she turned away.

Bill turned to Campbell with a sigh. "We should go down and brief Keith when he gets here."

"I don't think we ought to leave her alone," Campbell whispered.

"You stay with her then. I'll go and meet Keith." He walked wearily down the stairs.

"Mrs. Standish." Campbell touched her arm, and she pivoted toward her. "Let's go downstairs, shall we?"

"What happens next?" Tears filled her bleak eyes.

"They'll ask for a medical examiner. It might

be some time before he gets here. Is there anyone I can call for you? Do you have family nearby?"

"My son. But he'll be at work."

"Can we call him at work?"

She hesitated.

"This is very important," Campbell said.

"Yes. Of course. This way." She led Campbell down the hall and into a large, airy bedroom. Picking up the receiver of a landline phone on the nightstand, she pushed a few buttons. "Dylan? Yes. You need to come over here. It's your father. He's—he's dead." Tears streamed down her face. "Just come home." She replaced the receiver and stood motionless, as if stunned.

Campbell heard the EMTs going down the stairs and faint voices from below. She stepped closer and put an arm around Colleen's shoulders. "Do you want to lie down?"

She shook her head.

"Then let's go downstairs. The police are probably here now."

"Wh-why the police? I understand about the medical examiner, but . . ."

"An unattended death."

"Ah."

As if that settled everything, Mrs. Standish walked stiffly out of the bedroom and along the hall to the staircase. Campbell followed her, trying not to hover too close but fearing the woman might collapse at any moment.

In the entry below, her father was talking to Keith and Detective Matt Jackson. When the victim's wife reached the last step, Bill said, "Mrs. Standish, these are Detectives Fuller and Jackson from the Murray Police Department. If you and Campbell would sit down for a moment in the living room, I'll take the detectives upstairs. Is there anyone you'd like—"

"She called her son," Campbell said. "He's coming over."

Bill nodded and headed upstairs with Keith and Matt on his heels.

"Come on." Campbell waved a hand toward the living room.

"I think I'd be more comfortable in the kitchen."

"That's fine. I can make you a cup of tea, or whatever would go down well for you right now."

They walked into the kitchen, and Campbell immediately felt a flash of jealousy. The kitchen in their old house had perhaps been updated thirty years ago, but this one was marvelous, with up-to-date appliances, a work island topped with gorgeous tile, and a glass patio door leading out onto a deck and a huge backyard.

Colleen sank onto a stool at the island. "There's tea in the fridge."

Campbell opened the door and saw a glass pitcher of iced tea with floating slices of lemon, worthy of a photo in a homemaking magazine. She set it out on the counter. Her hostess had turned to gaze back the way they'd come, so she cautiously opened a couple of upper cabinet doors and found the glassware. A minute later, she carried a tumbler of tea to Colleen and placed it in her hand.

"Oh, thank you." She sniffed and looked around. Campbell followed her gaze to a box of tissues on the counter and hurried over to fetch it.

"Here you go."

"Thanks. I'm sorry." Colleen yanked out a tissue and swabbed it over her cheeks then wiped her nose.

"No need to be sorry," Campbell said.

"Mom?" a loud voice carried down the hall.

Colleen shifted on her stool. "In here, Dylan."

A young man wearing a shirt and tie under his winter jacket, his rumpled hair the only thing marring his handsome features, strode into the room. He went to Colleen and gave her a hug. "What happened?"

"I don't know. I went to the store, and when I got home, this young lady was here, with her father. They came to see Brad. But he hadn't come to the door, so I let them in. And he was up in his study—dead." She stared bleakly into her son's eyes. "They've sent for the medical examiner, and there are police detectives up there."

"What?" Dylan shot a questioning glance at Campbell.

"That's right," Campbell said. "I'm very sorry."

Dylan shook his head. "I just—I can't believe it. Did anyone try to revive him?"

"EMTs came," Colleen said vaguely.

"I think he was beyond that," Campbell said softly. "Oh, here's my dad. He may be able to tell us more."

Bill walked into the kitchen and darted a quick look around.

"Dad, this is Colleen's son, Dylan."

"Hi. Bill McBride." Her father shook Dylan's hand.

"You came to visit my dad?" Dylan asked.

"Yes. We had an appointment."

Dylan frowned. "What happened to him?"

"We don't know for sure, but when your mother let us in, he had already passed away."

"But—" Dylan jerked around and stared at his mother. "How long were you gone? He couldn't have been lying there long."

"I was gone a couple of hours," Colleen said. "I met Maureen for brunch, and then we went shopping." She sobbed and clutched a tissue to her face, her shoulders heaving.

Resting a hand on her shoulder, Dylan looked at Bill. "Why are the police here?"

Bill lowered his voice. "They need to be sure it was a—a natural death."

Dylan's face blanched. "You mean . . . Is there any doubt?"

"There might be."

"What—"

"Let's let the police discuss that with you. I'm very sorry, Mr. Standish, but I'm glad we were here to help your mother. Now that you're with her, I think my daughter and I should leave."

"Wait! How do I know—how can I get in touch with you?"

Campbell expected her father to whip out a True Blue Investigations card and hand it to him. Instead, he told the young man, "Detective Fuller can tell you that if you need to contact us later." He looked pointedly at Campbell. "We should go."

"Yes." She straightened, feeling awkward. Normally, she'd tell the distraught woman beside her to call if she needed anything at all, but it seemed her dad wasn't crazy about giving out their contact information. She pressed Colleen's wrist for a moment. "Again, I'm very sorry."

She and her father let themselves out as Dylan alternated between swearing and making clumsy attempts to comfort his mother.

"Why didn't you give him a card?" Campbell asked as soon as the door closed behind them.

"He seemed to have no clue why we were there, and I'm not sure Mrs. Standish did either. If I'd told him we were private detectives, that would have brought on a rash of questions. He needs to get his information from the police, not from us. It's in our client's best interest to keep quiet around other people."

Our client. Campbell had almost forgotten for a few minutes that they'd come to this house as employees of Leila Abbott. The Standishes had owned the house where Leila's grandmother lived. Did Colleen even know about the painting? Surely her husband had told her. But perhaps not the son. She shook her head.

"You're right. I had lost some of my focus in there. It was quite a shock."

They'd reached the car. Bill clicked his remote to unlock it, and they both got in.

"I don't know if you saw, but there was some blood," he said. "Not a lot, but enough to make me think he didn't die of a heart attack."

"What then?"

Bill's face tightened. "Shot, maybe? I'm not sure."

She caught her breath. "Okay, so now what?"

"We wait for Keith to do his job. Maybe later he'll be able to tell us something. I told him about our appointment, so maybe he'll be willing to share."

"But we asked for the appointment, not Standish."

"Yeah." He made a face and started the engine. "We may have to wait a few days and then talk to Mrs. Standish again. I assume she and her husband owned the rental house together."

"But we don't know how much she had to do with the tenants." Campbell raised her eyebrows. "Hey, maybe we should ask Leila. She must have dealt with the Standishes at some point. I mean. Didn't she pay her Grandma's bills?"

"Yes, and that's a good thought. Let's see if we can talk to her about it."

"She must have known who he was," Campbell said.

"I can't speculate, but it seems as though she didn't have much personal interaction with him. We can ask her about that."

Chapter 8

Nick was coming from the kitchen with a thick sandwich on a plate when they returned home.

"Hope you don't mind," he said with his rascally smile. "I brought chips."

"If we've got food, you're always welcome to help yourself," Bill said.

Campbell would not have been so amenable, but she could hardly contradict her dad. Besides, Nick was already wolfing the sandwich down. She and her father had already eaten, but that was two hours ago. They went to the kitchen, and she fixed herself some crackers and cheese. Bill opted for a piece of leftover pie, and they carried their plates into the dining room, where Nick sat at the table with an open bag of sour cream and onion chips before him.

"So, boss," he said as Bill settled in with his pie and glass of iced tea, "I finished up my assignment, and I was looking at those files you put in the Abbott case folder."

"Right. The attorney sent me those. Find anything interesting?"

Bill had already seen the files, and Campbell knew he wouldn't miss anything obvious within them, but he often treated his younger colleagues as students, letting them figure out for themselves what was important. As a former teacher, she appreciated that, though sometimes she got frustrated and wished he would just tell them the salient points.

"Well," Nick said with half a mouthful of chips. He chewed, swallowed, and took a drink from a plastic bottle of Coke. "It seemed like the uncle, Jacob Abbott, was a pretty suspicious character. He went against Leila in some of her decisions—didn't like the way she was handling the estate."

"I think that's accurate," Bill said. "He definitely wanted the assets distributed quickly, and he objected to time-consuming valuations of things Leila thought could be worth a significant amount."

"And he got a third of everything."

Bill nodded and took a bite of his pie.

"The estate wasn't that big," Campbell said. "Mrs. Abbott didn't own her house, and her savings were minimal. She was on Social Security."

"Uh-huh." Nick took a generous handful of chips and held the bag out toward her with a questioning look.

"No, thanks." Campbell concentrated on her crackers. They'd had leftovers for their early lunch, and she wished Rita was there to cook for them again today. They'd made arrangements with the per diem housekeeper to come in twice a week, starting on Monday. Campbell could hardly wait. Rita's cooking was far superior to her own, or to most of the take-out meals they frequently consumed.

"So, anyway," Nick said, "I thought I'd take a closer look at Jacob Abbott. Seems he's got a record. Most recently, drug possession, but before that, he's got a string of thefts and— *ta-da*—an insurance fraud case."

"You don't say." Bill took a sip of his tea.

Campbell wondered if this was old news to her father, but surely he'd have put it in the file if he'd known. She hadn't had time to go over the files Soule had sent them, and her dad had probably done only a quick run-through.

"I linked it to the folder." Nick was clearly looking for praise, and Bill obliged.

"Nice work. I'll look at it after lunch."

Nick smiled. "So, what did y'all find out this morning?"

"We found a dead body," Campbell said.

Nick's jaw dropped.

Campbell looked at her father to see his reaction. She hadn't intended to steal his thunder, but she couldn't resist.

"Really?" Nick stared at her for a moment, then turned back to Bill, as if waiting for him to laugh and deny her statement.

"Yeah, we did." Bill took another bite of his pie.

"Unbelievable!" Nick shook his head and

turned to Campbell in accusation. "How do you do it?"

"Do what?" She tried to sound innocent, but she knew what he meant. This wasn't the first body she'd found. "You do it too."

His face scrunched up. "That one time. And you were with me."

She shrugged. "Do you think we should go talk to Mr. Abbott next?"

"Maybe so," Bill said.

Nick got that hangdog expression. "This time, can I go with?"

Her father caught Campbell's eye with just a flicker of inquiry.

"I wouldn't mind staying here this afternoon," she said. "I can catch up on those files Mr. Soule sent and maybe do a little more digging on the rest of the family."

"Good idea," Bill said. "We don't know much about Cathy Abbott, Leila's mother. I think her sister's out of it. She's off at college. But then there are the three cousins."

"Anna, Blaine, and Corey," Campbell said. "Yeah, we should definitely find out more about them."

"Wait a sec," Nick said. "You found a dead guy. I assume it was the landlord. You went to see him this morning, right?"

"That's right." Bill launched into an explanation of what they'd found at the Standish house, and

Campbell placidly stacked sliced cheddar on her crackers and ate them.

"So Keith's on it?" Nick asked.

"He and Matt Jackson were both there when we left," Bill said. "I thought we'd give them a little space to do their job. We'll know soon enough if they find any evidence of who did it."

"You're pretty sure it was a homicide then?"

"I didn't see a weapon, and believe me, I looked while we waited for the EMTs to get there."

Campbell thought about that. "So it wasn't suicide or accidental."

"Probably not," her father corrected. "I suppose it's possibly an accident, but that seems very unlikely."

"All right. I'm ready to go see Mr. Abbott," Nick said. He threw a hopeful look at Campbell. "Unless you've got more of that pie."

"I think Dad got the last piece, but there are still some of Rita's cookies in the cupboard."

Nick grinned and hopped up, snagged his plate and soda bottle, and disappeared toward the kitchen.

"That kid's got a cast iron stomach," Bill muttered.

Campbell refrained from commenting on the multiple cups of coffee he drank daily.

"What about Standish, though?" she asked. "We may never find out his angle. He may have known about the painting. In fact, he could have put it there without the Abbotts ever knowing."

"Yes. Well, we'll see how forthcoming Jacob Abbott is. If he won't talk to us, we'll have to come at this a different way. But we need to give Colleen Standish some time before we try to get any more out of her."

"I agree. She was in shock today."

"Yes. I'm glad her son arrived when he did."

Campbell drew an uneasy breath. "I don't think Dylan knows anything about the situation."

"He must have heard about it if he lives in town. The court case, at least."

"But would he know his father was involved?"

Bill shrugged. "The story's been in the *Ledger and Times*, and it was on the local news out of Paducah one evening. But I suppose he might not realize the people were tenants of his father's. He wasn't called to testify, was he?"

"Not while I was in court. Did Brad Standish own other rental houses?"

"I haven't had time to look into it. You could do some checking this afternoon."

"Would Nell Calhoun be a good person to ask?"

"Check our online sites involving real estate titles first. But yeah, she might know something."

Nick came in from the kitchen with his mouth full and two cookies in his hand.

"Ready?" Bill pushed back his chair.

Nick nodded and swallowed. "I'll get my laptop."

They were gone in two minutes, taking Bill's Camry, and the house settled into profound quiet. Campbell put the dirty dishes in the dishwasher and wiped down the counter where Nick had made a sandwich. As she ambled toward her desk, her cell rang. Keith.

"Hi," she said with a big smile that raised her inflection.

"Hey there," Keith said. "Just wondered how you and Bill are doing. We didn't get a chance to say boo this morning."

"That's the job. But we're fine. Dad and Nick just left to go and see if they can talk to Jacob Abbott. I'm here to browse for information on the Abbott family and poke around Brad Standish's business. Do you know if the Abbotts' house was his only rental?"

"I don't. We didn't get into that with Mrs. Standish. I recommended that her son call their family practitioner. She was pretty shook up."

"You can't blame her."

"No."

"Listen, I know you're not the M.E.," Campbell said, "but Dad says he thinks that was homicide and that he didn't see any sign of a weapon in the room. But he did see some blood."

"Yes, a chest wound. We didn't find anything either, but I'm telling you that on the Q.T."

"Sure. I understand."

"It looked like a gunshot wound."

"Hmm."

"Yeah," Keith said. "We've got a lot of work to do on this one. Matt and I are grabbing a late lunch."

"Are you going to keep working together on the case?"

"Unless something else comes up that one of us has to handle."

"I thought you were investigating the credit union robbery."

"That's mostly done. We got security video of the robber, and he's in custody." He paused. "So, are you glad you're not in court today?"

"Yes."

"I love you."

Her heartbeat sped up. "Same here. It's so comforting to know you're out there and that you feel that way about me."

"If the job gets too rough for you, or too depressing . . ."

"No, I'm good. I'd say it's usually boring, but we've seen quite a bit of action since I started working with Dad."

"You sure have. But my job's that way too. Some days are all paperwork or research or sitting in court. Others are . . . well, like today."

She chuckled. "I'm praying for you. I know your job is stressful." A question they'd all wondered about flitted through her mind. "Keith, do you know who that painting belongs to now?

104

I heard on the news that it was owned by a man named Nelson."

"That's right. David Nelson, otherwise known around here as 'the tobacco millionaire.' He died ten or twelve years ago."

"So, who inherited from him?"

"Well, he has children, but it seems he wanted that painting to go to a museum."

"He wanted it to go? Does that mean it wasn't designated in his will?"

"You got it. The kids say that was just a whim, and if he'd truly wanted that, he'd have put it in writing. I went back to the old records that tell about when the theft was investigated."

"Did he live here in Murray?"

"Yes. He owned a lot of land in Calloway County and some in Marshall. The theft happened before I was a detective. In his statement, Mr. Nelson said he was planning to donate the painting to a museum in Louisville. He'd actually talked to a representative of the museum. He told his kids about it, and it was stolen that night."

Campbell let out a puff of air. "Well, that's pretty conclusive, isn't it? That he meant to donate it, I mean. He'd contacted the museum already."

"Yes, but when the detectives on the case contacted the museum, the curator said they'd had a phone conversation about it as a possibility. He wasn't sure if Mr. Nelson had made up his mind. And that curator retired three years later."

"So, what now?"

"There are four children, all equal heirs. Three of them want to donate it to the museum."

"And the fourth?"

"Is the executor."

"Oh, brother. This sounds more and more like the Abbott case."

"It *is* the Abbott case," Keith said. "But I know what you mean. I told my folks that if they dared to make me their executor, I'd move to Argentina."

Campbell laughed. "I'm afraid I'm stuck with the job for my dad, but at least I don't have any hard-headed siblings to deal with."

"My folks named Nicole, and when the time comes, I'll remember how I bullied them into it and do whatever Nic wants."

The things Keith had told Campbell nudged her into new paths of research. She browsed the websites of art museums in Louisville and found that one already owned two paintings by Elroy Banitier. Keith hadn't said as much, but she suspected this was the one David Nelson had contacted about his prospective donation.

Next she delved into the Nelson family and found the names of all four children in his obituary. This led her to other sites, where she gleaned bits of information. She added them to the file on Leila's case. An hour had passed. Nick and her dad must have found Jacob Abbott. Was he cooperative or belligerent?

With a sigh, she turned to the real estate question. She soon learned that Brad Standish owned three rental houses in Calloway County, and one apartment building that held four units. To her surprise, she found that Colleen's name was not on the deeds.

Again she noted the time. A wave of apprehension went through her as she recalled the tragic ending to the interview she and Bill had attempted that morning. What was keeping Nick and her father?

Bill pulled up in front of a small hotel. It was in a quiet neighborhood, and their website declared it was cozy and secure, with twelve comfortable, immaculate rooms. He and Nick got out of the car and sauntered into the small lobby. No one was at the front desk, so Bill rang the bell.

After a short delay, a woman in a cotton housekeeper's uniform appeared from a hallway.

"May I help you?" She stepped behind the desk.

"We're here to see Jacob Abbott."

"He took a late lunch today, I'm afraid. He should be back by two."

Bill glanced at his cell. It was twenty minutes till. "And when does he get off?"

"The shift ends at three."

"Okay, thanks. We'll come back."

They walked outside and toward the car.

"Are we going to wait?" Nick asked.

"Yeah. Did you bring your laptop?"

"Uh-huh. I guess we can do some research. But he's not at his house, and he's not here."

"I think he'll be back, like she said."

"Seems funny to go to lunch and come back only an hour before your shift ends."

"Well, yeah, a little. But they probably have three eight-hour shifts, and it got busy around noon, so he took his break late, like she said."

"Okay." Nick climbed in on the passenger side.

Bill ignored Nick's fidgeting and checked his messages. One was from an insurance agent he sporadically did work for. The other appeared to be garbled. He frowned and examined it more carefully.

"Another code."

"Huh?" Nick looked up from his laptop.

"Oh, I've got a text that looks as though it's in code."

"You said *another* code. Is this a recurrence?"

Bill arched his eyebrows. Was Nick upgrading his vocabulary? If so, was he hoping to impress Campbell?

"Yeah, we got a Christmas card in the mail the other day, and it had a similar message inside."

"Can I see?"

Bill handed him the phone.

Nick scowled at the screen and scrolled up and

down. "Nah, I think someone just had their finger on the wrong keys."

"In a text?" Bill took the phone back and looked at it again. "I figured the card was a nostalgic prank from my brother or something. But Richard doesn't text much. And if you were texting a coded message, you'd have to be really careful not to spell anything wrong."

"Like I said, it's a mistake."

"I don't think so, but I'll find out." Bill glanced up as a pickup truck entered the parking lot.

"Is that our guy?" Nick asked.

Bill waited until the driver got out and headed for the hotel door. He noted the short-cropped blond hair and lined face. "Yup, that's Abbott." Bill got out of the car and caught up to the man just as he reached to open the door. "Mr. Abbott."

Jacob Abbott pivoted toward him. "Yes?"

Bill sensed Nick just behind him. "Bill McBride. This is my associate, Nick Emerson. We're private investigators. May we have a moment of your time?"

Abbott's eyes shuttered. "I'm working. I need to get back to my job."

"This will only take a minute," Bill said easily. "Besides, we've been in there, and it seems pretty quiet right now. I doubt we'd bother anyone if we talked in the lobby."

"What's this about?"

"We'd like to ask you a few questions about the court case."

"Court—you mean Leila? I don't have anything to say."

"We hoped you could tell us a little bit about your relationship with your mother."

"Forget it. And if you harass me at work, I'll call the cops." Abbott shoved the door open and stalked inside.

Chapter 9

Campbell was in the kitchen when her father and Nick came in through the garage.

"Whatcha doin' with the cookies?" Nick demanded, frowning at the small foil-lined box she was filling.

"Relax. I left you some. I thought I'd take a few over to the new neighbor."

Nick scowled. "Why?"

"Because that's what nice neighbors do."

"What if she turns out to be an axe murderer?"

"Oh, hush." She closed the box and turned to Bill, who was filling his favorite mug with coffee. "What did you find out from Jacob Abbott?"

"Zilch."

"Oh. That's disappointing."

Bill shrugged. "He didn't want to talk to us."

"At all," Nick added. "He threatened to call the cops if we harassed him."

"That fits," Campbell said.

"What do you mean?" Nick asked.

"Well, I learned a few things about Jacob Abbott today. For instance, his first wife claimed he beat her, and she divorced him."

"I saw that his wife took out a restraining order on him," Bill said, lifting his mug to his lips.

"Oh, that was Wife Number Two, after the

neighbors called the police on him for the second time. That bout put her in the hospital."

"So he's got a violent past," Nick mused. "I did see domestic calls on his police record. I guess he wasn't kidding about us leaving him alone."

She nodded. "Probably a good idea."

Bill's eyebrows pulled together. "I wonder how that fits in with his current job. He's a desk clerk at a small hotel."

"Maybe they don't know," Campbell said with a shrug.

"Or he knows the owner, and they're giving him a chance." Nick turned toward his desk.

"Did he do time?" Bill called over his shoulder as he headed for his office.

"Yes. A few months, some for the old drug bust, and he went back inside after the domestic thing. But that was a couple years ago." Campbell ran after her father to keep up with him, clutching the box of cookies.

"Any kids?" Bill asked.

"No, from both marriages."

"Okay, so if he had died, his share of Teresa's estate would go into the pot to be divided among his five nieces and nephews."

"I guess so."

Bill placed his mug on his desk, sat down, and tapped a computer key to wake up the machine.

"I also found out about David Nelson's family," Campbell said. "He's the man who owned the painting when it was stolen. I put the new info in the file."

"Good. I'll take a look. Go ahead and do your good-neighbor thing, but don't stay too long, okay?"

She studied his face, trying to decide what he was thinking.

"I don't have to do it if you want me here, Dad. I just needed a break, and to be honest, I was a little worried about you and Nick. This seemed like a good distraction."

"Oh, we had to wait for Abbott to come back from his late lunch. It was nothing."

"Okay." Campbell looked down at the box she'd prepared.

"Go," he said.

She went out to the entry, put on her jacket, then tucked the cookie box under her arm. What if their new neighbor was Marissa Chilton, the private investigator? No, her dad would have discovered that by now. No doubt he had the addresses of both Ms. Chilton's home and office. He probably had the new neighbors' names too.

As she approached the light-colored brick house, she glanced toward the front windows. A woman stood inside, polishing the glass. Campbell hesitated, then waved and smiled. The woman saw her and waved back.

The front door opened as Campbell climbed the steps. Her heart skittered, which was silly.

She shouldn't be nervous over meeting the new neighbor.

"Hi. I'm Campbell McBride, from next door. I thought maybe you could use some cookies." She held out the box.

"Oh, how nice!" The woman reached for it. "I'm Allison Peele. Won't you come in?"

Well, that's one thing I don't have to worry about. She's not Marissa Chilton.

Campbell stepped inside and drew the door shut after her. "Chilly today."

"Yes, it is." Allison led her into the living room and set the box on the coffee table. Several cartons were stacked against one wall, and her cloth and bottle of window cleaner sat on the rug below the picture window. "Sorry about the mess."

"You just moved in. It actually looks pretty organized in here. I'd say you've got things under control."

"Thanks. I took a week off from work to do this, but I have to go back Monday. Would you like something to drink?"

"Oh, no thanks," Campbell said. "I can't stay long. I'm taking a work break myself."

"Where do you work?" Allison asked.

"At home—my dad has his office there."

Her expression brightened. "I saw your sign. Investigations, is it?"

"Yes, we're P.I.s. I just passed the exam a couple of months ago, and I work with my dad full time."

"Do you enjoy that?"

"Oh, I love it."

Allison's brow puckered. "And I've seen a young man go in and out of your house. Is he your brother?"

"No, that's Nick Emerson, an employee."

"He looks about my son's age."

"Does your son live with you?"

"Yes, or he will now. He's taking his degree in Computer Science at Murray State."

They sat down, and Campbell learned more about Allison's son, Greg, who seemed to be the light of her life.

A cuckoo clock came alive, with the little bird popping out three times, and Campbell realized twenty minutes had passed.

"I need to get going. Dad wanted me to look into something this afternoon." She rose, reaching for her jacket.

Allison jumped up. "It was nice to meet you, Campbell. And thanks for the cookies."

"You're welcome."

She stepped out into a cold wind and wished she had gloves in her pockets. The garage door was down, so she jogged to the porch steps, even though that path was a little longer. Inside the entry, she shut the door and pulled off her jacket, her face tingling.

"Hey." Nick leaned against the doorjamb in the opening to their office.

"It's cold out there." Campbell gave an exaggerated shiver.

"I heard on the radio it might snow tonight."

"Really?" It seemed awfully early for that in western Kentucky. "Is Dad in his office? I think he had something he wanted me to work on."

"He's in there. I read the notes you put in the file while we were gone. Interesting about the Nelson family. Everybody wants that painting."

"Or wants to sell it," Campbell said. "I don't think the Nelson kids want to donate it to the museum, because they want the money."

"Could be. I know I would."

"Hey, the lady next door asked me if you were my brother." She laughed.

"Would that be so funny?"

Campbell wished she hadn't told him. Wouldn't he just love to be Bill's son? But she really didn't think he'd want her as a sister.

"What's her name?" Nick asked.

"Allison." She turned toward her dad's office and knocked on the door.

"Come on in," he called. When she entered, he laid aside a manila folder and reached for his cell phone. "Oh, good, you're back. This probably has nothing to do with the case we're on—don't see how it could, actually—but take a look."

Campbell took his cell and studied the screen. He'd opened a text that was made up of jumbled letters. "Another coded message."

"Yes. And that means the sender not only has my address but also knows my phone number."

"It must be someone you know. I mean, anyone could get our address online, but we put the landline number on the website, not your cell."

"True, but I give it to a lot of people. Most of our business contacts have it."

She passed the phone back to him. "Don't rule out family and friends."

"You think it's a joke?"

"Don't you? When you got the card, you thought it might be from your brother, remember?"

"Richard and I did dabble in simple codes when we were kids." He eyed her speculatively.

"What?" Campbell asked.

"I've known you to enjoy solving cryptograms."

She couldn't deny it. In fact, she'd thought about taking a whack at the encrypted message on the Christmas card, but she hadn't gotten around to it.

"Where's the card?"

Bill opened a desk drawer and pulled it out.

"Send me the text message." She took the card from him. "Anything else?"

"No, just keep doing what you're doing, kiddo."

"Okay. I'll take a crack at the codes after work. We should at least be able to tell if they use the same key. If it's a simple substitution, we should be able to solve it quickly. If they're getting fancy, that's beyond me."

She went back to her desk itching to jump into code solving, but she couldn't do that on company time. Instead she decided to see if she could turn up anything her dad had missed on Jacob Abbott. His first wife wasn't hard to locate—she now lived in McCracken County. His second wife was a little harder to trace, but eventually she learned the woman had remarried and resided in Tennessee. She speed-dialed her dad on the house phone.

"What's up, Soup?"

"Jacob Abbott's second wife—the one he injured so badly—lives in Franklin, Tennessee, now. She remarried last summer, after she and Jacob had been divorced a year and a half. I just wondered if we could find out if he bothered her after she moved to Tennessee."

"Might be worth looking into."

"Maybe Keith would check on it?" She hated to ask Keith for favors, but this might be loosely related to the murder investigation he was now leading.

"I know someone in Nashville who might be able to help us," Bill said. "I don't like to ask Keith about active cases if I don't have to. And anyway, he might have solid leads by now in a totally different direction. I think I'll call Leila first, though. Maybe our client can tell us more about her uncle's history."

At five o'clock, Nick left. When Campbell

approached her father's office, she could hear him talking on the phone. She about-faced and went back to her desk. Now was the time to work on the codes.

Both messages seemed to use the same method. She couldn't be positive they used exactly the same mechanics, but simple substitution seemed likely. She noted the most frequently used letters and a few educated guesses. Within half an hour a flash of insight hit her, and she rushed to write out the solution. Just as she finished, her dad walked into the room.

"Are you still working? I thought we'd go out for supper."

"Sounds good." She grinned at him and held up her worksheet. "I've got it, Dad! It's a Caesar shift."

"A what?"

"Every letter in these messages is shifted over four spaces. It could be any number, but in this case, they used four. So an *A* became *E,* a *B* became *F,* and so on. Are you ready?"

He stepped closer, his face slack as he considered what she was saying. "Yeah. What do they say?"

"Well, the card came first, right? It says, 'GOOD LUCK FROM YOUR NEW COLLEAGUE OR RIVAL.'"

"What?" Bill grabbed the paper from her hands. "New colleague or rival?" His featured hardened.

"This has to be from that Marissa Chilton."

"That's what I think. And the text message says, 'TWO NEW CASES HERE. HOW ABOUT YOU?' Something tells me she's a cheeky show-off."

Bill stood frozen for a moment, scanning the paper. "What does she want?"

"How do you mean?"

"Why is she taunting me?"

"She wants to take away your business."

He scowled. "Good luck with that. She might pick up a few background checks and women who want their cheating husbands surveilled, but all the good lawyers and insurance agents in town know we're the best. She's not going to poach any of our repeat clients."

"Yeah, I don't think we have anything to worry about. Your business contacts are rock solid." Campbell smiled. "Want to send back a message?"

"Why would I give her the satisfaction?"

"I dunno. Maybe to show her you're smarter than she thinks? We could send it in a different code."

He shook his head. "I don't want to waste time playing games. Let's go hit the Sirloin Stockade. I'm hungry."

Over their meal, Campbell listened avidly as Bill related his earlier conversation with Leila Abbott.

"Seems our client is almost deathly afraid of her uncle."

"What's he done?" Campbell asked.

"She says he's threatened her numerous times, but never when anyone could hear, and it's his word against hers."

"So, he never laid hands on her?"

"No. Well, she said he grabbed her shirt once and got right in her face, but no bruises or anything."

"No evidence. He must have learned a thing or two after the jail time he earned beating his second wife." She put the last bite of perfectly cooked steak in her mouth and chewed. She could never learn to cook this well. "You want dessert?"

Bill had cleaned his own plate, and he gazed at her with placid green eyes that were her legacy. "I shouldn't."

She chuckled. "But you want to."

"That pie is calling to me."

"Go for it."

He shook his head. "No, if I don't cut back on the calories, I won't be able to chase a suspect."

"Eh, you hardly ever have to do that. Not since you retired from the police force."

"Maybe not, but I'd like to think I could if the occasion arose." He sobered. "There's one more thing I learned tonight. There's a warrant out on Jacob Abbott in Tennessee."

"What for? And why don't they come get him?"

"I have a feeling it's a ways down their list. It's for violating the protective order."

Campbell's jaw dropped. "Wife Number Two, when he sent her to the hospital?"

"No, it was after that. He didn't physically harm her—at least, not that time—but he went to her house and barged in on her. She called the cops, and he ran."

"He sounds like such a charming fellow." The bleakness of it made her consider eating a piece of pie herself. But no, she was trying to confine sweets to the days Rita cooked for them. "Come on, Dad. Let's go home and unwind. No more work tonight."

"Deal."

She reached for her purse. "You must have something recorded that we can watch together."

"Sure."

As they walked out into the crisp evening air, stars glittered overhead. They strolled side-by-side toward Bill's Toyota but halted in their tracks when a young man burst out from behind the front end of a pickup.

"McBride!"

Campbell's heart skipped a beat. Her dad put out a hand and shoved her behind him.

"What do you want?"

Chapter 10

Swallowing hard, Campbell peered over Bill's shoulder. She didn't recognize the man who accosted them, but she quickly cataloged his appearance in case she needed to describe him later. Five-nine or so, lean, with hair that looked dark in the glare of the streetlights. Wearing jeans and a camouflage jacket.

"That landlord's son is claiming that painting belonged to his father."

"Who are you?" Bill asked.

"Corey Smith."

"You're Leila Abbott's cousin."

"Yeah. Leila called me and asked me to find you. She's scared."

"What happened?" Bill asked.

"She saw someone outside her house, and when she opened the door, he ran away. Then she discovered her tires were slashed."

"Now?"

"Well, a few minutes ago—no more than half an hour. She tried to call you and couldn't get you, so she called me."

That's right, Campbell thought. *We both put our phones on silent when we got to the restaurant.*

"Hold on." Bill pulled his cell from his pocket and tapped it.

She took out her own phone and quickly checked her messages. Nothing there. But her father was speaking again.

"Okay, I see she tried to reach me. I'll call her and find out what's what."

Corey hesitated. "That's it?"

"I told you, we'll do something. Tonight."

His shoulders relaxed. "Right."

Bill held out a hand. "Here's my business card. You can call me if anything else comes up. And thanks for the heads-up."

Corey took it and muttered something as he turned toward his truck.

"How are you doing?" Bill asked Campbell.

"I'm okay. You handled that well."

He smiled. "I thought it was Jacob at first."

"He does look a little like him."

"But twenty years younger." Bill chuckled. "I'm just glad he wasn't coming at me with a gun. Let's get in the car, and I'll call Leila back."

While her father placed the call, Campbell watched Corey drive out of the parking lot and head north. With Leila's permission, Bill put his phone in speaker mode so Campbell could hear the conversation.

"Thank you for calling, Mr. McBride. I didn't know what to do."

"Campbell and I are only a couple of minutes away. Would you like us to come over?"

"That would be great," Leila said. "I'm still nervous."

"We'll be right there."

He started the engine and drove a few blocks, into Leila's apartment complex. She had a single unit in a row of attached dwellings. Bill parked next to her Chevy and grabbed his flashlight from the back seat. He stooped to examine the cuts on a couple of the tires.

Leila opened her front door, and Campbell hurried toward her with her father close behind.

"Thanks so much," Leila said, stepping back to let them in. "I'm sorry it's kind of messy."

"Don't worry about it." Campbell touched her arm. "Are you all right?"

Leila nodded. "Just a little spooked, I guess."

"Your cousin Corey just popped up at us in a parking lot," Bill said. "How did he know where we were?"

"I called your office when you didn't answer your cell, and some guy answered. Nick Somebody."

Bill's eyes widened. They hadn't expected Nick to go back to the office tonight.

"He's my employee."

"Right," Leila said. "He told me you'd gone to Sirloin Stockade."

Campbell nodded at her father. She'd texted Nick with their location just in case they were needed.

"Tell me about the vandalism," Bill said.

"There are always people around on this street, but I heard something that sounded like it was right outside my window. Kind of a clunk." Leila nodded toward the large front window that was now covered by olive green drapes. "I saw a man out there."

"You're sure it was a man?" Bill asked.

"Pretty sure. But I didn't recognize him. It's dark out there. I didn't have my outside light on. I don't put it on at night unless I'm expecting someone."

"Okay. What was he doing?"

"He was crouched down by my car. I rapped on the window. Maybe I shouldn't have, but I didn't want anyone messing with my car." She pressed her lips together and shook her head. "Too late."

"Did he see you?"

"Yeah, he looked over at me when I knocked on the window. Then he bolted. I was scared to go outside at first, but after a few minutes, I did, and I saw what he'd done to my tires. I figured the noise I heard must have been a tool dropping or something. Mr. Bill, he cut all four tires! I need my car to get to work tomorrow. What am I going to do?"

"Maybe your mom can help you out until you get this sorted," he said gently.

"That's—yeah, she probably will." Leila swiped a sleeve across her tear-filled eyes. "I haven't told her about this yet. She'll have a conniption."

"What did you do after you saw the damage?" Campbell asked.

Leila seemed to refocus on the crime. "I was furious. And then I got scared. I ran in here and locked the door, and I tried to call you."

"Not the police?" Bill asked.

She hesitated. "Police aren't the most welcome in this neighborhood. And I thought, with my being arrested over the painting and all, I'd rather keep them out of it."

"I understand," Bill said, "but this was a crime, Leila. You need to get the police involved so you can tell your insurance company, if nothing else. But also, there may have been other incidents in this neighborhood. They'd know if this is one of a string of cases. In a way, that wouldn't be so bad for you. If it's an isolated incident, though . . ."

"It means I was targeted deliberately."

Bill nodded. "Let's sit down for a minute. Do you mind?"

Leila shook her head and moved a pile of laundry off the couch and carried it into another room. She returned as Campbell settled on the sagging sofa beside her father.

"Okay," he said once Leila was seated in a chair opposite them, "is there anyone who might want to scare you or punish you?"

She shook her head almost automatically.

"Think hard, Leila," Campbell said softly. "Who's angry at you?"

"I—I can't think of anyone. I haven't done anything."

"Are your cousins and your uncle satisfied with the way the court case turned out?" Bill asked.

Leila jerked her chin up. "Well, nobody's happy that we don't get the painting, but I think they realize it will be the right thing for them to give it back to the owners."

"Right. Is there anyone else? Has anything happened to tick someone off lately?"

Her face crumpled. "I can't think of anything except this whole painting fiasco. It was a nightmare."

"But the police took the painting," Campbell said.

Bill shrugged as if weighing the fairness of life. "There are still people who might blame Leila for losing them some money—and remember, she's still poking around about it. She hired us to look into it. Some people might see that as prying."

"Who?" Campbell looked from him to Leila. "Who's still upset, Leila? Your cousins? Jacob? Craig?"

"Any of the above." Leila's voice shook. "I was only trying to find out if the estate had something valuable."

"We know that," Campbell said softly.

"But I really do think you should call the police now," Bill said.

Leila sniffed and nodded. "Okay. Will you stay until they get here?"

"Of course."

Half an hour later, Campbell at last climbed into her father's Camry. A patrolman had come and taken Leila's statement and examined the damage. On Bill's advice, he'd called Detective Matt Jackson, who was on duty. Bill had a private word with Matt and then told Campbell they could leave.

"This is really weird," she said as he turned the car toward home. "What were you huddling with Matt about, if I may ask?"

"You heard him say there hadn't been any other incidents of tire slashing reported for at least a few weeks. I wanted to make sure he kept Keith informed on this. I pointed out to him that this could be related to the Standish murder case."

She blinked. "How do you figure?"

"Well, we don't know why Brad Standish was killed or why Leila's car was vandalized, but they're both connected to the painting incident."

Campbell let out a big breath. "You're right. It's too coincidental. Do you think Standish put the Banitier in the Abbotts' attic?"

"I don't know. Brad Standish is dead, so he can't tell us what really happened. It certainly seems as though he'd have spoken up before the trial if he had a legal claim to the painting."

"Agreed." Campbell scowled and watched out

the window as they headed toward Willow Street.

"Do me a favor," her father said. "Call Nick and find out why he was in the office tonight. I didn't see any new messages from him when I checked my phone for Leila's."

Campbell took out her cell. "Hey, that's another thing, Dad. Leila could have called the restaurant and asked to speak to you instead of sending her cousin to ambush us in the parking lot."

"That might have been a little more genteel. I expect she panicked when she couldn't get me."

Campbell huffed out a breath. "*She* panicked? I almost had a heart attack when I saw Corey." Her frequent contacts appeared on her phone, and she punched Nick's and hit speaker. A moment later, he answered.

"Yeah, Professor?"

She frowned but didn't bother to remind him that he'd promised not to call her that anymore. "Hey. I'm with Dad, and we've been to Leila Abbott's."

"Oh, good," Nick said.

"She told us you answered the phone at the office. Are you working tonight?"

"Well, I came back after supper. The boss had me checking on the family that used to own the painting this whole flap is about."

"The Nelson family?"

"Yeah."

"I did some work on that," Campbell said stiffly.

130

"I saw your notes in the file, and they were helpful. The police records from when it was stolen said Nelson told his kids it was going to a fancy art museum, and that night someone stole it."

"That did seem fishy, but they never pinned it on any of his children."

"Right," Nick said. "And how did old Mr. and Mrs. Abbott get it? That's what we're trying to find out, right?"

Bill turned in at their driveway, where Nick's Jeep sat.

"We're home," Campbell said into the phone. "We'll be right in, and we can talk about it."

A few minutes later, the three of them were settled near the fireplace. Nick had kindled a small blaze, and it felt good. The fire's warmth and the scents of the burning wood and their coffee lulled Campbell. She sat back in one of the recliners with a cup of decaf nestled in her hands while her dad filled Nick in on the tire slashing.

"So, did you find out anything interesting about the Nelson children?" Campbell asked.

Nick made a face. "Children. The youngest is, like, forty-five. The oldest one's over sixty."

"Well, you know what I mean. They're still David Nelson's children."

"Right." Nick had apparently fixed a large bowl of popcorn before they drove in, and he reached to scoop a portion into a cereal bowl. "I didn't find any criminal records, but I started looking for a connection between them and the Abbotts."

Bill's eyebrows shot up. "And?"

With a satisfied smile, Nick said, "Bingo." He tossed a piece of popcorn into his mouth.

"Mr. Nelson knew Leila's grandfather?" Bill asked.

"Better than that. Both Abbott boys worked summers on his tobacco farm back when they were high school and college age."

"Wait," Campbell said. "When you say 'both Abbott boys,' do you mean—"

"I mean Jacob Abbott and his brother—Leila's father, Randall Abbott."

"Who is now deceased," Bill said.

Nick nodded. "Right. But ol' Jake is still with us."

"And didn't want Leila to sell the painting."

"If he knew about it, why didn't Jacob speak up and say Mr. Nelson gave it to him, or that he used it to pay the boys for their work one summer?" Campbell asked.

"Maybe he *didn't* know about it," Nick said.

"Then why was it in his parents' house? I mean the house they rented." Campbell sighed with frustration. "You know what I mean!"

"Yeah, we know," Bill said. "And that is exactly what we need to find out. That, and why Dylan Standish is suddenly stepping forward and claiming the painting is his."

Campbell took a cereal bowl from the stack Nick had brought in and scooped out a portion of popcorn. They sat in silence for a couple of minutes, Bill sipping his coffee and the younger investigators pensively eating popcorn.

"What if . . ." Campbell broke off and frowned.

"What if what?" Nick demanded.

"It's kind of crazy, but I was thinking of different scenarios about the painting."

"And?" her father prompted.

"What if the Abbott boys stole the painting while they worked for Mr. Abbott? They could have hidden it in their attic—their parents' attic—and just left it there, thinking that once the brouhaha from its being missing calmed down, they could quietly sell it. Only they didn't realize Banitier was a big-deal artist and that if they tried to sell it, someone would recognize it and turn them in."

"So they just left it there for twenty or thirty years?" Nick sounded incredulous, but he wore a thoughtful expression.

"Did the Abbotts live in that house back when it was stolen?" Bill asked. "I guess that's another thing we need to check on. But we don't want to ask Jacob."

"Leila might know," Campbell said.

"Maybe. I suppose she could have heard family stories about when her father and Jacob and their sister were young."

"Marcella," Campbell said absently. She'd pored over the Abbott family tree so much she had it memorized. "It's a shame that Jacob's the only one in that generation still alive."

Bill straightened his shoulders. "What about Leila's mother? She married the older son, right?"

"Right." Campbell studied his face, unsuccessfully trying to read his thoughts.

"So, she'd know if Grandma and Grandpa—"

"Teresa and Stanley," Campbell murmured.

"Lived in that house when she married Randall."

Campbell nodded. "That's true. If the Abbotts lived somewhere else when she and Randall were dating, Cathy would remember. Let me check on what year they were married." She set aside her popcorn and strode to her desk. A quick look at the family tree told her what she needed to know.

"Jacob was only nineteen when Randall and Cathy got married."

"Okay," Bill said. "Cathy is on Leila's side, so she ought to be cooperative. She can tell us if the Abbotts were renting Standish's house then, and if Jacob and Randall were still working for Mr. Nelson then. So tomorrow, we interview Dylan Standish and Cathy Abbott."

"Tomorrow's Saturday," Nick said.

"That might make it easier to pin them down for a talk." Bill grimaced. "Everyone willing to work tomorrow? I'll give you each an extra day off next week."

"You shouldn't promise us that until we see what next week brings," Campbell said. "But sure, I'll work tomorrow." She did a lot of work on weekends anyway.

"I'm game." Nick scooped another bowlful of popcorn. "Where do you want me?"

"I think I'd better tackle Dylan myself," Bill replied. "Maybe you and Campbell can go and see Cathy. Leila might sit in on that."

"We should call her tonight and set it up." Campbell glanced at the clock. "It's not nine o'clock yet. Is it too late to call?"

"Go ahead," Bill said. "I'll try to hit Dylan Standish cold, I think. He might not be happy to see me."

Chapter 11

On Saturday morning, Nick arrived at the McBride house at nine thirty, and Campbell greeted him at the front door.

"Hey! Want coffee? Cathy expects us at ten. There's time."

"Sure. Is your father in?"

"No, he left already, to beard Dylan Standish in his den if he can. Why?"

Nick shrugged. "I was just going to tell him that this morning I drove past that tobacco farm David Nelson used to own. Only the Nelson family doesn't own it anymore. They sold it after the old man died. Part of it's in winter wheat now."

"What about the rest?"

"A housing development."

Campbell blinked. "That sounds lucrative."

"Yeah. I don't know about the land he owned in Marshall County." Nick fixed himself a mug at the single-serve coffeemaker, and Campbell gathered her notebook, purse, and laptop, just in case something came up they wanted to check on during the interview.

They took Nick's Jeep, and almost immediately Campbell wished she'd driven. Not only was her car more comfortable, but she hated the way Nick sped up for yellow lights and zoomed through intersections a split second after they turned red. When he arrived at Cathy Abbott's house, he parked decorously behind Leila's car in the driveway, and Campbell exhaled, relieved that they'd made it in one piece.

Cathy Abbott met them at the door with a smile and took them into the sunny living room, where her daughter sat in a recliner. A fully decorated Christmas tree stood in one corner—artificial, but a good one—and holiday decorations graced the mantelpiece and side tables.

"Good morning," Leila said cheerfully. "I take it this means you've made some progress."

"Some," Campbell said. "This is Nick Emerson, my coworker."

"You've met my mom," Leila said. "I guess Mr. McBride's not coming?"

"He's out hoping to interview Dylan Standish this morning. We'll keep you in the loop as to what happens there."

"Good!"

Cathy nodded. "That's a big relief. I couldn't believe it when Leila told me what he said to her last night. Where does he get off, anyhow?"

"We hope to find out." Campbell opened her notebook. "Cathy, we're especially hoping you can give us some insight about the Abbott family's past. Leila's told us some things, but since you've been part of the family since before she was born, we thought maybe you could answer some other questions that have come up."

"I'll try." Cathy sat down between Nick and her daughter. "What do you want to know?"

"Think back to when you and Randall were married," Campbell said. "Was Randall still working for Mr. Nelson at the time?"

"Chopping tobacco?" Cathy shook her head. "No, that had been his summer job when he was in school, but by the time we got married, he had a steady job with the Chevy dealership in town. Trust me, he liked that a lot more than being out in the sun all day. And the car salesman job was year-round, of course."

Campbell made a note. "I believe his brother Jacob was nineteen at the time you were married.

"Yes, Jake was one of the groomsmen at our wedding."

"Was he still working on the farm?"

Cathy's forehead wrinkled. "I think he did chop tobacco that summer. He was taking classes during the school year—he thought he'd be an electrician for a while. But he gave that up. Never finished the course."

"Now, what about their parents," Campbell said. "When you got married, were Stanley and Teresa Abbott living in the house where Teresa was living before she died?"

"Oh, no." Cathy leaned back in her chair. "They had a place over on Sycamore Street."

"Did they own it?"

"Well, yes and no. They had a mortgage on it. But the place burned down."

Nick's eyes widened. "That must have been a shock."

"It was. There was insurance, but their equity wasn't very high at the time." Cathy frowned. "They couldn't buy another house. They'd lost everything and had to start over. They decided to rent for a while. And, well, they just kept on renting. After Stanley died, I don't think Teresa wanted to buy another house. The maintenance would have been too much for her. She had health issues, even then."

"Do you remember when the fire happened?"

"Oh, my." Cathy closed her eyes for a few seconds. "I think Danielle was a baby." She calculated the year. "It was then or the next year."

Nick was working on his computer, and Campbell figured he was looking for news reports of the fire. She smiled at Cathy.

"Had you ever been up into the attic at the rental house?"

"I don't think so."

"And had you ever met the landlord?"

"Mr. Standish? Yes, I was at the house once when he came by to take a look at the sink. They were having problems, and he wanted to see it before calling a plumber."

"And did he? Call a plumber, I mean."

"Eventually. But Teresa was without water for two or three days. Maybe longer. I took her some bottled water and brought some of her laundry home to do it up for her. He wasn't the most sympathetic landlord. In fact, Teresa called Randall one time when they had a chimney problem."

"Why didn't she call the fire department?" Nick asked.

"I don't think she wanted to cause problems if it wasn't necessary. Randall checked it out. I guess it wasn't real serious, but he called Standish and told him the chimney was plugged and needed cleaning. I don't think the fire department came."

"And did Standish have the chimney cleaned?"

Cathy frowned. "Actually, I think Randall called someone and had it done and told them to bill Mr. Standish. I never heard any more about it, so I assume he took care of it."

"So, more people in the attic," Campbell mused. "Mrs. Abbott, did you ever meet Mrs. Standish— Colleen—or their son, Dylan?"

"You know, I did meet Colleen through the Women's Club. I didn't realize at first that she was the landlord's wife. She was very nice. Likable."

"Did you ever talk to her about the rental?"

Cathy sighed. "When I first learned who she was, I asked about it, but she kind of brushed off my question. She said that was her husband's business, and she didn't really have anything to do with the rentals or the tenants."

"So, you knew they had more than one rental unit?"

"I assumed so, but I never thought much about it. And I don't think I ever met the son."

"Okay." Campbell looked at Leila. "Can you add anything to what your mom's told us?"

"Well, I did know that Mr. Standish had other rentals. One time Grandma wanted something minor done—replacing the screen door, I think. But he said he couldn't right then, since one of his other houses needed a roofing job and it was taking all his resources at the moment."

Campbell wrote it down, but she'd seen Standish's own house, and she doubted he was ever too strapped for cash to buy a screen door for an elderly tenant.

She smiled at Mrs. Abbott. "I assume you'd never heard anything about the stolen painting?"

"Heavens, no. Not until Leila got in trouble over it and called me from the police station. That was a shock, I'll tell you."

Leila winced. "I'm sorry, Mom."

"I know you are." Cathy leaned over and gave her a quick hug. "You don't have to keep apologizing. I hope it's all in the past now. In fact, if I were you, I'd just forget about it and move on."

"I can't." Tears glistened in Leila's eyes. "I can't stand it that people thought I did something underhanded, or that my grandpa was a thief. I'm sure he wasn't."

Campbell thought for a moment. "I assume you've gone through all your grandmother's papers since she died?"

"Definitely. I started out looking for anything about those antique dishes. I didn't find anything that mattered. But after I found the painting, I went through all her old tax records and check registers—everything—looking for—I don't know what. A receipt, maybe? Or some mention of the artist? I hoped I'd find some little thing—anything that would put Grandpa and Grandma in the clear. She'd kept a lot of paper, but I couldn't find anything significant."

"Do you still have all of that?"

Leila sighed. "I kept the tax returns, but I couldn't see keeping box after box of old receipts and paid bills. I'd have had to rent a storage unit. But they were honest people."

Nick spoke up once more. "Did you throw all that stuff in the trash, or what?"

"No way. Well, I did throw away some that seemed anonymous. But I didn't want to put anything like bank statements with account numbers out in the trash. When they came around with that Super Shredder thing, I carried about six boxes of stuff to that and had it all shredded."

Campbell wasn't sure if that was a good thing or a bad thing. While Leila had probably been wise to downsize the clutter, it was possible she'd gotten rid of documents she didn't recognize as pertinent.

She asked a few more questions but learned nothing new. Finally she pushed back her chair. "Thank you both so much. Leila, we'll keep you posted on the investigation."

Nick rose when she did. Cathy also jumped up.

"I'll walk out with you. And if there's anything else you want to talk about, feel free to come back or give me a call."

They ambled out to Nick's Jeep, and he headed home.

"She didn't even offer us tea," he grumbled.

"Oh, well. We can have some when we get home."

Campbell felt the bleakness of the office when they walked in. She'd thought it was homey after she'd hung a few photos and a Matisse print, but after the Abbotts' cheery living room, it seemed stark. They needed a tree, she decided, and soon. Christmas was only two weeks away. When they emptied her dad's storage unit, she'd found the box of figurines her mom had loved—nativity sets and porcelain carolers. Definitely decorations tonight.

She was typing up her notes, and Nick was settling in at his desk with a tall glass of iced tea, when Bill walked in.

"Hi, Dad. Can we get a Christmas tree?" She

stopped with her smile frozen on her face. Her dad looked terrible. His left eye was swollen shut, and the skin around it was red and purple.

"What happened to you?" She ran to his side.

Bill held up both hands. "Take it easy. I'll be okay. Just get me an ice pack."

Nick walked toward them frowning. "Should you see a doctor?"

"No, nothing's broken. It just hurts like the dickens." Bill sank into Campbell's swivel chair.

"What's the other guy look like?" Nick actually smirked, and Campbell could have brained him.

She shoved her hands to her hips. "Did Dylan Standish do this to you?"

"He did, and Officer Ferris is taking the particulars from him now."

"Is he going to arrest him?" Campbell asked.

"I doubt it. I told him I didn't want to press charges." He looked up at his daughter. "Ice?"

"I'll get it." Nick strode into the hallway.

"Okay, spill it," Campbell said sternly. "Why did he hit you?"

"I might have implied that he was a little precipitous in wading into the landlord position."

"What do you mean?"

Bill sighed. "Before I went to Dylan's house, I stopped by his father's unit of four apartments. The tenants there told me Dylan raised the rent this morning."

"What?" Campbell's blood heated. "His father only died yesterday, and he's going around raising the rent today?"

Nick entered as she gave this shrill summary. He handed Bill an ice pack they used in their picnic cooler and a clean dish towel. "That does sound a little callous. Did you hit him back?"

"No, I decided I was better off retreating to my car and calling the cops. Of course, I *was* on his property, and I offended him."

"That doesn't give him the right to sock you," Nick said.

"I don't think so either. I figured a stern talking-to from Mel Ferris would give him second thoughts. How'd you two make out? You don't look any worse for the wear."

"We talked to Cathy and Leila," Campbell said. "We got a few details. The Abbotts started renting that house about eighteen years ago, after their own home was destroyed by fire."

"So, they weren't in the rental until a couple of years after the painting was stolen." Bill wrapped the ice pack in the towel and held it gingerly to his face.

Campbell nodded slowly. "I guess the question is, did the painting move in with them? Or was it already there?"

"Or did someone put it there later," Nick said.

"Do you really think so?" Campbell scrunched up her face.

"It could be," Nick insisted. "The person who stole it may have hidden it some other place for a while, but then, if he wanted it out of his possession, he might have figured that would be a good place to stash it."

"But . . ."

"That's a possibility," her father said. "What it tells me is that it wasn't in the Abbotts' old house. It would either have burned up, or they'd have had to grab it when the fire started, and someone else would probably have seen it."

"Hmm." Campbell strolled to one of the chairs she kept to one side of her desk for clients to use and sank into it. "I guess you're right. If either Stanley or Teresa put it in the attic of the rental, it had to be after their move."

"Unless they had it stashed in another place before the fire and decided to bring it there," Nick said.

She shook her head. "If your house just burned, would you put something valuable in your new digs?"

"No, but that painting's probably too big for a safe deposit box."

"There are large ones," Bill said. "But the Abbotts weren't wealthy. They may not have had a safe deposit box. I think it's more likely the painting was put in the attic by someone else."

"Like the landlord," Campbell said.

"Or his son," Nick added. "If he considered

it his, that would make him mad enough to clock a guy who came snooping around about it."

"Dylan would have been a child when that thing was stolen," Campbell said.

Bill's lips twitched. "A very young child."

"But he might have known about it and moved it later," Nick insisted.

"I doubt it—not without his father knowing about it."

Campbell looked at Nick, then at her dad. "What about Colleen?"

With a sigh, Bill sank back in the desk chair. "I don't know. She clearly stayed out of Brad's rental business, whether at his insistence or her own volition. Do you think she'd risk hiding a valuable item in one of his properties that she supposedly had nothing to do with?"

"It might be the perfect place." Inspiration flickered inside Campbell. "If Brad found it, he'd have no idea she put it there."

"He'd think it belonged to the tenants," Nick said.

"Well, what if Colleen put it there and the tenants found it, and they went and asked Brad about it. He would assume it wasn't theirs." She wasn't ready to let go of the idea.

"And he'd probably claim it for himself at that point."

"Exactly," Campbell said.

Silence hung in the air for several seconds, and

then Bill slapped the desktop. "I'm not buying it. I don't say it's impossible, but I don't think that attic is a place where Mrs. Standish would hide something she hoped to keep from her husband. For one thing, the tenants say she never came there while they lived in the house."

"The tenants are dead," Campbell said gently.

"Yes, but Teresa's daughter-in-law and granddaughter, her caregivers, said she never came around, right?"

Reluctantly, Campbell nodded. "Cathy said she met Colleen through the local women's club, but she didn't know her well. And Leila . . ." She let out a sigh.

"Let's be logical about this," Bill said. "Who is the most likely person to have put that painting in the attic, no matter when?"

"Stanley Abbott," Nick said immediately.

"Right. Or someone in his immediate family."

"You mean . . ." Campbell sat up straight. "One of his kids might have done it."

"It's possible," Bill said. "Cathy's husband, Randall, was alive when his parents moved into that house, right?"

Campbell nodded. "Yeah, I'm pretty sure. He was married and all, but he was still living in town."

"Leila and her sister were tiny when their grandparents moved into the rental," Nick said.

"Right. But their parents were on the scene.

Cathy told you she knew nothing about the painting, but that doesn't mean Randall didn't."

"What about the other kids?" Nick asked. "Randall's sibs."

"Marcella and Jacob," Campbell supplied.

Bill smiled. "I doubt Marcella Abbott Smith had anything to do with it. She had her hands full with three young children when her parents' house burned and they made the move. But Jacob . . ."

Campbell could see a clear path to where he was going. "Jacob's in his mid-forties now. He was early twenties then. Maybe in a mess with his first wife."

"And we know he did some illegal things when he was younger," Nick put in.

"He could have put that painting there anytime after the folks moved in." Campbell spread her hands. "If he got hold of it somehow, he might consider that a good, safe hiding place. His parents didn't go up there much. Especially his mom. If he hid it after his dad died . . ."

"It would still be a risk," Bill said. "If his parents or one of his siblings or nieces or nephews went up there for whatever reason—to stow things, to hunt for something . . ."

"To clean," Campbell suggested.

"Or to play," Nick said.

"Right. Any of them could have found it. But it's unlikely anyone else would, and Jacob is a brash fellow who's willing to wing it. He'd come up with some explanation on the spot if that happened."

"So you think Jacob hid it there?" Campbell asked eagerly.

"No."

"Oh." She slumped in the chair, like yeast dough when Rita punched it down.

"I think Stanley is still our most likely candidate," Bill said. "But if not him, I'd put my money on either Brad Standish or Jacob Abbott. But I'm not counting Randall out."

"What about Teresa?" Campbell asked.

"Grandma?" Nick asked disdainfully.

"She was only in her forties when they moved into that house. She was still spry, and she probably put most of those boxes and things up in the attic, or supervised their storage. It wouldn't have been too difficult for her to sneak that painting up there before her health made it harder for her to climb the stairs." Campbell looked to her father for agreement.

"She's not completely in the clear," Bill admitted. "But I think Stanley, Brad, and Jacob are our main suspects."

Campbell stood. "I'll fix us some lunch, then I think you should have a nap, Dad. Later, we can talk about how we can dig out something definitive about all this."

Nick smiled at Bill, his eyes twinkling. "You

going to show up in church tomorrow with that shiner, boss?"

Bill tipped his head to one side, still holding the ice pack against his cheek. "I can't show up without it, now, can I?"

Chapter 12

After church the next day, Keith picked Campbell up to take her out to the lake for dinner with his parents. On the way, she told him how her father got his black eye.

A cold wind blew over the water, shoving up whitecaps, and it was too cold to sit outside or on the screened porch. After the meal, they moved to the living room with Angela and Nathan, before a crackling blaze in the fireplace.

"When is Nicole arriving?" Campbell asked.

"Not until the twenty-third." Angela smiled. "They'll stay five days. I can hardly wait."

"I'm eager to meet her and Todd."

Keith said, "They want to meet you too. And your dad."

"I hope we'll have this Abbott case wrapped up by then." Campbell shot an anxious glance at Angela, in case the hostess objected to shop talk during the visit.

"It would be nice if you had some free time while they're here," she said.

Campbell nodded. "I'd like to see it laid to rest for the family's sake."

Nathan picked up the poker and jabbed at the logs in the fireplace, sending up a burst of sparks.

He tossed another log on the blaze and replaced the poker then turned to look at her. "I've taken the liberty of getting tickets for all of us, including Bill, for Playhouse in the Park."

"Yes," Angela said with a grin. "They're doing a Christmas musical, and I thought it would be fun if we all went together."

"How nice! I'll love it." Campbell had seen ads for the show, and she knew it was true. Her father, however, wasn't a great fan of musical comedy. He preferred mysteries. But she was sure she could talk him into going and spending the evening with the Fullers and their children.

"The tickets are for the night after Christmas," Nathan said.

"Terrific." Already, Campbell was planning how to break this news to her father. Somehow, she hoped she could spin things so he would like it. He always enjoyed Nathan and Angela's company. But Keith had taken her to several musicals at the community theater, and Bill always bowed out.

"So, anything new on your murder case?" Nathan asked his son.

Keith shrugged. "Nothing I can talk about."

"Isn't it always the wife?" Angela's eyes widened in expectation.

With a laugh, Keith shook his head. "Not always, Mom."

"I know."

"The day Brad Standish died, his wife was in shock," Campbell mused. "I really thought it was genuine."

"Well, she seems to be letting her son take over his father's business," Keith said, frowning.

"I take it you're not sure that's a good idea?"

"We'll see, eventually."

Angela rose. "Who wants more coffee?"

"I'd take some," Keith said.

"Are there any more brownies?" Nathan asked.

Angela swatted playfully at him. "You know you shouldn't."

"Me? I was asking for Campbell, in case she wanted another one." He threw a sheepish look at Campbell.

"Oh, no, thank you," she said quickly. "They were delicious, but I've reached my limit."

Angela took Nathan's coffee mug and headed for the kitchen.

"I guess you and old Bill can't work on the murder." Nathan eyed Campbell keenly.

"No, but we're still working on the stolen painting. I guess you know the murder victim owned the house where it was found."

"Yeah, I followed it when the trial was on. Too bad they dismissed you from the jury."

She shrugged. "I'm just as glad."

Angela returned and handed her husband a steaming mug. "So, is Bill seeing anyone now?"

154

She sat down cozily next to Campbell on the couch.

"Not really. The last woman he dated . . . well, that didn't end well."

"You mean Jackie?" Keith asked.

She nodded. "They're still speaking, and she's still attending our church, but no more dates. I think Dad decided she wasn't his type after all." She didn't want to get into Jackie's troubled past, so she turned the conversation on a dime. "So, Nathan, I guess your repairs are all finished? Is the upstairs as nice as it was before the tornado damage?"

"Better," he said, his eyes sparkling.

"Oh, you haven't seen it," Angela said. "We decided to remodel the upstairs bathroom, since it needed a lot of work anyway. Come on, I'll give you a tour."

Later, Campbell and Keith had a few minutes to themselves in the living room.

"Did you decide what to give your dad for Christmas yet?" Keith asked.

She frowned. "No, and time's running out."

"I got my dad a new fishing rod the last time I was in Nashville."

"That gives me an idea. Dad's always hankering to go fishing with Nathan or with his old friend Mart. Not in the middle of winter, of course, but . . ." She gave him a big smile. "Thanks for the inspiration."

Keith shrugged. "I didn't do anything, but if you really want to show your appreciation . . ."

She slid into his arms.

When she got home, Campbell wasn't surprised to find her father busy at his computer. His mind wouldn't stop working for a weekend.

"Hey." She held out a paper plate covered with aluminum foil. "Angela sent you some brownies. They're really good."

"Oh, thanks." He took the plate and set it on his desk without opening the foil, which signaled Campbell that he was deep into whatever he was working on.

"Uh, they've invited us to go to the theater with them on Boxing Day."

He blinked at that. "The twenty-sixth?"

"Yeah, Keith's sister and her husband will be here. Nathan and Angela thought it would be a fun outing."

Bill shrugged one shoulder. "I guess. As long as they're not trying to set me up with some woman."

She smiled at that. "Aw, Dad. There was no mention of bringing a date for you."

"Good." She studied his injured eye and cringed. The dark skin was a deep black beneath the socket, and it puffed out with blood collecting there. "Are you sure you shouldn't get that eye looked at?"

"I can see out of it just fine."

"Are we going to Bowling Green on Christmas Day? Keith asked me what we were doing, and I told him I wasn't sure yet."

"Yeah, I called Mart and told him we'd be over. I hope that's okay."

"It's fine. I'll be happy to see everybody over there." She edged around the desk so she could see his screen. "What are you working on?"

"I'm reading up about that fire. The one that destroyed the Abbotts' house."

"You think it's significant?"

Bill leaned back in his chair with a sigh. "Maybe not. It's just that it happened a year or two after the painting was stolen. If someone connected to the Abbotts had it, it could have been in that house that burned."

"If it was, they rescued it."

"Right. And then they needed another place to put it."

"They lost all their furniture and clothing—everything," she said.

"Yes. It seems unlikely they saved the painting from the fire. Even if it was the first thing you'd grab, someone would have noticed, wouldn't they?"

"It seems likely." She pulled over another chair and sat down. "I know we considered this before, but what if someone else in the family had it? Randall, maybe. When his folks had to move, he stuck it in their attic so that it couldn't be found on his property."

"That's a thought."

"Was Jacob still living with them when they moved?"

"I don't know." He looked over at her and smiled. "So, kiddo, what do you want for Christmas? You know me—I'm a last-minute shopper."

She laughed. "Nothing special."

"Maybe I want to give you something special."

"That works both ways, you know."

He nodded. "I guess it does. A new history of Calloway County was published last summer. I wouldn't mind having a copy of that."

"I'll ask Santa if he has any in his stash." She couldn't help smiling as she thought about the idea Keith had given her. No way would she tell her father, though.

"How about you?" he asked.

She made a face. "I think I need some new tires."

"That's not a special Christmas present."

"Sure it is. It would stop me from thinking I'm going to have a flat someday. Those tires are pretty old."

"I'll take a look at 'em."

"Would you? Thanks! Oh, and some new pens."

"Pens?" He stared at her.

"Yeah. Not fancy ones, just functional. I've had

two run out of ink on me in the past couple of days." She brightened at a thought. "Hey, maybe we should fill stockings for each other. We haven't done that for a long time." Her parents did it for her when she was young, but the tradition had fizzled after her mother died.

"Stockings?" Bill frowned.

"Yeah. You know, put a bunch of little stuff in them. Like pens."

"Hmpf."

She smiled. "I know you're not much of a shopper, Dad. But I think I'll make one for you." A stroll through a stationery store and a hardware store would give her plenty of ideas for his stocking stuffers.

"I'll think about it."

"Or you could just get me some new socks."

He laughed and shoved back his chair. "Come on. Are we going to eat out tonight?"

"If you want to. Or I could make waffles."

"Hey, that sounds good." He put his arm around her shoulders, and they walked toward the kitchen together.

On Monday morning, Nick surprised Campbell when he arrived with a fir tree sticking out the back of his Jeep.

"Is that for you or for us?" she asked.

"You. The boss asked me to stop by the farm store and pick out a nice one."

"Wow. Thanks!"

"No probs. Where do you want it?"

She pointed. "Over there. Not too near the fireplace."

While he went out to carry the tree in, she crossed the hall to Bill's office.

"Hey, Dad. Nick brought us a tree."

"Oh, good." He pushed his chair back. "Where's that box of ornaments?"

"I stuck it in a corner of the dining room. I'll get it."

By the time she returned to the office with the carton, the two men were releasing the ties that held the fir's branches close.

"I hope the tree stand is in there," her father said.

Campbell set the box on her desk and rummaged. "Yeah, it's here. So are the lights."

While they wrestled the tree upright and wound the light strings around it, she gently set out the ornaments she loved. Many were from her childhood.

"I think the box from the storage unit is up in the attic," her dad called across the room.

"I'll go look."

Feeling lighter than she had in weeks, Campbell hurried up the two flights of stairs. It didn't take her long to locate a medium-sized carton marked "XMAS." She remembered the day they'd emptied her dad's storage unit and found it among boxes of dishes, books, and her mother's keepsakes.

She carried it down to find the tree glorious in its blinking lights and silver garland. Nick and her father were gingerly hanging a few ornaments on the branches, and Rita Henry, their house-keeper, was helping them.

"Rita! Happy Monday morning," Campbell cried.

"Thank you. I'm glad to be here."

"Didn't you work for someone else on Mondays?" Nick asked.

"Just four hours, and she was willing to let me move that to Tuesday."

"We really appreciate it," Bill said, reaching for a reindeer ornament.

In the box she'd just retrieved, Campbell found more things she remembered and some she didn't. A few vintage glass bulbs were hand-me-downs from her grandparents. One small container held cross-stitched ornaments her mother had made. Tears filled her eyes as she gazed down at them. Bill must have found it too painful to get them out over the last few years.

Rita peered over her shoulder into the box. "Precious memories."

"For sure." Campbell smiled at her.

"I'm going to go and get started on some laundry," Rita said. "I'm glad to see y'all are getting into the holiday spirit together."

Campbell whispered a heartfelt thank you. She'd truly been blessed since she came back to Kentucky and made her home with her dad.

She turned back to the box of decorations. A tiny pillow stitched with "Campbell's 1st Christmas" and a teddy bear caught her eye. She held it up. Yes, she remembered that. She'd always been allowed to hang it herself when they got their tree. She carried it over to where the guys were working. Bill had just hung a little sled made of popsicle sticks with "Best Dad Ever" painted crudely across it.

She laughed. "I see you found my handiwork."

He smiled fondly. "Don't make fun of your immature self. I love that sled."

"Well, I love this. May I hang it?" She held out the cross-stitched ornament.

Bill took it gently in his hand. "Oh, yeah. Emily made that the year you were born." He smiled and looked up. "I'm glad you found it."

They spent another enjoyable fifteen minutes decking out the tree. The house phone rang, and Campbell picked it up. A man inquired if Bill McBride was available. Campbell pointed to her father, and he hurried toward his private office. A few seconds later, he answered, and she hung up. She took small boxes containing nativity sets from one of the larger cartons.

"I think we'll put one of these on the mantel and one in the dining room." She frowned. "I'm not sure about the third one. What do you think? I could ask Dad if he wants it in his office, but he doesn't really have a good place for it."

Nick waved a hand toward their coffee station. "How about over there? We'd all get a good look several times a day."

"Good thinking." She selected the one with ceramic children as the main figures in the set.

"Where do you want these boxes?" Nick asked.

"Can you take them up to the guest room? We can leave them there until we take the tree down. We're not expecting any overnight company in the next couple of weeks."

He hefted the nearly empty boxes and headed up the stairs. Campbell sat down at her desk with a sigh. Back to the real world now. She opened the file on the Abbott case.

Her father came to the office doorway, and Campbell looked up. Nick came down the stairs, and Bill moved aside enough for him to enter the room.

"We're taking on a new case," Bill said.

"What about the Abbott case?" Campbell asked.

"The new one's not urgent. I arranged to meet with the client and get the details on Wednesday. I told him we couldn't start work on it until next week. He said that was all right, that we could even postpone it until after the holidays."

"What kind of case is it?" Nick asked. "Insurance fraud?"

"No. He believes his business partner is stealing from him. He's had a forensic audit done, and he found evidence that money's being siphoned off. It's up to us to find where it's going."

"The accountant couldn't do that?" Campbell asked.

"Apparently not."

"Well, Nick's pretty good with computers," she said. "But if it's going into a foreign, encrypted bank account—"

"He doesn't think that's the case," her father said. "Anyway, I hope to find out more on Wednesday. If I think it's beyond our capabilities, I'll tell him. I haven't signed a contract yet."

Campbell drew in a deep breath. She glanced at Nick, who looked relieved but hadn't spoken out. "Well, what's on the agenda now?"

Bill scowled. "I'm pretty sure there's more to this business with Dylan Standish."

"Dad, you can't go back there. He assaulted you."

He held up a hand. "I know, I know. And I gave Keith all the information I had about him and his harassment of Leila Abbott."

"So, Keith is looking into that?"

"If he has time."

"What do we do?" Nick asked.

"I'd like to talk to Jacob, but I'm not sure he'll talk to me."

They were silent for a moment, then Campbell

said, "I wasn't with you when you and Nick went to the hotel. I could go at the end of his shift and ask if he'd give me a few minutes."

Her father frowned. "His shift was ending at three the other day, but we don't know for sure if he's working today."

"We could call—"

"No." Bill cut her off.

Nick said, "I can swing by there and just see if he's on the desk. I stayed in the background the other day. If he's there, Campbell could go by there at three."

"I don't think we should confront him at the hotel again," Bill said. "We don't want to make him angry."

"Do you have his home address?" Campbell asked. "If he's working, I could go by his place later this afternoon, when his shift is over."

Nick's face brightened. "I could follow him when he leaves the hotel, in case he goes someplace else. And if he does go straight home, Campbell can be waiting there. If not, I can call her and tell her where he is."

"I don't know," Bill said slowly.

"Dad, we have to talk to him," Campbell said with a bit of wheedle in her voice.

He sighed. "Okay, but if you go, I'll be in the car with Nick. I don't want any funny business. If he goes home, we can park down the block and keep an eye on you."

Now it was Campbell's turn to hesitate. Still, her dad was an expert at tailing suspects, and he could be discreet, even if Nick was sometimes lacking in that area. His black eye notwithstanding, she had faith in her father's skills.

"That sounds like a plan."

Chapter 13

A few snowflakes settled gently on Campbell's windshield as she drove toward Jacob Abbott's house. His home, it turned out, was a small cabin east of town—not on the lake shore, but near it. He had lake access without paying the exorbitant taxes commanded by shorefront property.

The snowfall wasn't intense enough to hamper her driving, and she sang Christmas carols along with the radio as she drove. At five minutes after three, her GPS told her she was close. She slowed and located the right dwelling. After driving past it, she turned around and parked a little way beyond his driveway. She picked up her cell and called her dad.

"I'm right beside his driveway. It looks like no one's home."

"Leila says he lives alone, and we've got him in sight. We're just leaving town. No stops so far."

She left the engine and the heater running, as well as the radio. Jacob's cabin didn't have any Christmas lights, and no decorations graced his yard or rooftop, but still, she would have voted for it as a Christmas card image with the falling snow embellishing the log structure.

After half a dozen more carols, her phone rang.

"Yeah, Dad?"

"He's on the road where you are. We're only about a mile from you. We're hanging back, so he doesn't catch on that we're following him. We'll stay out of sight for a few minutes then move in a little closer."

"Thanks." She stuffed the phone in her pocket and turned off the radio, peering through the snow, back along the road where she'd driven in. A truck's headlights came into view.

Jacob slowed and stared at her before turning into his driveway. He parked and got out of the truck. Campbell unbuckled her seatbelt, but before she could open her door, he was striding toward her.

"You looking for me?" he demanded as she got out of the car.

"Yes. I was wondering if I could talk to you for a minute."

His eyebrows drew together in a frown. "Are you police?"

"No."

"Then who are you?"

"My name is Campbell McBride, and I'm trying to clear your father's name."

"What are you talking about?" His scowl deepened. "Oh, I get it. Leila sent you."

"Not exactly."

He glared at her for a long moment, his tight expression marring his natural good looks. Finally, he shrugged. "It's cold out here. Let's go inside."

Campbell swallowed hard. Ordinarily she wouldn't enter a private space with a man she didn't know, especially one she knew could be violent. There were the two ex-wives to consider. On the other hand, her father and Nick were a stone's throw away. She couldn't help darting a glance back along the road from town. Nick's Jeep wasn't in sight. She sent up a quick prayer.

"Okay. This shouldn't take long."

He grunted and swung around, setting off in long strides toward his cabin. She hurried to keep up with him. The light snow hadn't covered the ground, but it made the pavement a little slippery, and she staggered once, jarring her knee. She said nothing, but regained her balance as quickly as she could and jogged a couple of steps. She caught up as he unlocked the front door.

The interior of the cabin was surprisingly inviting. The front half was one great room with the kitchen to the right and a decent dining table with four chairs nearer the door. To the left sat a blue tweed sofa and matching recliner, facing a fieldstone fireplace. A couple of bookshelves, a coffee table, and lamps completed the furnishings. Campbell was glad to see some interesting prints hanging on the walls—and books. If he liked to read, he couldn't be all bad.

"Have a seat." He hung up his jacket on a row of hooks behind the door.

Campbell perched on the sofa and unzipped her jacket. Jacob went to the recliner and plunked himself down.

"What is it you think I can do for you?"

"I hoped you'd tell me a little about your family. I've learned your parents' house was destroyed in a fire when you were in your early twenties. Were you living with them at the time?"

"No, I was married."

He didn't offer more, and Campbell assumed he was thinking about the period of his unhappy first marriage.

"You and your wife had your own home, then?"

"Yeah, we had an apartment."

She nodded, itching to take notes. But she didn't want to scare him into clamming up. She decided to jump in deep.

"Did you know about the stolen painting that was hidden in their attic?"

Jacob's jaw tightened, and his color heightened. "I did not steal that painting."

"But did you know about it? You were in the house the day Leila was going to clean out the attic." That was sort of the truth. She waited, watching his eyes harden.

"I was there to see if we needed to do anything before the family handed the keys over to Brad Standish."

"You haven't answered the question."

"I told you. I. Did. Not. Steal. The painting."

Campbell pulled in a breath to steady her rioting nerves. "But did you know about it?"

He looked away, jerking his head to the side. "I think it's time for you to leave."

"Jacob," she said softly. "Leila's afraid her grandfather was a thief. If you know otherwise . . ."

He sat forward, coming halfway out of his chair and glaring at her. "My father was not a thief."

"And you know this . . . how?"

Running a hand through his hair, he bowed his head. Campbell sensed that he was close to breaking. What could she say to keep him talking? She made herself take three slow breaths.

"Okay. I was doing a favor for a friend." He grunted and looked away. "I don't want to go to jail for this."

Campbell wished she could reassure him, but she couldn't. Jacob was involved. But how?

He swore. "I don't know why I'm telling you this."

"Because you want it to be over," she said gently. "Just like Leila, you want the authorities to leave your family alone. And you don't want the world thinking your father was an art thief."

"He wasn't!"

"I believe you."

Jacob let out a big sigh and slumped back in his chair.

"Who did steal the painting?" Campbell asked.

"You were working for Mr. Nelson at the time."

"So were a lot of people."

She waited half a minute, but he didn't speak, so she said, "You mentioned a friend. You did a favor for a friend."

Jacob licked his lips. "He was working there too."

"And . . . he stole the painting?"

He shook his head vehemently. "No! He didn't take it. But . . ." He closed his eyes.

"You don't want to get your friend in trouble," Campbell said. "I can understand that."

"He's not my friend anymore."

"Then why protect him?"

As she waited for him to respond, she wondered what her dad and Nick were thinking. Were they worried about her? Someone had killed Brad Standish. Was her father afraid Jacob would kill her? But what if the theft of the painting had nothing to do with Standish's death? A sudden thought hit her.

"Was your friend Dylan Standish?"

"What? No. Dylan was just a kid then."

She nodded. "You know, it won't take the police long to figure out who it was—someone working with you at Mr. Nelson's farm at the time of the theft." She didn't think there'd been more than twenty or thirty people—although Nelson had considerable holdings at the time, and he might have employed migrant workers. That would complicate things. Still, Jacob had said it was a friend.

Finally he met her gaze. "Okay, look, it was Craig."

"Craig . . ."

"Smith, all right? My brother-in-law. *Ex*-brother-in-law. But he didn't steal it."

"I don't understand." In her mind, she was clicking through the family tree. Craig Smith had been married to Jacob's sister Marcella. They'd had three children, Leila's cousins Anna, Blaine, and Corey. The children must have been very young when the theft occurred. "You're saying Craig got you involved in the theft, but he wasn't the one who actually stole it?"

"He didn't get me involved in the theft. I didn't know anything about it until later. Neither did Craig. All he got me into was hiding the stupid thing." He raked his hand through his hair once more. "I never should have agreed to take it for him."

"Why did you?"

Jacob huffed out a big breath. "I was stupid, that's why. They had a small house, and Craig said he couldn't have it there any longer. Marcella almost found it. He had to get it out of the house. So he came to me."

"And you took it and put it in your parents' attic?"

"Well, I couldn't very well put it our apartment,

could I? Emma would have seen it for sure. We were already having trouble, and I had to find another place for it. I figured if I hid it way in the back of all that junk in their attic, it would be okay for a while. If Craig asked for it back, I could make some excuse to go up there and dig it out. Only he didn't."

"He never asked for it back?"

Jacob shook his head. "He and Marcella got divorced. I don't know, maybe he forgot about it. But it sat there for years. Mr. Nelson died. I thought at the time I might hear something, but no. Then my father died. I figured it was safer then. It could stay right where it was for a long time. My mother wasn't big on cleaning attics."

Campbell thought about that. She straightened and got to the point. "Jacob, who gave that painting to Craig and asked him to hold it for them?"

He held her gaze for a long moment. "You'll have to ask Craig."

"I'm asking you."

He pushed himself up from the chair. "All I need to tell you is, I didn't steal it. I told you how I got it. If you want to know how Craig got it, go track him down and ask him."

"You don't know where he lives?"

"Nah. I see him once in a while in town, so I think he's still in the area, but we don't stay in touch."

Reluctantly, she rose. "Okay. And thank you."

"Are you going to tell the cops I put it there?"

She hesitated. "Probably, but I don't know yet."

"Terrific. Just terrific." As he swung toward the door, a knock sounded on its panels. Jacob froze and stared at her. "Did you bring cops?"

"No. But . . . it could be my father. He was going to pick me up."

"You had your own car."

"Okay, that wasn't quite the truth. I'm sorry. But he was worried about me coming here to talk to you alone. He . . . may have come out here to check on me."

Jacob's eyebrows lowered, and he grabbed the knob and swung the door open. Bill and Nick stood on the doorstep.

"You!" Jacob's stare drilled into her father's face. "You came to the hotel Friday."

"That's right. You couldn't talk to me then."

Jacob whirled and poked an accusing finger at Campbell. "*He's* your father?"

"Yes," she said shakily. "We mean you no harm, Jacob. We only want to find out the truth."

"Well, I told you. I didn't steal the painting, and my father didn't either. Now get out."

She was grateful to step out into the fresh, crisp air. The snow had stopped, leaving just a dusting on the grass.

Turning back, she said quietly, "Thank you for your honesty, Jacob."

He glared at her and then at Bill. "You're going to tell the cops, aren't you?"

Bill glanced at Campbell then back at Jacob. "Only if we have to."

"He hid the painting for a friend," Campbell said softly.

"I see." Bill raised his chin a fraction of an inch. "Our intention is to serve our client, Mr. Abbott. But if we uncover a crime, we do have to report it."

"A crime—like what?"

"Accepting stolen property, maybe?"

Jacob slammed the door.

Chapter 14

Campbell sat anxiously in her father's office, waiting for him to read the notes she'd written up. Nick had ridden back to the house with her from the cabin. While Campbell told him everything Jacob had said, as nearly as she could remember it, he'd frantically typed it in on his laptop. As soon as they reached home, Nick made coffee while her dad paced, and Campbell went over the file, corrected typos, and added a few tidbits.

Finally, Bill looked up. His hand moved toward the coffee mug Nick had set on his coaster.

"So, Craig Smith."

"We never considered him," Campbell said.

"If Jacob's telling the truth, this sheds a whole new light on things."

Nick sat down in a straight chair near the bookshelf. "We can probably confirm that Smith worked on the farm that year without much trouble."

Bill nodded pensively. "I'll see what I can find out. I don't want to approach the Nelsons yet if I don't have to."

"Why not?" Campbell asked.

"Somebody stole that painting. Jacob says it wasn't him or Craig, but somehow Craig got hold of it. If someone in the family took it, they might have passed it off to a worker they trusted, so that it wouldn't be on the premises when the theft was reported and the police came."

"Okay." She mulled that over.

"We don't know it was a family member," Nick said.

"No, we don't." Bill scrolled up on his computer screen. "We need to find out if Craig Smith is still alive."

"Jacob thinks he is, and that he's in the area. But Craig and Marcella got a divorce." Campbell squeezed her lips together. "That family seems to have gone through a lot of death and divorce."

Her father sat back. "It has. Two of the siblings—Randall and Marcella—dead before they reached fifty."

"Do we know how they died?" she asked.

"You look into that," Bill said, "although I doubt it was murder. I'd have heard about it. Nick, you check on Craig Smith's status. I'll try to get a list of people working on the tobacco farm the year the painting was stolen. And Nick, if you find Craig Smith, give me his contact information. He might be able to give us some names."

"There's a good chance he won't want to talk to us," Campbell said. "And he'll be furious if he realizes Jacob gave him up."

Bill sighed. "I'll try another angle first. I think Nelson had a foreman who worked for him for several years. If I can locate him—"

"If he hasn't kicked the bucket," Nick said.

Campbell glared at him. "That was unprofessional."

Nick shrugged. "There are no clients listening in."

Bill took a big swallow of coffee and plunked down the mug. "He has a point. All right, you two. Get to work, and I'll see if I can find out who the farm's foreman was. I might be able to locate some old payroll records or something, if I'm lucky."

"Pray first, Dad," Campbell said with a smile.

"Right."

As they walked over to the main office, Nick shot her a sidelong glance. "The boss is always telling me not to rely on luck."

"Wise advice."

"He said God is in charge of everything, and luck and coincidence are just ways we explain why things happen in ways we can't understand. I was kind of surprised to hear him say 'if he was lucky.' Were you?"

"Not really. It's an expression, Nick."

"Yeah."

She stopped near her desk and looked him in the eye. "I was a little flippant to remind him to pray, but . . . Maybe we should pray before we do our assignments too."

Nick stared at her. "You mean, like, out loud?"

"Dad told me you've been talking to him about

the Lord. He even told me he's prayed with you a few times."

His jaw clenched. "I don't know, Professor. I don't think I'm ready for that. With you, I mean."

"Okay. But I'll ask God to help us clear up this case. You could do the same. Silently, I mean. Then we'll see how we do."

He pulled in a big breath. "You're on."

She sat down smiling and closed her eyes. *Lord, I don't know exactly where Nick is spiritually right now, but he's come a long way. Thank You. Help me to be more patient with him. And please, Lord, help us to find the information we need.*

When she opened her eyes, Nick was seated behind his desk across the room. He hadn't opened his laptop yet. His eyes were shut, and his face scrunched like a crumpled piece of paper.

Thank You.

She set to work.

In less than ten minutes, she found obituaries for Randall Abbott and his sister, Marcella Smith. She typed her findings into the case file.

"You got something?" Nick asked.

"Randall had a heart attack while he was at work. He was only forty-one. Marcella, it seems, was an asthmatic. She caught a bad case of the flu or something like that. It went to pneumonia, and she died a couple of years ago, at the age of forty-five."

"Wow."

"Yeah. Jacob's forty-five now."

"If he makes it through this year, he'll have outlived the rest of his family."

"Well, their parents were older when they died."

Nick grunted.

"How about you?" she asked. "Any success with Marcella's ex?"

"I haven't found any evidence that he's dead. And there are a lot of Smiths."

Campbell chuckled. "You speak true. I'm going to pop over and tell Dad what I found and see how he's coming along."

Bill looked up with a grin as she entered. "I struck gold. My accountant did some work for David Nelson. I told him I didn't want any financial information, I just wanted to know who worked on the farm twenty years ago. He put me in touch with Nelson's old business manager, who was able to give me a list of people on the payroll that year."

"Fantastic. That makes my news seem insignificant. It seems Randall and Marcella both died of natural causes. Oh, and Nick thinks Craig Smith is still alive."

"All right. We're making progress. Tell Nick to keep trying to trace Smith. I'll give you half the list of employees besides Jacob and Craig."

"Do I contact them?"

"Not yet. Let's just find out if they're still alive

181

and still in the area. With the questions we're asking, I think we'd do better to see them in person."

"Okay." She took the list of seven names he handed her. It included a cook-housekeeper, a year-round farm hand, and five summer employees.

When they quit for the evening, Nick went home. Campbell and her dad went to the kitchen, where Rita had left them a savory beef stew in the slow cooker and fresh corn muffins, with homemade custard in the refrigerator.

"Hiring Rita for a second day every week was a brilliant decision," Bill said, grinning as Campbell ladled out two bowls of stew.

"Then pat yourself on the back. It was your decision. But I agree. And she did up all the laundry today."

"Let's eat out here." Bill moved toward the small pine table by one of the windows. Eating in the kitchen was so much cozier than in the dining room.

When they'd finished, Bill went off to watch the evening news in the sitting room upstairs. Campbell put their dishes in the dishwasher and went to her room. She'd picked up a box of Christmas cards, and she addressed several to their extended family members and closest friends.

After stamping the cards, she opened her laptop. Now was the perfect time to arrange for her dad's Christmas gifts. First, she looked up the book he'd mentioned. She liked to support local businesses, so she placed an online order through a local bookstore. Then she searched for "Kentucky trout fishing."

By noon on Tuesday, they'd determined that, of all the workers for David Nelson when his Banitier painting was reported stolen, several had moved out of state. Three were migrant workers who had long since moved on and didn't currently show up in western Kentucky searches. One young man had married and lived in Graves County, but after a chat with him on the phone, Bill was convinced he had nothing to do with their case.

They still hadn't decided about Jacob and Craig.

"Okay," Nick said as they settled around the dining room table with sandwiches and leftover stew, "where does that leave us?"

"It leaves me heading for court this afternoon," Bill said. "I'll be a witness in an insurance case."

"Just today?" Campbell asked.

"If it goes the way Barry McGann thinks it will, they should wrap it up today." Barry was an attorney friend of Bill's, and he often sent work their way.

"What should Nick and I focus on?" Campbell asked.

Her father took a bite of his sandwich and chewed it slowly, staring off toward the antique oak buffet that had come with the house. "It seems to me that we need to find out who gave that painting to Craig to hold for him."

"Or her," Nick said.

"Right." Bill reached for his coffee. "Did you get an address for Craig?"

Nick winced. "Not exactly. But I think I have his email. We might be able to contact him that way."

Bill paused with his mug an inch from his lips. "No phone?"

"I got sidetracked. I think I can find it, though."

"You get on that." Bill took a sip. "Look, as soon as we're done here, I need to get changed and get over to the courthouse."

"If Nick finds a phone number, do you want us to call him?" Campbell asked.

He hesitated. "You'll have to be careful."

"We can't tell him how we got on his trail as far as the painting is concerned." Campbell remembered Jacob's cagey interview.

"Did you promise Jacob you wouldn't?"

"Well, no. He said don't tell the cops. But when I asked him who gave the painting to Craig, he said, 'You'll have to ask him.' So I guess . . ."

Her father nodded. "There you go. He didn't tell you not to reveal your source to Craig. And even if he did, Jacob's not our client, remember?"

"Yeah."

Bill drilled his gaze into Nick. "You be careful. If you two try to go see this guy, you take care of my daughter."

"Da-ad!"

Campbell's protest came out at the same moment as Nick's solemn "Yes, sir." She turned and scowled at him.

"I'm an adult, Dad, and I must say I've been in some dicey situations this past year, and I've come out of them all right."

"Yes, you have," Bill said smoothly. "You've handled yourself well. Nevertheless, men who are bullies with women alone tend to watch their step better when she has a male escort."

"You think Craig Smith is a bully?" Nick asked.

"I don't know, but I know he and his wife divorced while their kids were still fairly young. I don't know why, but it's a red flag. I don't like to send my daughter alone to interview a man with an uncertain past, as you know."

"Everything went fine yesterday with Jacob," Campbell reminded him.

"Yes. But he's involved in a crime, and this man is one step closer to it."

Campbell could see there was no sense in continuing the heated discussion with her dad. She would always be his little girl, even if she could serve on a jury and confront criminals. She was surprised he hadn't insisted she take a self-defense course—which she wasn't opposed to. In fact, maybe she'd sign up for one before he got the idea. It might give her a little more confidence, and it would give her father a bit more peace of mind.

Bill shoved back his chair. "All right, you two. I've got to get moving."

"No dessert?" Nick had an injured air.

"There's custard in the fridge and ice cream in the freezer," Campbell said, a bit annoyed with him. "Dad, give me a call when you're done, okay? If we're on the road, at least we'll know what you're up to."

"You mean *I'll* know what *you're* up to." He smiled. "Oh, and while Nick's running down Smith's contact info, you can do some more research on the Standish matter. We can't investigate the murder exactly, but I want to be certain Brad and Dylan weren't mixed up in this mess."

Chapter 15

When Campbell carried their dishes into the kitchen, Nick was seated at the pine table with a dish of black cherry ice cream in front of him. She put the dishes into the dishwasher and scowled at him.

"I'll be at my desk." She wheeled toward the hall, feeling guilty. She thought she'd gotten over being annoyed by everything Nick did. Eating a bowl of ice cream wasn't a crime. In fact, if he hadn't been there, she might have taken some herself. Did she want to feel superior to him?

Lord, please help me to conquer my pride. Without squashing it out of me, if possible. I really want to change. She settled at her desk and bowed her head, eyes closed to block out distractions. She could see Nick digging a big cherry out of his ice cream and carrying it to his smiling mouth. *Father, I like ice cream too. Please help me to quit looking down my nose at Nick.*

She opened her eyes and started trolling online for bits of information on any of the Standish clan. Accessing legal sites available to private investigators for a fee, she learned that Brad Standish had taken three renters to court over the years to recoup money for damage to his property. All had happened at least three years previously, and none amounted to more than five thousand dollars' worth of repairs. She couldn't imagine that was enough to kill someone over.

She came across an ad Brad had placed in August for a vacancy in one of his apartment units. The fact that he'd paid for an ad surprised her. One would think a landlord would have a waiting list for rentals in this college town.

Nick breezed into the room, sans the ice cream. She opened her mouth to ask if he'd put his bowl in the dishwasher but clamped her lips firmly shut.

"Find anything yet?" he asked.

"Nothing that seems pertinent."

He sat down at his desk, and she turned her attention back to the Standishes. Mentions of Colleen seemed confined to social blurbs and community briefs. Helping out at the Women's Club's annual iris show. Serving on a committee for a local food pantry. Volunteering at a fund-raiser for a homeless shelter.

Dylan had worked at the hospital, but in a non-medical capacity. He'd been supervisor of the food service for a year, and before that he'd worked in the kitchen for three years. However, when Campbell called the hospital and asked for him, she was told that he no longer worked there.

She hung up and sat frowning at the phone.

"Something got you down?" Nick asked.

"Yeah. Dylan Standish apparently quit his job at the hospital recently."

"How recently? Since his father died?"

"I don't know."

Nick lifted one shoulder in a casual shrug. "Maybe he feels he needs to concentrate on his father's business now."

"Maybe. But I don't see that he worked with his father before. The job he held at the hospital was full time."

"Well, I've got something. Craig Smith lives in Aurora. Want to take a ride?"

"Sure." Campbell almost said, "If we can take my car," but she caught herself. No need to be bossy about it. "Want me to drive?"

"If you don't mind. I'm a little low on gas today."

"Let's go." She grabbed her purse and a jacket, and soon both were in her Fusion, heading out Route 80. Using his phone, Nick guided her onto 68 North for a few miles, and then onto a side road to the west, away from Kentucky Lake.

"It's nice out here," he said, gazing at the farmland and hardwood forests they passed.

Campbell kept her eyes on the road. "I like living in town."

"So you can shop easier?"

She bit back a snarky retort. "That's part of it. I can see the sense of being in a central location for a business like ours. And I'll admit, I like being close to certain amenities, like the hospital and the library. Call me a fuddy-duddy, but knowing the fire department and the police station are only a few blocks away gives me a little extra feeling of security."

"Huh."

She glanced over at him. "I suppose you'd be a hermit if you had a choice."

"No, I like socializing. But I like the peaceful countryside too. Not isolation, just . . . space."

She considered that as she drove past a large farm with cattle in the pasture, browsing languidly on the winter grass.

"It should be up here on the right," Nick said.

Another farm? Campbell squinted into the lowering sun and wish she had her dark glasses.

"I think that's it." He tapped his window, and she saw it then, a one-story wood-frame house near the road, backed by a large, fallow field. No vehicles sat in the driveway.

"He's probably not home," she said.

"Maybe. We can at least look around."

"He remarried, right?" Campbell turned in and parked on the gravel drive.

"Yeah, not long after he and Marcella split. I'm not sure what the status is now."

They both got out, and Campbell perused the attached garage as they approached the porch. The overhead door held two small windows, but she couldn't tell if a car was parked inside. A cold wind blew off the field and made her shiver.

There was no doorbell, so Nick knocked. They waited. When no one answered, Nick raised his eyebrows. "What time is it?"

She checked her phone. "Almost three."

"He might not be back for a couple hours. Want me to take a stroll around back just for drill?"

"Wait." She turned at the sound of an approaching vehicle.

A red Dodge Ram slowed as it neared the driveway. As the pickup swung in toward them, Nick muttered, "Well, what do you know? We timed it right after all."

Campbell's stomach clenched at the thought that she should have called her father and told him where they were. Still, he'd told her he'd call when he got out of court. If he was still in the session, he wouldn't answer a call from her. Her cell was in her hand, and she whipped off a quick text message to Bill. "N and I at C Smith's in Aurora." She hoped that was enough. Craig was now out of the truck and walking toward them, wearing a puzzled frown.

"Can I help you folks?"

"Yeah." Nick stepped toward him.

Campbell quickly cataloged the man's appearance. He must be nearly fifty, she knew from her research. He was good-looking—he must have been a doll in high school. His dark hair had just a sprinkling of gray, and the intent gaze from his brown eyes would melt chocolate. When they married, Marcella probably thought she'd caught the man of the year.

Meanwhile, Nick was giving his spiel.

"I'm Nick Emerson, and this is Campbell McBride. We're private investigators."

Craig's back stiffened. "Investigators? Oh, don't tell me. Leila? I heard she was in trouble, but honestly, she's only my niece by marriage. I really don't—"

"This isn't about Leila," Campbell said quickly. "We need your insight on something that happened a long time ago."

"How long?"

She swallowed hard, wishing she could put off the moment when the gears in his brain started turning. "About twenty years."

He stood very still, but his eyes darted back and forth, from her to Nick and back.

"You said *private* investigators?"

"Yes."

"May I ask who's behind the investigation?"

"We're not allowed to reveal client information," Nick said.

"But you're not working for the police?"

"That's right." Campbell gave him what she hoped was a reassuring smile. "This is strictly private, for our client's satisfaction. We hope to uncover a few facts about the past, for the client's peace of mind."

Still he hesitated. After a moment, he walked past her with his keyring in his hand.

"All right, I guess. But come inside. It's cold out here."

"It sure is," she said. "Thank you."

Nick gave her a subtle nod as they waited for Craig to open the door. He let them in and closed it.

"On the left. Have a seat." He started to remove his coat but didn't offer to take theirs.

When he joined them, Nick leaned forward in his armchair and seemed ready to take the lead, so Campbell kept quiet.

"We understand you worked for David Nelson when you were younger," Nick began. "Back in the tobacco farm days."

"Yeah. It was just a summer job, but he paid pretty good." Craig sighed. "Hardly anyone grows tobacco around here anymore."

"I guess other crops are more profitable now." Nick glanced at Campbell then said, "And you were there working the year a valuable painting was stolen from Mr. Nelson's house."

Craig's eyes widened. "I thought this wasn't about Leila. I mean, isn't that what she got in trouble over? That painting?"

"Well, yes, it is, but the charges against her have been dismissed. We're just trying to find out what really happened with the painting."

"I . . . don't really see what that has to do with me."

"What did the other people you worked with say about it? Did you hear any guesses on what happened to the painting?"

"No. Other than, someone took it."

Campbell felt they were getting nowhere and it was time to be more direct. "Mr. Smith, we spoke to your former brother-in-law, Jacob Abbott. He was working there as well at that time."

Craig's lips twitched. "Well, yeah. He was there that summer."

"Jacob was kind enough to tell us that he hid the painting in his parents' attic," Campbell said, ignoring the glare Nick shot at her. Was she revealing too much? She didn't think so, given that they wanted more information from this reticent man. "He said you gave it to him and asked him to hold on to it for him. Is that true?"

He hauled in a shaky breath but said nothing.

Nick cleared his throat. "Look, we're not interested in your part, other than who you got the picture from."

"What picture?" Craig asked.

"The Elroy Banitier painting," Campbell said, struggling to control her frustration. "Jacob told us that if we wanted to know where you got it, we'd have to ask you. So, here we are. We'd like to know who gave you the Banitier—that is, if you didn't steal it yourself."

"What? No! I didn't steal it."

"Then who did?" Nick asked.

Craig glanced toward the doorway, as though contemplating his chances of escape.

"Look, I was hoping to put that behind me. I mean, it's been twenty years."

"Leila Abbott almost went to prison over it," Campbell said evenly. "Don't you think it's time you told the truth?"

Craig clenched his fists on the arms of his chair. "I did not do anything illegal."

Nick scratched his chin. "Receiving stolen property."

The color in Craig's face drained. "No. You can't make that stick."

A rogue thought hit her, and Campbell caught her breath. "Yes, the D.A. *can* make that stick, unless you can prove one of two things."

"What's that?"

"Either the painting belonged to you, or it was given to you by the owner to hold for him."

Nick's eyebrows shot up. "Did Mr. Nelson give you that painting?"

Craig's mouth moved, but no words emerged.

"Okay, listen." Campbell leaned forward. "At the time it was reported stolen, that painting belonged to David Nelson. Period. If he gave it to you as a gift, you need something that will prove that—a receipt, or a witness. Something along those lines. If he handed it over to you to keep out of sight for him for a while—say, because he thought someone might take it—then you need to be able to prove that."

"I'm not buying it," Nick said almost casually. "If that happened, he'd have asked for it back once things calmed down and he was ready to take it to the museum. Nelson wouldn't have left something like that hanging for years, until he died."

Campbell jerked her chin up. "Did he mention the painting in his will?"

"How should I know?" Craig jumped up. "We're done here. I'm not answering any more questions."

Campbell stood reluctantly.

"In that case," Nick said as he unwound from his chair, "maybe you'd better get yourself a lawyer. Because more questions will be asked, I can guarantee."

Craig herded them to the front door and closed it behind them, and Campbell heard the deadbolt turn. She followed Nick down the steps and to her car.

"So, what do you think?" she asked as they clicked on their seat belts.

"I think he's calling Jacob this very minute to rant at him for ratting him out."

"When you think about it, it was a pretty mean thing to do to a friend."

Nick shook his head. "I'm guessing Craig had no idea how valuable the painting was when he gave it to Jacob, or he'd have fenced it someplace like St. Louis or Nashville once Old Man Nelson died."

"You could be right. But since Jacob had it, Craig would be afraid to rock the boat."

"He didn't want to go to jail then, and he doesn't want to go to jail now," Nick said.

"Hey." Campbell hit the brake at the end of the driveway and looked over at him.

"What?"

"Assuming Craig didn't actually steal the painting, and assuming Mr. Nelson didn't give it to him for whatever reason . . ."

"Yeah?"

Campbell huffed out a breath. "I was just thinking. If you were in Craig's position then, and you found out the hot painting was worth north of forty thousand dollars, wouldn't you see that as an opportunity to make a little cash?"

"You mean . . ." Nick's gaze met hers. "He might have been blackmailing whoever really stole it."

She nodded. "He never asked Jacob to give it back. But what if the person who gave it to Craig asked for it back?"

"We know he didn't give it back," Nick said slowly. "If they gave him some money to keep quiet, he'd have to either return it or explain."

"Not necessarily. What if he didn't promise to return it? What if he said he'd take it to the police if he wasn't paid . . . oh, I don't know. Say, ten thousand?"

"I'm with you now," Nick said. "And later, he could have gone back and demanded more money."

"He could have extorted more than the painting was even worth," Campbell said, turning onto the pavement, "and never gone near it himself. Whoever gave it to him would live in fear of being reported. They might keep on paying him indefinitely."

"The scumbag."

Campbell sighed. "It's only speculation."

"Yeah, but what other reason could he have for not asking Jacob to give it back? It was perfect. Jacob had no idea of the value—"

"Oh, I think he did," Campbell said. "The theft was reported in the newspapers, remember? I'll bet it was on the TV news too."

"But Jacob was afraid to touch the thing once he'd hidden it, in case he was blamed. And the thief was afraid to pressure Craig too hard to give it back, or it would all come out. Let's run your theory by the boss, Detective."

Campbell smiled. "If you think we should, Partner."

Nick grinned back at her. "I definitely think we should."

As soon as her car was back in the garage, she called her dad's cell, but there was no answer.

"Still in court, I guess," she told Nick.

They went into the office and fixed coffee.

"What do we do now?" Campbell asked. "There's no way to research whether or not Craig Smith was blackmailing someone."

"True." Nick frowned and took a sip from his mug. "Have we talked to his kids at all?"

"Just Corey, when he accosted Dad and me in the parking lot at the Sirloin Stockade. He and Dad exchanged a few words. But I did see Anna when she testified at Leila's trial."

"Hmm."

"What are you thinking?"

"They might be able to tell us something."

Campbell grimaced. "You think so? It seems to me they're well out of it. They were kids when this all started."

"And their parents split up. Marcella's dead, so she can't tell us why, but I'm thinking the kids could give us an earful about why their parents divorced."

"And it could have to do with the painting?"

"I have no idea, but I think it's worth asking them."

Campbell thought about it for a moment. "We should ask Leila first. It might have nothing to do with this."

Nick shrugged. "Let's check the date of the

divorce." He moved to his desk and opened his laptop.

"I know they were still married when Craig gave the painting to Jacob," Campbell said, looking up at the ceiling while she taxed her memory. "He said Marcella nearly found it, and he wanted it out of the house. That was sixteen years ago."

"Okay, hold on." Nick tapped away at his keyboard.

Campbell waited, sipping her coffee.

After a few minutes, Nick raised his head. "Got it. They divorced a year later."

She stared at him across the room. "That makes it seem . . . possible it's connected. If she found out about it, or even suspected her husband was up to something, that could have sparked a lot of arguments. Until finally, she'd had enough. She no longer wanted to be married to a liar and a criminal."

Nick looked a little skeptical. "Or maybe he just found a younger woman he liked better. I think we should ask the kids."

"Okay." She set down her mug. "I'll call Leila and Cousin Anna. You take the boys, Blaine and Corey."

"All right, but I don't think it's something we should just call up and ask them cold. Leila, maybe. You know her better, and it wasn't her folks."

"That makes sense. I'll call her first, and then if we need to, I'll try to see Anna in person, and you can find the guys." Campbell picked up the desk phone's receiver and hit Leila's number.

Chapter 16

"Oh, wow, I was only eight or nine when they split up."

Campbell could hear the strain in Leila's voice. "I don't want to stir up bad memories, but this could shed some light on our investigation. Just tell me, if you can, what was going on between your aunt Marcella and her husband."

"All I know is, Anna was a disaster. Just shattered. She stayed over with us quite a lot, and she shared our room with Danielle and me when her mom died." Leila let out a sigh. "I remember she told me her parents fought a lot, especially at night. They both worked during the day, but as soon as Uncle Craig got home from work, Aunt Marcella would start in on him. Anna had to start supper before they got home, so she heard a lot of it."

"Did she tell you why they were fighting?"

"I'm not sure she knew. Her mother seemed to be mad about something Uncle Craig did. Maybe a lot of things. I know he drank a lot. If he stayed out late and came home drunk, Anna just cringed in her room. That's part of why she liked to stay with us so much. I don't know what the boys did. They were younger, but I'm sure it affected them too."

"Is it possible Craig was cheating on your aunt?"

"Sure. Anything's possible."

"Anna's older than you," Campbell said.

"Yeah. She was around twelve then." After a moment's silence, Leila said, "That was really rough on her."

"And, by extension, on you and your sister."

"Yeah. Danielle was . . . what, five? But she was scared too. After she was asleep, Anna would tell me stuff she didn't want Dani to hear."

"What kind of stuff?"

"I only remember bits and pieces. I've tried to forget about it. Anna seems happy now, with Pete."

"I'm so sorry. I don't like raking it all up, but it might help us."

"Okay." Leila sniffed. "Uh, she said her mom screamed a lot at her dad. And one time—yeah, I'm pretty sure she said one time her father hit Blaine. He'd done something stupid or clumsy—I don't remember what. Spilled something, maybe. And Craig hit him."

"Was it bad?"

"I don't think he had to go to the hospital or anything like that. But Anna wondered about her mom."

"You mean . . ."

"If he hit her too."

Campbell drew in a deep breath. "Was there

ever anything that made you think he might have, other than what Anna told you about them fighting?"

"I came home from school one day, and Anna and the boys got off the bus at our house. My mother or Aunt Marcella—somebody—had called the school and said for them all to get off with me. So I thought, this is nice, my cousins are going to have supper with us. We all played for a while and ate together. Finally Aunt Marcella came to get them, and . . . Her face was a mess." Leila sobbed. "She said she'd fallen down and smacked her face, but . . ."

"But you didn't believe her?"

"Anna ran to her and hugged her and said something like, 'Mom, you can't put up with this any longer.' I think it wasn't long after that when Uncle Craig left."

"He moved out?"

There was a moment's silence. "I think he just left. Maybe Aunt Marcella threw him out. I don't know exactly what happened, but it was a shock to the kids. One day, he was just gone. Anna told me at school he'd gone and he wasn't coming back. The boys . . . Little Corey looked shell-shocked. He cried a lot after that."

"Do you know if your cousins have contact with their father now? Because he lives in Aurora. I'm sure he's in Murray now and then," Campbell said.

"Yeah, he went away for a while, but then I guess he moved back and bought that old farmhouse. Anna doesn't see him, I'm sure. I don't think she's spoken to him in years. She was her mom's rock. They were very close, even after Anna and Pete got married. She never had a good word to say about Craig."

"What about her brothers?"

"I don't know."

They signed off soon after, and Campbell looked up at Nick. "I have to wonder if Anna knows a lot more about this than she's let on to Leila. She was her mother's closest and final confidant."

"But didn't she testify against Leila at the trial?" Nick asked.

"Yeah." Campbell frowned. "That's problematic. Why would she do that if she knew the painting in question was stolen?"

"Well, it's possible she didn't know specifically about the painting. Her folks yelled a lot. Her mother could have told her that Craig was involved in a theft—or maybe just something illegal, not specified."

"True. I guess we'd better talk to her. The boys, on the other hand, could know something."

"Leila called one of them when she couldn't get hold of Bill after Dylan Standish threatened her."

"Corey." Campbell grimaced, recalling the

encounter in the parking lot. She pushed back her chair. "Since Craig's back in the area, it's entirely possible he's reached out to his boys over the years—or vice versa. But that doesn't mean they know any more about the theft, or about why he and Marcella divorced."

"He'd try to spin the divorce if he could," Nick said with certainty.

"Make Marcella out to be the bad guy, so to speak?"

"The shrew, the judgmental harridan."

Campbell nodded. Before she could speak, her cell rang. She glanced at the screen then answered with a smile. "Hey, Dad."

"Hi. Just out of court and heading home. What are you two up to?"

"Well, we went to see Craig Smith. He wasn't happy, and he insisted he didn't steal the painting, but he wouldn't tell us how he got it. I just talked to Leila to see what she could tell us about Craig and Marcella. That marriage ended badly."

"I'm not surprised."

"Me either. I was going to try to contact Anna. I think she works days. Our plan is for me to try to talk to her, and Nick will try to see her brothers, Corey and Blaine Smith."

"Assuming they're all working today, let's hash this over first," Bill said. "I'll be there in five, and you can give me the details."

"Okay, I'll have your coffee ready."

• • •

When the three of them were seated together near the fireplace with a cheerful blaze warming them, Nick gave a rundown of their visit to Craig, and Campbell related the high points of her conversation with Leila.

"So, Smith says he didn't steal it, but he admitted having it and then giving it to his brother-in-law to hold for him." Bill took a sip of his brew.

"Yeah," Campbell said. "If he was telling the truth, we think it's possible he might be blackmailing whoever gave it to him." She explained what she and Nick had talked about.

"That's possible," Bill said. "But I think you've overlooked an alternative."

"What?"

Bill pulled in a deep breath. "Just suppose that David Nelson gave the painting to Craig—"

"I don't think he just gave it to him," Nick said. "Not as a gift, anyway."

"Neither do I. But what if Nelson was planning to claim insurance for a stolen artwork?"

Campbell frowned, thinking about that. "You're saying Mr. Nelson may have committed insurance fraud?"

"His insurer did reimburse him for the value of the painting. That would be a pretty good motive for blackmail, wouldn't it?"

"Well, yeah," Nick said. "But Mr. Nelson died ten years ago."

"Twelve," Campbell corrected. "So, why would the blackmailer leave the painting in the attic after his source of income died? Why didn't he sell it at that point?"

"I can think of reasons." Bill took another drink from his coffee and set the mug on the end table. "Just suppose Nelson reports the painting stolen—"

"But he told his kids the day before that he was donating it," Campbell protested. "Why tell them that, if he was going to claim it was stolen?"

"It threw suspicion on them."

She gazed at her father, trying to follow his reasoning. "If it was me, I wouldn't have said boo in advance. I'd have just hidden it and reported it."

"David Nelson had four children. If there was infighting in that family, that made a pretty good field of suspects, don't you think?"

Nick leaned over to take the poker from its stand. "And if none of them was really guilty, nothing could be proven on any of them, so there was no danger of really ruining their lives, but it would sure make them uncomfortable for a while." He jabbed at the burning logs and added another to the blaze.

Campbell shook her head. "We don't know that there were any hard feelings between him and his kids, and I'm not sure how we could find out. But it still seems more likely to me that the painting was really stolen. By someone else."

Her father sighed. "Well, as far as we know, David Nelson was an honest man. I did check his record earlier. He was never arrested for anything. I didn't find so much as a traffic ticket. And I don't think he needed the money."

"There's that," Campbell said almost triumphantly. "Nelson was a rich man. If he was desperate for cash, wouldn't it make more sense for him to sell his painting legitimately than to pretend it was stolen and take the insurance valuation?"

"You're right. I'll do some more digging into his financials around that time."

"Do we have a copy of his will?" she asked.

"Not yet." Bill checked the time. "I'll see if I can get one tomorrow."

Nick looked from him to Campbell and back. "So, where do we stand?"

"I think your blackmail theory is a good one," Bill said. "It's one Craig Smith could have instigated by himself, whether he stole the painting or someone else did and then asked him to hide it."

Campbell spread her hands. "As far as we know, nobody else knew where the painting was."

"They wouldn't have to know to blackmail Nelson or the thief," Nick said. "They could bluff it."

"If Mr. Nelson wasn't behind it—if someone really stole that painting from him—why would someone blackmail him?" Campbell asked. "They couldn't. He'd tell the police someone threatened him. They'd only be putting themselves in danger. But if the person who had the painting—or at least knew who took it—did the blackmailing, that would make more sense."

"There'd be an extra layer of protection between the blackmailer and the target." Bill nodded. "You're right, Soup. The blackmailer would feel pretty safe, I'd think. He didn't take the painting, and he was once removed from the theft. It would be hard for the victim to figure out who was doing it."

"Guess you'd better look for some large payments between the time of the theft and Nelson's death," Nick said.

Bill pushed himself up from his chair. "Time to get to work."

"Should we still try to see Craig's children?" Campbell asked.

"Not yet." Bill paused in the office doorway. "Oh, I saw Hayden Nesmith at the courthouse. He wants us to do a little job for him. It probably won't take more than half a day. It's almost quitting time for today, but you two can work on that while I muck around in Nelson's finances. If Hayden's sent me the details, I'll email them to you both. Campbell, you can open a new case file, please."

"Sure, Dad. You want more coffee?"

"That would be nice."

She smiled and picked up his empty mug.

Keith rang the doorbell at True Blue just before seven o'clock. He'd gone off duty at three and taken advantage of some free time to do a little grocery shopping, followed by some cleaning at his house. His visit to the McBrides was for a dual purpose, to discuss their findings in the Abbott case, and to see Campbell.

The door was usually left unlocked during the day so that clients could walk in, but after five they locked it. Campbell opened it and smiled when she saw him.

"Hi! Come on in."

"How's it going?" Keith asked.

"Fine. Dad's upstairs. I'm guessing you want to talk to both of us."

"Eventually." At the bottom of the stairway, Keith leaned down for a kiss.

When he released her, she smiled up at him. "Can I bring you anything? I'm getting Dad some sweet tea to keep him from drinking coffee this late."

"How is he with decaf?"

"Not so good. But I can fix you some if you want."

"No, I'll take the tea as well. Thanks."

He knew the way up to the sitting room, and he climbed the stairs as she hurried off toward the kitchen. The TV was on, and the sound of a videoed shootout grew louder as he approached the doorway.

Bill looked up and hit the remote to pause the program. "Hi! Have a seat."

Keith settled on the end of the couch nearest Bill's recliner. "I hate to interrupt your show."

"It's taped." Bill shrugged. "I'm sure what you have to say will be much more interesting."

The skin around Bill's left eye was still distended, with varying hues of purple.

"How's the eye? Still painful?"

"Some, but don't tell Campbell I said that." He glanced toward the doorway. "Where'd she get to?"

"Refreshments." Keith wondered if he should have gone with her and offered to carry the tray.

"How are you coming on the Standish case?" Bill asked.

"We've made some headway. We know what type of gun was used, but the ballistics tests don't show a match in the system. It seems to be an unregistered, but legal, handgun."

"There are a ton of those around. You don't have to register handguns in Kentucky."

"Yeah," Keith said. "We hoped to match it in the system with one that's been used in another crime, but nothing's come up."

Bill clicked the remote and shut the television off completely as Campbell entered the room.

Her tray held three tall glasses of iced tea and a plate of peanut butter cookies.

"Those look good," Keith said.

"Help yourself. Yesterday was Rita's day—her first Monday for us. We didn't see much of her, but she was busy." Campbell set down the tray and took a seat beside Keith. While both men were chewing their first bites of cookies, she said, "So, Keith, we're looking hard at the Smith children—Leila Abbott's cousins. Their father is involved in this somehow. He swears he didn't steal the painting from Mr. Nelson, but he won't tell us how he got it."

Bill swallowed. "The latest theory is that Craig Smith or some other person was blackmailing the thief."

"Mr. Nelson collected a cool forty-five thousand dollars from his insurance company after that painting was stolen," Keith said. "It's worth even more now."

Bill gave a low whistle.

Campbell explained why they didn't think Mr. Nelson was being blackmailed, and her father gave his agreement.

"I don't think he committed insurance fraud," Bill said. "However, I am going through everything I can get on his financials. No red flags so far."

"Do you think Craig Smith was blackmailing him?"

"I think somebody—maybe Smith—was black-

213

mailing the actual thief, not Mr. Nelson. Because Smith knew where the painting was all that time. Very few people did."

"Do you have evidence that he received payments?"

Bill shook his head. "Not yet. He's living in an old farmhouse in Aurora."

Keith took a swallow from his glass and sat back on the couch. "It's an interesting theory, but so far it sounds like it's just speculation."

"It is," Campbell admitted. "It's not like he's living far above his income or anything like that."

"Well, I find it very interesting that Brad Standish's son took a swing at your father."

Bill put a finger gingerly to his cheekbone. "These two cases have got to be tied together somehow."

"I think you're right. And blackmail is one possible connection." Keith reached for another cookie.

"What does your schedule look like for next week?" Campbell asked.

With the holidays coming, officers were scrambling to get certain shifts off on Christmas Eve and Christmas Day, to have time with their families. Keith had talked to his parents and managed to get the hours off that they most wanted for him.

"I've got the twenty-third off, and I work the day shift Christmas Eve," he said. "I volunteered to do the four-to-midnight on Christmas Day. That will give me the chance to eat a big dinner with the folks and Nicole and Todd before I go in. And that way, I get the twenty-sixth off."

Campbell smiled. "The day of our theater party."

"Right. Have you decided what you're doing Christmas Day? Because you're always welcome with us."

"Thanks," she said. "We accepted the Bradys' invitation. We'll have our own tree and gifts here the night before."

"What about Nick?" Keith asked.

"He's going to Florida on Friday and spending the weekend with his parents."

Bill took another cookie. "I told him to go and spend a few days down there. Since Christmas is on a Monday this year, I told him I won't expect him back in the office until Wednesday. That'll give him an extra day for travel."

"Are you going to work Tuesday?" Keith asked.

Bill shrugged. "We'll just tie up loose ends, if there are any. We're doing a couple of small jobs, and I hope to wind up this Abbott thing by then. We've already gone beyond Leila's budget, but with things shaking down the way they are, we can't just drop it."

Keith nodded with a frown. Bill was a pit bull when it came to his cases. No way would he stop investigating until they knew exactly what happened and who was responsible.

Chapter 17

Campbell was having a ball Wednesday morning. Her shopping was done, and she was setting up a detailed family group sheet for David Nelson. His four children had all married and given him grandchildren. The younger generation and the three great-grands were well out of the theft and blackmail sphere, she was sure. She filled in their vital statistics but went light on details for them.

The four adult children claimed more of her attention. They were all between forty-five and sixty. The eldest, David Nelson, Jr., had settled in the southern end of Murray, where he had a large estate and owned several pieces of farmland. He didn't appear to work the land himself, but leased out the parcels to several sharecroppers. If his upscale house and expensive cars were any indication, he did well.

The oldest daughter, Charlotte, had married a doctor and now lived in Franklin, Tennessee, outside Nashville. The online view of her house looked to Campbell like a palace.

Diane, the next child, was now fifty-three. She'd been married twice, but with her second husband, she'd settled in Marshall County, just to the north. The couple jointly owned three farm stores in the area and appeared to be well-heeled. Diane was featured often in society page stories in the local newspaper. Campbell thought she recognized her from a couple of events she'd attended.

The youngest, Edmund, or "Eddie," was now forty-five. He'd been married fifteen years and produced two youngsters. He and his wife, Sally, owned and ran a doughnut shop that was popular with MSU students and locals. Their home off Sixteenth Street looked like an average brick ranch built forty or fifty years ago—nothing special, but adequate for a typical family.

Campbell looked up as her dad walked into the room.

"We should stop by Eddie's Donuts and sample the merchandise," she said.

Bill and Nick both perked up.

"Why is that?" her father asked.

"It's owned by one of David Nelson's sons and his wife. They make the doughnuts themselves."

"Definitely worth a visit," Nick said with a grin.

"Well, thanks to a friend who owed me a big favor, I've got news," Bill said. "In the last part of David Nelson's life—from the theft of the painting until he died eight years later—I couldn't find any evidence that he was making blackmail payments. No unexplained large withdrawals, no repeated payments to one person without a good reason."

Campbell nodded. "So if there was a blackmailer, the target was someone else, as we thought."

"The thief," Nick said.

With a frown, Campbell gazed up at her dad. "We're guessing. Maybe there wasn't any blackmail."

"Could be." Bill sighed.

"Do we just give up?" Nick had a hang-dog look, as though he didn't want to let go of his bone.

"Not yet," Bill said. "There's one more thing. A few minutes ago, I took a call on my cell phone. It was Cathy Abbott, Leila's mother."

"What did she want?" Nick asked.

"She just had a little morsel of news she thought might interest us. Her Women's Club group had a meeting yesterday. She heard through the grapevine that the Nelson family is having a big holiday bash."

"This weekend?" Campbell asked, mentally zipping through their own social commitments.

Bill shook his head. "New Year's Eve. A week from Sunday."

"Ooh. A private party?"

"Well, yes, but a large one."

Campbell looked at her screen and the information she'd collected on the Nelson family. "Where are they holding it? And who's hosting?"

"David, Jr., at his place down in south Murray."

She nodded. At least it wasn't Charlotte, over near Nashville. And she hadn't figured on Eddie,

218

in his small house. "What else do you know? Who all is invited?"

"All four siblings and their families and probably some friends and business associates."

"Hmm."

"They wouldn't invite you," Nick said, eyeing her scornfully.

"They don't know I exist. But maybe someone we know has an invitation." She looked eagerly at her dad.

"I'm not privy to the guest list, but we can ask around," Bill said.

"David, Jr. owns a lot of farmland, and his sister Diane and her husband own three farm stores."

Bill smiled. "Perfect. I'll make a list of large-scale farmers we've met, along with the county extension agent and the Department of Agriculture rep."

"Hey, I know someone who works at Tractor Supply," Nick said. "I could probably talk to the manager."

"I'm not sure how much we can learn by chatting up their employees, but I guess it's worth a try." Bill gave Nick a hard look. "Just steer clear of Diane Block and her husband. We don't want them to know we're sniffing around. Just casually see if the people working at the store know about the party and who's going."

Campbell went back to her family research on the Nelsons with new verve.

At noon, they gathered in the dining room over sandwiches and salad. Nick's trip to the farm store had netted him nothing. Bill had learned that the extension agent and his wife were, indeed, invited to the Nelson party. He couldn't help with getting one of the True Blue staff invited, but he did promise Bill that if one of them showed up, he wouldn't give away their investigation.

"How exactly would going to a party help us?" Nick asked. "I mean, other than champagne and caviar?"

Campbell scowled at him. If any of them got to go it should definitely *not* be Nick.

"We need to get closer to the family," Bill said. "Maybe we'll crack this thing before New Year's—I hope so. But if not, it would give us a close-up view of the siblings and their attitudes toward each other."

"None of them took over their dad's business," Campbell said, "and none of them work together now."

"I think all his farm property was sold when he died," Bill told her. "The older son is into farming now, but in a different location. Oh, and I have that new client coming in this afternoon, so I'll be tied up here. Campbell, could you go by the county courthouse for me?"

"Sure, Dad. What am I doing there?"

"Picking up a copy of David Nelson, Sr.'s will. They'll have it with my name on it at the clerk's desk. I told them I'd pick it up or my daughter would."

Campbell was relieved to have something to do other than hunch over her computer all afternoon.

"Okay if I swing by Plantation Place first? I ordered something, and they texted that it came in."

"No problem," Bill said.

Campbell loved the gift shop on Twelfth Street. She went in and browsed for a few minutes before approaching the counter. She'd ordered a special hand-painted trinket box for her friend Reagan Brady's Christmas gift. The smiling clerk brought it out for her. She looked it over and nodded with approval.

"It's perfect. And I'd like these." Campbell laid a pair of embroidered tea towels on the counter. They would be her hostess gift for Angela when they went to the Fullers' for dinner before the play the day after Christmas.

Pleased with her purchases, she drove downtown to the courthouse. When the oversized envelope was placed in her hands, she itched to open it. She told herself to be patient and drove back to the house on Willow Street.

"Did you get it?" Nick asked as soon as she walked in.

"Yeah. I saw a car out front. Is Dad in conference?"

Nick nodded. "He's with the client. I got the

impression we might be doing some more work on that case after the holidays."

"There's that embezzlement case he talked about too. Something tells me we'll be busy."

Campbell ran her shopping bag up to her room and came back down ready for some coffee. As she prepared it, she looked over at Nick. "Travel plans all sorted?"

"Yup, I'm flying down from Nashville."

"Oh, I thought you were driving."

"It takes too long, and it's really boring when you're alone." He flashed a grin. "You don't want to go with me, do you? The folks would love to see you."

She chuckled. "No, thanks, but say hi to them for me."

"Oh, come on. Road trip!"

Campbell shook her head and carried her mug to her desk.

He rose and came closer, lowering his voice. "Listen, while you were gone, we found out Dylan Standish is being, like, the crazy landlord. Raising people's rent Christmas week."

"Nice gift for the tenants," Campbell said with a sour tone. "We'd heard that already, though."

"Yeah, well, we heard he's also doing spot inspections of each unit."

"What?"

He nodded. "One of Bill's lawyer friends tipped him off. He knew we were interested in the Standish killing. Well, apparently one of the tenants called the attorney to ask if Dylan could do that."

"Can he?"

"Apparently so. He wasn't sure about all the others, but this particular tenant took him a copy of the lease, and he said it was perfectly legal, though not nice, for Dylan to announce a substantial increase starting in January and inspect any time he felt like it."

"Ouch."

"I don't know why he's inspecting," Nick said with a frown. "Maybe looking for excuses to evict people?"

Campbell froze for a moment then looked up at him. "Or looking for other contraband in their attics. What if he thinks his father put that painting in the Abbotts' attic?"

"You mean, like he stole it?"

"I mean, like Dylan thinks he stole it. And that maybe his father stole other stuff too."

"And hid it in other rental units." Nick broke out in a grin then sobered. "But he'd be wrong."

"Would he?"

"Well, as far as we know, Brad Standish had nothing to do with the theft."

"But somebody stole it and gave it to Craig Smith, who gave it to Jacob Abbott to hide. What if the first someone was good old Brad?"

"He wasn't working for David Nelson."

"So?"

They looked at each other for a long moment.

Nick shook his head and broke the stare. "I don't know. It seems a little too off-the-wall to me."

"Maybe so."

"But I do think you should write books."

Campbell eyed him suspiciously. "What?"

"You come up with these crazy scenarios. Why would somebody like Brad Standish steal a valuable painting and hide it for twenty years? A guy like him—he'd just sell it. Forget the blackmail."

She heaved out a deep sigh. "Okay, but—" She broke off as Bill's office door opened and voices told her he and his client were emerging into the hall. Her dad showed the guest out then strolled into the room.

"What's the verdict?" she asked.

"We're all set on that one. If he needs anything else, he'll contact us after New Year's."

"Hooray. I've got the will, Dad."

"Great. Let's have it."

She took it from her shoulder bag and handed it to him. Bill looked across the room.

"You should be in on this, Nick. Let's all have a seat." He led the way to the sofa near the fireplace, and Campbell and Nick joined him.

"All righty." Bill drew several sheets of folded paper from the envelope and smoothed them out on his knee. His eyes darted back and forth as he scanned the introductory paragraphs.

"Looks about as expected." He turned a page. "Uh-huh. He sold off some of the land before he died. The remainder, as well as the main house and outbuildings on the estate, was to be sold and divided among his four children."

"Equally?" Nick asked.

"No. It looks like a rather unequal split, as a matter of fact." Bill frowned and flipped to the final page. "David, the oldest son, got forty percent. The two girls got twenty-five percent each. The younger son, Edmund, got only ten percent."

"I wonder why that was," Campbell said.

Nick nodded. "Doesn't seem fair."

"I don't know."

"Wait a sec." Campbell sat up straighter. "In my family history research, I did see something this morning. Edmund Nelson was expelled from college for cheating on an exam."

"Is that enough for his father to dock his inheritance?" Nick asked.

"Maybe," Bill said. "Or maybe that was just the start of it. This will is dated about five years before Mr. Nelson died."

"So, after the painting was stolen." Campbell set her elbow on the sofa's arm and perched her chin on her fist.

"Keep looking at Edmund's past," her father said. "What school ejected him?"

"Vanderbilt."

Bill gave a low whistle. "See if he went back to college—maybe transferred to another school. And if he had a police record, either here or in Nashville, or wherever he ended up if he went back to school."

"Isn't he the one who runs the doughnut shop?" Nick sounded crushed, as if the last thing he wanted to hear was that the doughnut man was a criminal.

"He is," Campbell said, "but we're talking about his college days, Nick. He's forty-five now."

Nick scrunched up his face but said nothing further.

Campbell turned to her father. "Right. Keep investigating Edmund. Anything else?"

Bill shrugged. "There are a few charitable bequests in this will. The kids' inheritance was whatever was left after those were made and the estate expenses were paid. But I expect that was in the millions, with all his land and farm equipment and everything."

"Who was the personal representative?" Campbell asked.

Bill checked the last page. "His lawyer."

"Why a lawyer?" Nick asked. "Mrs. Abbott's executor was her granddaughter."

"Mrs. Abbott wasn't wealthy," Campbell said.

Chapter 18

"Look, I didn't kill my father. I have nothing else to say." Dylan Standish stared sullenly at Keith across the table in the interview room. Detective Matt Jackson also sat in on the session, but he was letting Keith take the lead.

"Where were you Friday evening?" Keith asked.

Dylan scowled. "Last Friday?"

"Yes. Between seven and eight o'clock."

After a pause, Dylan said, "I don't know. Home, I guess."

"Can anyone confirm that?"

Another pause. "Probably not."

"We were told you went to the apartments on Fifteenth Street."

"Well, whoever said that is wrong. Those aren't our apartments."

"I know they're not. But you paid a visit to the parking area there, didn't you?"

"What are you talking about?" Dylan's face had flushed, and he sat very still.

Keith placed a photograph on the table in front of Dylan. "This is Leila Abbott's car. You slashed her tires Friday night."

"No."

"Yes."

Dylan's face went scarlet. Keith could almost

hear the gears turning in his brain. He shouldn't have gone out with his friend Saturday night. He shouldn't have had so much to drink. He should have kept his mouth shut at the bar. He'd throttle Gary.

"You've taken over your father's business," Keith said calmly.

"So? I'm his only son."

"Didn't your mother inherit the business?"

"Yes, she's the sole owner now, but she doesn't want to take on the hassle of actually running it. She asked me if I'd step in." Dylan seemed on firmer ground now and glad for the change of subject.

"So you quit your job and dove into it."

Dylan nodded.

"Do you expect it to be profitable?"

"I hope it is."

"You raised the rent on the tenants immediately."

With a shrug, Dylan said, "I gave notice of an increase when their present leases expire. Some end this month, some in the spring . . . it varies."

"Why did you do that?"

"It had been a while since Dad raised the rates, and I thought it was warranted."

Keith frowned. "Your first day on the job, you made that decision."

"I'd done a lot of work for my father over the years. I was familiar with the basics."

"When did you first hear about the Banitier painting?" Matt asked.

Dylan's head jerked up, and he stared at the second detective. "When it was in the news."

"This year, you mean, or back when it was first stolen?"

"I don't remember that."

Keith leaned forward and clasped his hands on the table. "Dylan, as far as we can see, you're the only one who has a motive for killing your father."

"I wouldn't do that."

"Did you love him?" Keith asked softly.

After a long pause, Dylan said, "I love my mother. I wouldn't do that to her."

"I see."

"Look." Dylan's eyes flickered back and forth between the two detectives. "You're saying I'm a suspect?"

"Very much so," Keith said. "Do you have any evidence to prove you didn't kill him?" He still wasn't sure about the murder, but he could nail Dylan for the tire slashing. After the anonymous tip came in, he'd located two other people in the bar who'd heard him brag about it. Now was the time to press him about his father's death.

Dylan's breath came faster, shallower. "I . . ."

"Yes?" Keith caught his gaze and held it.

"I might have an idea of who did it."

Keith exhaled. "By all means, tell us."

They waited in silence for several seconds. Beads of sweat glittered on Dylan's brow.

"I found something when I went through my dad's desk," he said at last.

Campbell knocked on the door of her father's office. At his response, she and Nick walked in.

"I may have something on Eddie Nelson," she said.

Bill sat back in his chair. "Take a seat."

She and Nick took the two visitor chairs, and Campbell leaned forward eagerly.

"No arrest record for Eddie, but he and Sally had a baby four months after they got married."

Bill stared at her blankly for a moment then said, "You think that explains the discrepancy in his inheritance?"

"It could," Campbell said. "I think a lot of fathers would be disappointed. His son got kicked out of college, and then his girlfriend got pregnant."

"I wouldn't punish him for that."

"Dad!" She couldn't keep her exasperation out of her voice. "You only have one child."

"And I'd love you no matter what. You know what's in my will."

She smiled. "I know, and I love you too. But let's say I had a brother." She almost glanced at Nick but managed to control the impulse.

"And let's say I worked diligently with you for years, but my brother goofed off. He dropped out of school, got some traffic tickets, maybe a marijuana bust. Then he had a shotgun wedding, and you didn't like the girl. What would your will look like then?"

Her father gritted his teeth, and she pressed on. This time she couldn't help a quick look at Nick, and his eyes popped wide.

"Would my *brother* get as big a share of the biz as I did?"

"I don't know," Bill admitted. "Maybe I'd leave the business to you, but I wouldn't cut him out entirely."

Nick shifted uneasily. "It does seem a little off-kilter that David, Jr. has a huge estate now and Eddie has a doughnut shop."

"Okay," Bill said with a sigh. "I'll admit, Eddie may not have been his father's favorite when the will was written. But does it affect our case?"

"Probably not." Campbell slumped back in her chair.

Her father nodded. "Put the details in the case file and keep digging."

Nick and Campbell went back to the main office. Halfway to his desk, Nick whirled.

Campbell held up both hands to stop him from saying anything. "Don't worry. If you were my brother, we'd get equal shares."

"Maybe I'd get out of the business and open my own video game store."

She laughed. "Somehow, I think you and Eddie Nelson will get along."

"I wonder if he can sing." Nick's brow furrowed.

"Huh?"

"Wasn't Eddie Nelson an actor?"

She laughed. "That was Nelson Eddy. *Naughty Marietta* was my favorite. That and *Rose Marie*."

"Oh, yeah. The Mountie."

The desk phone rang, and she hurried to pick it up.

"Hi, it's Keith."

She smiled. "What can we do for you this morning?"

"I'd like to drop by after lunch if I may. We've arrested the man who slashed your client's tires, and I have other news that will interest you."

"Great," Campbell said. "Come and eat lunch with us if you want."

"I'm not sure when I'll be free. I have a lot of things to take care of here first."

"We've got potato soup in the slow cooker. Come when you can, and if you're not here by one we'll eat without you."

"Sounds good."

When she hung up, Nick was watching her from behind his desk.

"Keith's coming for lunch," she said. "There's plenty for you too. Soup and sandwiches."

"Dessert?" he asked.

Rita would come in the next day, but she hadn't been to the house since Monday.

"I think we're low on cookies, and I didn't bake anything."

"I could run for something."

Campbell shrugged. "Honestly, Nick, we're trying not to eat too many sweets. Why don't you grab something later for yourself?"

His face drooped. "But Keith is coming. I thought you'd want something special."

"We don't have to serve dessert every time Keith comes."

"Oh. Too bad."

Campbell clued her father in as to their lunch plans, and at twelve forty-five Keith walked in carrying a cardboard box. Campbell met him in the hall and kissed him.

"What's this?" She nodded toward the box.

"I stopped by Eddie's Donuts."

"Eddie's?" She stared up at him. "Did you question him?"

"Nope. I just thought it would be a good chance to take a look at him. And to get some doughnuts. We don't have to eat them now."

"Nick will kiss your feet. Rita's not working here today, and we don't have any dessert."

The four of them were soon seated in the dining room, and in between enjoying the welcome lunch of homemade soup, tossed salad, and assorted sandwiches, Keith related his morning interview with Dylan Standish.

"Dylan has been charged with slashing Leila Abbott's tires, to which he's confessed, and he's been released. He'll be arraigned for that on Friday."

"Glad to hear it," Bill said.

"You mentioned more news?" Campbell eyed him expectantly.

"Well, yes. Big news, actually. You were right. Someone was being blackmailed about the painting."

"Who?" Nick demanded.

Keith smiled. "Let me tell you a little story." He took a sip of his coffee and sat back. "Dylan's mother asked him to take over his father's landlord role. He started immediately, as you know."

"Yes, raising the rents," Nick muttered. "I'm glad I'm not in one of his apartments."

"It seems he went through his father's files that first day, and he also rifled through his desk."

Bill lifted his chin, his sandwich suspended in midair. "And?"

"He found something he thought was odd." Keith smiled. "Dylan might not be the smartest businessman out there, but in light of recent events, including his father's violent demise, it caught his attention."

Campbell squirmed with suspense, but she

wouldn't give him the satisfaction of asking what it was.

Nick, however, had no such compunction. "Come on, man. You're killing us."

"It was a sticky note. An old sticky note."

Campbell blinked and looked at her dad. They all waited for Keith to go on.

"He knew it was old because it was wrinkled, and the adhesive wasn't sticky anymore. It had picked up dust and what have you. But the hand-written words on it caught his attention. For one thing, they weren't written in his father's hand, or his mother's."

"Okay, I'll bite," Campbell said. "What did it say?"

"It said . . ." Keith smiled, drawing out his revelation. "Keep this until I ask you for it."

"That's it?" Nick scowled.

Campbell said with certainty, "It referred to the painting."

Keith nodded.

"But whoever stole the painting gave it to Craig Smith, not Brad Standish."

Keith just smiled at her.

"Brad must have found it in the attic," Bill said.

"You win the prize," Keith told him. "We think—Dylan thinks, and I agree—that his father at some point found the painting in the Abbotts' attic, and the note was with it."

"Still, how did Dylan know it referred to the

painting?" Bill asked. "That sticky note seems pretty generic."

"It was signed with initials."

Campbell caught her breath.

Maddeningly, Keith took a bite of his ham sandwich.

"Oh, come on," Nick spluttered. "You gotta spill it."

"Patience," Bill said quietly. "Work on your patience, Nick."

A dutiful daughter, Campbell spooned the last of her soup into her mouth. Nick really should have learned how to wait for the punchline by now, what with all the hours he'd spent doing surveillance.

Keith swallowed and took a drink. When he set down his cup, he said with heavy drama, "D.L.N."

"David Nelson," Nick cried.

Bill shook his head. "No, his signature on the will was David R. Nelson."

"His middle name was Richter," Campbell said. "It was his mother's maiden name."

They all stared at her, and she said, looking at Keith, "I did a detailed family tree on the Nelsons."

Nick's mouth sagged. "Then it can't be David, Jr. either."

"No." Campbell looked over at him and copied Keith in giving a melodramatic pause. "But it *could* be Diane Lorraine Nelson."

Chapter 19

"You're spot on." Keith smiled at Campbell and gave a little nod. "We're looking at Diane Nelson Block's finances."

"Find anything?" Bill asked.

"Nothing conclusive yet. What with the business and several separate bank accounts, it may take some time. I'll keep you posted if I can. In general terms, of course."

Campbell sank back in her chair. Were they close to solving this? Even if Keith and his team could prove Diane Nelson Block had made payments over the years, would that be enough? The case seemed too convoluted to unravel that quickly.

They continued to talk about the case over doughnuts and coffee, but as soon as he'd finished his maple glazed, Keith stood.

"I've got to get back to the station. We've got a forensic accountant coming in at two."

Campbell walked with him to the front door.

"Thanks for lunch." Keith leaned over to kiss her.

"You're welcome." She'd noticed that her father was careful not to say anything about what True Blue would do next, and she felt an unrelated topic would be best. "I'm looking forward to meeting Nicole."

"Yeah, she's excited about it too. We expect her and Todd on Saturday. Maybe we can get together then? I know you're going to Bowling Green Sunday."

Campbell nodded. "We'll see how it goes."

So far, she had only some gift wrapping and a bit more shopping for stocking gifts planned, but she was sure her dad was already mapping out what they'd do next in their investigation.

Back in the dining room, she freshened her coffee. Bill and Nick still sat where they'd been when she left the room. She knew they'd been discussing the case.

"So." She resumed her seat. "What do we do now?"

"We stay away from Diane," Bill said, and Nick nodded vehemently.

"Can we talk to Craig Smith again?" she asked.

"That's what I'm thinking."

Nick reached into the doughnut box for another treat. "These are really good. Maybe we should talk to Eddie."

Bill shook his head. "We've got ammunition for Craig now. Let's see if we can get him to admit he got that painting from Diane."

Campbell sipped her coffee. "What about Jacob? Now that we know . . ."

"Well, we don't *know*. We're still guessing, but

thanks to Keith, the odds are a little better that we know who stole it. Or at least, who gave it to Craig."

Nick frowned and swallowed his mouthful of doughnut. "You mean, another layer? Like, someone gave it to Diane, who gave it to Craig, who gave it to Jacob, who . . . ?"

"I'm not saying that." Bill drained his coffee mug and set it down with a thump. "If the police get good results from this audit they're doing of the Blocks, they'll surely want to talk to Craig again. I say we talk to him first. That wouldn't wreck their investigation."

"What if Craig talks to Diane?" Nick asked, his remaining half doughnut poised before his mouth.

"Why would he? He wants to stay out of it." Bill stood. "I say we get to him before he gets spooked and runs."

"What if we spook him?" Campbell looked bleakly at the table full of dirty dishes. "And what about the dishes?"

"It's a chance we'll have to take with Craig. We want to solve this thing for Leila." Her dad glanced at the table and reached for his plate and silverware. "Everyone put your dishes in the sink and let's go."

"All of us?" Campbell slid her chair back.

Bill frowned, thinking for a moment. "Nick, you go to the doughnut shop. See if you can talk to Eddie if he's not too busy. See what kind of a feeling you get for his relationships with his siblings."

"Got it." Nick was off, leaving his dirty dishes behind.

Campbell sighed and picked up his mug with hers and Keith's. Her father picked up his own and the coffee carafe.

"Do you think Nick will scare Eddie and alert the whole Nelson family?" she asked as she opened the dishwasher.

"Nick has pretty good instincts. Don't sell him short."

She tried to assimilate that on their way to Craig's house. After a few minutes of silent prayer and contemplation, she turned to her father, who was driving this time.

"Did we ever find out where Craig works?"

"He drives a school bus."

"Really? I didn't expect that, since we know he's not the greatest with kids."

"Maybe he's mellowed."

"Yeah, but . . ." Campbell's brain hurt. Didn't they do background checks on school bus drivers? "Does he have a record?"

"I couldn't find one."

"Which means his employers probably didn't either."

Bill nodded. "He may not be home now, but he works a split. Morning pickups, then afternoon runs. His schedule has him back at school at two. I'm hoping we'll catch him at home."

"I wouldn't think that was a very high-paying job," Campbell said.

"It's not."

"Child support?" she asked, thinking of the unsavory divorce.

"He spent some years at a lumber company. But the kids are all adults now, and his ex is deceased, so he probably gets by on less now."

She thought about their conversation with Keith. "Dylan slashed Leila's tires to warn her off from investigating about the painting. His father had to have something to do with the blackmail scheme."

"Keith's looking into that. He's probably busy questioning Diane Block this very minute."

"Yeah." She sat up straighter. "Wait a minute. Diane wasn't married when the painting was stolen?"

"I think she was."

"Then why did she use her maiden name initials on the sticky note? Did she keep her maiden name?"

"We'll have to look into that." Bill put on his turn signal and pulled into Craig Smith's driveway.

"I think Craig is a few years younger than Diane. You don't think there was something romantic between them, do you?"

"I have no idea." Bill braked and huffed out a breath. Craig's pickup was nowhere in sight. "We missed him."

"Looks like it. We had a late lunch."

"Yeah." He squinted at the front door.

Campbell followed his gaze and spotted something above the doorknob. "Hold on, Dad."

She hopped out of the car and jogged up to the doorway. A business card was stuck backward in the crack just above the knob. In cramped cursive, a note was written on the blank cardstock. *Call me if you need some help*. She frowned and pulled the card free of the door jamb and turned it over. Marissa Chilton, *private investigator.*

Adrenaline pumped through Campbell's veins. What was she doing out here?

She carefully put the card back the way it was when she found it and walked back to the car.

"What is it?" her father asked.

"Marissa Chilton's business card."

Bill's jaw tightened as he put the transmission in reverse and backed out of the driveway.

"What now?" Campbell asked.

"I'm thinking."

The next day passed slowly. Bill put Nick to work on a new case which involved short-term surveillance. Rita came in and went cheerfully about her cleaning and cooking tasks. While Bill slogged away at his end-of-year reports,

Campbell did more work on the Nelson and Abbott families. She didn't turn up much new information.

The highlight of her day was when Keith dropped by. He informed her and her father that he'd talked to Diane Nelson Block the previous afternoon.

"She arrived at the station with her lawyer," Keith said.

Bill grimaced. "So you didn't get much out of her?"

"The chief really wants to lay this thing to rest, and it's a twenty-year old crime. We finally offered her a deal—if she'd tell us everything, we wouldn't arrest her for stealing the painting."

"Isn't the statute of limitations past on that?"

"No, its value places it in the felony category, so there's no limit on it. The same with the extortion, by the way. It seems she paid out sixty thousand dollars over the past ten years or so."

"Ten years?" Campbell looked at her father.

"She was being blackmailed for ten years?" Bill's brow furrowed.

"Yes," Keith said. "We found large cash withdrawals from her personal bank account going back that far."

Bill leaned forward. "Did you find out for sure who was doing the blackmailing? We've been playing tag with Craig Smith, but I'm not convinced he was the one."

"The note was found in Brad Standish's desk," Keith said. "However, Diane said she didn't know who the cash was going to. She got her last demand in August. Nothing since then."

"How often did the extortionist tap her?" Bill asked.

"Once or twice a year."

"For ten years," Campbell said. "That's about the time Leila Abbott's grandfather died."

Keith nodded. "It is."

"So . . ." She met his gaze. "Do you think Brad Standish got wind of the painting in the attic around the time Stanley died?"

"It's entirely possible. He may have inspected the house then, or maybe he went over to talk about the lease with Teresa and poked around. Who knows?"

"If he did find it, he left it there." Bill rested his chin on his hand, frowning. "I guess that would keep suspicion off him so far as the blackmail goes. It wasn't in his house."

"Well, it *was* on his property," Keith noted, "but not where he lived, and in a spot nobody visited very often. I think Brad was the blackmailer. We've put in a request for a warrant allowing the forensic accountant to examine Standish's back records."

"Dylan won't like that," Campbell said. "And he gets mean when he's not happy."

"So, you've got Diane Block on the theft of the

painting, even if you can't arrest her?" Bill held Keith's gaze.

Keith gritted his teeth. "She didn't admit to it precisely."

Campbell jerked her head up and frowned at him. "If she didn't steal it, why on earth would she pay a blackmailer?"

"I asked the same question, but her lawyer told her to clam up."

"I'm sure," Bill said.

"We're assuming she's the one who stole the painting and gave it to Craig Smith to hold for her."

Bill nodded. "That got it off the farm. We know that sometime later—a couple of years, maybe—Craig handed it over to Jacob, who hid it in his folks' attic."

"Right," Keith said. "That's my train of thought as well. But we don't have proof."

"The fact that she's been making blackmail payments isn't enough?"

"Her lawyer kept it ambiguous and wouldn't let her say much. We had the financial statements, and she did admit someone was bleeding her for ten years. She wouldn't say directly that it was because of the painting."

"Hmm." Bill scowled. "The painting was stolen twenty years ago, and the blackmail began ten years later."

"Yeah," Keith said. "What if it was over something else? An affair or something else totally unrelated?"

Bill shook his head. "You got me."

Campbell's mind was spinning. How could the payments possibly be for anything else?

"The note," she said. "Isn't that the smoking gun?"

"We're trying to get samples of her handwriting to prove she wrote it."

"She signed her initials."

Keith gave a little shrug. "She was already married at the time."

"Yes," Campbell said with a smile. "But I learned today her first husband's name was Kyle Netherton. Her married initials were the same as her maiden name initials."

"That makes sense. And they weren't married long." Keith smiled grimly.

"Less than three years. I found the divorce record today. She didn't marry Travis Block until almost four years later." Campbell sighed. "I don't suppose you asked her why she never asked Craig to give the painting back."

"She won't admit she gave it to him. And if she thought he was blackmailing her, that would be a pointless exercise."

Keith went back to work, leaving Campbell frustrated and moody. Diane Block had to be the thief. There was no other explanation.

Midway through the afternoon, a client met

with her father. Campbell sat at her own desk, ruing the fact that her dad hadn't given her a new assignment and trying not to pull out her hair. After he and the client had been closeted for twenty minutes, just as she'd decided to do more research on Leila's cousins, Bill came out and entered the main office.

"What you doin', Soup?"

She winced. "I was going to look at Blaine and Corey Smith again—Craig's sons. Do you have something more pertinent for me? I feel like our hands are tied."

"They pretty much are. And Nick's leaving tomorrow for Florida. I think we should put this whole thing aside and relax over the holidays. Nothing will be open over Christmas anyway, and we're going to Bowling Green on Monday and spending the afternoon and evening with the Fullers on Tuesday. Let's just let it rest."

"I can't." Campbell flopped down in a chair. "My brain keeps going over and over the same ground."

He nodded. "You need to get away from it."

She looked up and met his gaze. "Have you tried Craig Smith today?"

"Several times. I expect he's working."

She checked her phone for the time. "He might be home now."

Bill shook his head. "I'm not driving all the way out there again today, Soup. Let Keith and his team figure it out. If it's still up in the air next week, we can consider doing some more investigating. Meanwhile, we've got plenty to do on other cases."

Hauling in a deep breath, she glanced past him toward the hallway and straightened her spine. "Did your client leave? I didn't see him come out of your office."

"No, he's still there. I thought you might want to come meet him."

"Who is he?"

"Christopher Powell, a junior associate of Lyman and Nesmith."

Campbell nodded at the law firm's familiar name.

"He has a small case for us to do a little digging on. But also, he's single."

She scowled. "Are you playing matchmaker, Dad?"

"No. If I was doing that, I'd have brought him in to meet you. But he mentioned the big wing-ding at David Nelson's place on New Year's Eve."

"So? He's invited?"

"Yes. He did a little work for Mr. Nelson Junior, and they sent him an invitation. He's allowed a plus-one."

"Dad. You didn't."

Bill raised his shoulders. "No obligation. When I suggested it might be advantageous to get one of our team members inside that party, he offered.

He says it's totally up to you, but he asked, if you're interested, to let him know by tomorrow."

"I don't know." She sat for a moment, mulling it over. She'd caught only a glimpse of the man. He was young enough to be believable as her escort. "It wouldn't be a real date, you know. I'm dating Keith."

"I know. I told him you're in a relationship, and he understood. But he also thought he might score some points if he brought a pretty lady to the shindig."

She made a face. "I'll think about it."

"Would you like to meet him?"

"Why not?" She rose a bit reluctantly. No use prolonging the agony, but she was embarrassed by the circumstances. As she followed her father across the hall, she swiped a hand through her hair. Maybe he'd change his mind after he saw her.

"Campbell," her dad said, turning halfway toward her inside the office, "This is Christopher Powell, of Lyman and Nesmith. Chris, this is my daughter."

"Hi." She extended her hand, hoping her smile didn't come across as a grimace.

"Hi, Campbell. Glad to meet you." Chris's smile seemed genuine. He wasn't the most handsome young man she'd ever seen, but he wasn't bad either. Before the pause got too awkward, he added, "Your father explained to me that your firm is investigating the Nelson family."

"Yes," she said. "It wasn't our main path of investigation—not at first. But I guess you know what the client wants us to do."

"Your father said it's directly related to the Nelsons, and you'd like to get more insight into the family."

"That's right." Apparently her dad had respected client confidentiality and not told him the whole story.

"Well, I'd be happy to escort you to the New Year's Eve party. You wouldn't have to stick to me all evening if you didn't want to. I'd understand if you followed your own agenda once we're inside."

"That's very generous of you."

"No problem. I was wondering how embarrassing it would be to show up without a date. Now I don't have to worry about that. If you're willing to go with me, that is."

His smile was mostly neutral, with just a hint of wistfulness. Campbell made up her mind in an instant.

"Sure. And thank you."

Chris nodded. "Shall I pick you up here around six thirty that night?"

"That would be great."

Her father showed Powell out and came back into his office, where Campbell had slumped into a chair.

"So?" Bill said.

"So, my father set me up for an undercover date. Oh!" She gasped and fumbled in her pocket for her cell. "I have to call Keith and explain this to him."

"You can blame me if it helps."

Campbell didn't see Keith as the jealous type, but it wouldn't hurt to have her father on tap to add his spin on the non-date. "Thanks," she said. "I'll hold you to that."

Chapter 20

Friday dawned clear and cold. Campbell found herself a little blue. She actually missed Nick coming in whistling at eight o'clock. He'd covertly slipped two wrapped gifts under the Christmas tree the day before, and she hadn't spotted them until he left to do surveillance. He was headed for the airport in Nashville this morning. They wouldn't get a chance to thank him in person until he returned next week.

"Chin up, kiddo," her father said over breakfast.

She made a wry face. "I don't feel very festive today."

"Do something Christmasy."

She cocked her head to one side. "Nick left presents for us. We could open them today."

"Christmas Eve is tomorrow."

"So. He wouldn't know."

Her dad smiled. "I think we can wait. You're a big girl."

With a frown, she peeled her banana. "What am I working on today?"

"Chris Powell wants us to do some preliminary work on a court case he's preparing. You could go to Hapwell, Inc., and get some employee records."

"Will they just give them to us?"

"Chris got a court order. They should have received it by now."

She took a bite of the banana.

"Or I could go get them," Bill said, "and you could take the neighbors some of the Christmas cookies Rita left us."

"Give away all our cookies?"

"She made a ton of them, and we're going away Monday. I hope we won't each eat two or three dozen apiece over the next two days."

He had a point. "Okay. I guess I can take Mrs. Peele a few, and the Hills."

"And maybe Miss Louanne."

"We don't want to give away *all* our cookies."

Bill laughed. "Take her half a dozen. And a dozen each for the Hills and the Peeles."

"Think that's enough?"

"Sure. It beats nothing."

At that moment the doorbell rang.

"I'll get it." Campbell got up and headed for the hallway, tossing her banana peel in the trash on her way out.

When she opened the door, Allison Peele stood on the porch holding a foil-wrapped rectangle.

"Hi. I hope I'm not calling too early."

"No, come right in. Dad and I were just finishing up our breakfast. We usually unlock the door for clients right after we eat."

Allison stepped inside and held out her offering. "I wanted to bring you a fruitcake. I always

253

make half a dozen and give most of them away. I don't have many people to give them to since we moved, but I made them anyway. It's one of Greg's favorites."

"How nice." Campbell took the package with a smile. "As a matter of fact, I was going to bring you some gingerbread cookies later. Can I give you a dozen now?"

"Ooh, that would be fantastic. I know Greg will love them. I'll try not to get into them before he comes home from school this afternoon."

"He's not on vacation yet?" Campbell asked.

"No, the university lets out today. Their break will be a full two weeks, though. Greg has two finals today, then he's off."

They went into the kitchen, and her father rose when he saw Campbell's companion.

"Dad, have you met Allison Peele?" Campbell asked.

"No. You must be our new neighbor."

"This is my dad, Bill McBride."

Allison shook his hand. "Pleased to meet you."

"Same here," Bill said.

"She brought us a fruitcake." Campbell held up the package.

"Oh, I love fruitcake."

"I'm going to give her those cookies we were just talking about." Campbell didn't want to seem stingy, so she placed a dozen and a half of the cleverly decorated gingerbread men and reindeer in a plastic container while Bill and Allison chatted.

"Ooh, those look scrumptious," Allison said as Campbell rummaged in the cupboard for the container's lid. "I'll be sure to get the box back to you soon."

"Take your time," Campbell said. "We're having Christmas dinner with some friends, so I'm not doing a ton of cooking this weekend." She'd promised Mart a pecan pie and some fudge, though, she reminded herself. That would take up some of her dragging time on Saturday.

"I didn't see that young man's Jeep out front this morning," Allison said.

"Oh, he's gone to spend Christmas with his folks." Campbell found the lid and snapped it onto the cookie box. She held it out to Allison. "What are you and Greg doing?"

"We're heading to Louisville after his tests. We're all packed. My parents live over there, and various aunts, uncles, and cousins."

"Why did you move to Murray?" Bill asked. The question struck Campbell as a bit snoopy, but Allison didn't seem to take offense.

"I was offered a job over here, and being close to the university allows Greg to live at home. It's a lot cheaper than when they live in the dorm."

Bill nodded. "Welcome to western Kentucky. I hope it goes well for you both."

Campbell walked Allison to the door and then returned to the kitchen.

"Have you seen her going to work since she moved in?" her father asked as soon as she entered the room.

She stopped and thought about it. "Now that you mention it, no. She just said she was offered a job. Maybe she hasn't started work yet."

"I suppose she could be starting after the holidays." Bill sipped his coffee. "Another odd thing—where was her son living before they bought Tatton's house? He certainly wasn't commuting from Louisville."

Campbell frowned. "You're right. I took it he was in the dorm up until then."

"Wouldn't he finish out the semester there?"

"Maybe he is. I mean, I've only seen him at the house once or twice. If he lived in the dorm and was helping his mother move into her new house, he wouldn't be around much. But she implied he'll be living there with her. I suppose she meant after the semester break."

"It still seems fishy to me." Bill stood and picked up his mug. "I'll be in my office."

As she divvied up the cookies, Campbell thought about what her father had said. Greg Peele's status according to his mother did seem odd. A few minutes later, she ventured across the street with a dozen gingerbread men in a plastic zipper bag and knocked on her friends' door. Frank Hill opened it.

"Campbell! Come on in."

As she stepped into their cozy living room, Vera came from the kitchen. "Well, hello, sugar!" She pulled Campbell into a hug.

"I brought you these." Campbell held up the cookies. "Dad and I will be away Christmas Day, and we wanted to wish you happy holidays."

"How sweet. Sit down, honey. Cup of tea?"

"No, thanks. I should get back." Campbell glanced out the picture window. The house that now belonged to Allison Peele was just across Willow Street. "Have you met the new folks in Ben Tatton's house?"

"I've met Mrs. Peele," Vera said.

Campbell decided she could spare a few minutes. Vera could spin out a yarn. She sat down on the couch. "What about her son?"

"No, I haven't had the pleasure. But I've seen him a couple of times, going in or out."

"Didn't she say he's a student?" Frank asked, sinking into his recliner.

"Yes," Campbell said. "The semester ends today, so you may see him again—although Allison said they're going to Louisville this weekend to spend the holidays with family over there."

Vera nodded sagely. "She did tell me they were from Louisville."

"Say, isn't one of your grandchildren a student at MSU?" Campbell asked.

"She sure is." Frank practically beamed.

"Lydia," Vera said.

"Maybe she's met Greg Peele," Campbell suggested.

Vera looked puzzled. "I suppose it's possible."

"I just wondered if we could find out a little more about him. His major, for instance, and if he's been living in the dormitory."

"You could ask his mother," Frank said.

"Well, yes, I could, but—"

"But she doesn't want Mrs. Peele to know she's asking questions." Vera gave her husband a pointed look then turned back to Campbell. "You're investigating, aren't you?"

"Not really. Just being nosey."

"I guess we could ask Lydia next time we see her," Frank said.

"I'll do better than that." Vera reached for her cell on the end table next to her chair. "I'll text her."

Frank made a face. "All this texting. I don't get it."

Campbell smiled. "Some people find it convenient."

"Kids." Frank shook his head.

"She may be in class," Vera said absently as she tapped away at the phone.

"I think today is the university's last day of finals," Campbell said. "She could be taking an exam right now."

Vera glanced up at her. "Lydia taught me to do this, you know."

"Texting?" Campbell chuckled. "Isn't that what grandchildren are for?"

"That's right. To teach us the new technology." Vera sighed. "She's not answering right away, but I'll let you know when she does." Her phone chimed. "Oh, there she is! Good girl."

Campbell watched her face as Vera read the new message. The older woman was certainly enjoying this, both the contact with her granddaughter and being part of something exciting. She was in her element.

Vera's mouth drooped. "She doesn't know him. Oh, but she says she'll ask some of her friends."

"That's great." Campbell stood. "I'd better go. I've got a bag of cookies for Miss Louanne."

"Oh, tell her I'll be over later to watch Jeopardy with her." Vera pushed up out of her chair, fumbling so she wouldn't drop her phone. "Thanks again, Campbell."

"Yeah, thanks." Frank was also old school, and he stood until she was out the door.

Campbell smiled to herself and hummed "Jingle Bells" as she crossed the street again and ambled past the Peeles' toward Louanne Vane's house. The old woman and her special Persian blue cat were extra-good friends of Campbell.

Miss Louanne greeted her with so much enthusiasm that Campbell felt obligated to step inside for a few minutes. Blue Boy, the enormous Persian blue, didn't bother to get off his favorite rocking chair, but he winked one eye at the visitor before sliding back into his nap.

"No, I haven't met them," Miss Louanne said in reply to Campbell's inquiry. She leaned toward her and whispered, "Do you suppose they know what happened to Ben Tatton in that kitchen?"

"I expect the real estate agent had to disclose it, but it didn't come up in my conversations with Mrs. Peele." Campbell sat down on the sofa.

"Can I get you a glass of sweet tea, dear?"

"No, thanks. I should get home. I left Dad all alone this morning, and he may have a job for me. I just wanted to bring you the cookies."

Miss Louanne smiled at the bag of gingerbread on the coffee table. "We'll certainly enjoy those, won't we, Blue Boy?"

The cat's tail twitched, but he didn't deign to open his eyes.

"And we have a gift for you." Miss Louanne reached over beneath a tabletop Christmas tree that had replaced the tall lamp that usually sat there but was now relegated to the floor. "Here you go, my dear."

"Thank you." Campbell accepted the small package wrapped in poinsettia-sprinkled paper. "Should I open it now?"

"Please do. I like to see people's faces when they open their gifts, don't you?"

Campbell didn't answer. Sometimes that was

a gratifying exercise, but other times . . . She steeled herself to don a delighted expression, no matter what.

"Oh!" She gave a genuine smile as she gazed down at the formal portrait of Blue Boy, sitting up and wearing a red bow tie. The cat eyed the camera with disdain. "How lovely. It's him to a *T!*"

Miss Louanne's pleasure radiated from her wrinkled face. "I knew you'd love it."

"I'd love a photo of you sometime too," Campbell said, eyeing her expectantly.

"Oh, no. I'm not nearly as photogenic as Blue Boy."

"Well, it's very sweet. Or should I say dignified?"

They both laughed. Campbell rose and gave Miss Louanne a hug.

"Are you going away for Christmas?" her hostess asked as they moved toward the door.

"Dad and I are going to Bowling Green for the day. How about you?"

"My daughter is coming for me."

Campbell paused in surprise. "All the way from Arkansas?"

Miss Louanne waved a hand. "It's not that far. A few hours each way. She could visit more often."

A change of subject was in order, Campbell could see. "Are you all packed?"

"Yes. She's coming this afternoon."

"Well, I hope you have a good visit. When are you coming back?"

"Tuesday, I expect. Would you or your father come by once or twice just to check on things?"

Campbell patted her arm. "Of course we will." No doubt Frank Hill had also been enlisted. "What about Blue Boy?"

"He's going with me. He won't like being in the carrier that long, but he'd hate being left home even more."

The urge to tell her to make sure he didn't escape her daughter's house while they were in Arkansas was strong, but Campbell didn't voice it. After her recent adventures with Blue Boy, Miss Louanne would be extra vigilant without a reminder.

She strode quickly up the sidewalk, passing Allison Peele's home with barely a glance, and found a pickup truck sitting in the front yard of her home. She entered the Victorian house through the front door. As she walked down the hall, she heard faint voices and realized her dad had someone in his office with him. Another new client right before Christmas?

Heading for the stairway, she passed the door. It was partway open, and her father called out to her.

"Campbell, could you come in here for a minute?"

"Sure, Dad." She turned and stepped into the office. The man sitting in the visitor's chair turned his profile toward her, and she stopped.

Craig Smith had come to True Blue voluntarily?

Chapter 21

"Mr. Smith was just telling me a little more about his role in holding the Banitier painting for Diane Block," Bill said as Campbell pulled over another chair to join them.

"Since you know now," Craig said, throwing her a cautious glance.

"Yes, it's official. I believe the police are asking for Mrs. Block's help on this now." Campbell wasn't sure why her father had called her in, but she wasn't sorry to hear the truth from Smith.

"Diane brought it to me as I was leaving work one evening," Craig said.

"So, she was the one who stole it."

"I'm pretty sure. But she never asked for it back."

"Did you ask her why?" Campbell glanced at her dad. He'd probably already asked that question and heard the answer.

"No. I just wanted to forget about it and not be blamed. In that first year or two, I did ask her if she wanted it back, and she said, 'Not yet.' So I let it ride. Then, after I gave it to Jacob, I kept thinking she'd ask for it, and I'd have to go get it back from him. But she never spoke to me about it again. Then she and her new husband, Travis, were building a business empire, and I just kept my mouth shut."

"At that point, it probably would have caused her more harm than good to have it in her possession," Bill said.

"You won't tell the police, will you? That I had it?"

Bill frowned. "I'm not sure I can make that promise, Mr. Smith. You're not our client."

"But I didn't do anything wrong."

"It's been so long," Campbell said, gazing at her father. "If Mr. Smith accepted the painting, knowing it was stolen, would they still charge him with accepting stolen goods twenty years later?"

"The value of the painting makes it grand larceny," Bill said with a sigh. "They might."

"What if I didn't know it was stolen?" Craig said. "I mean, she brought it to me, and at that point, all I knew was that it belonged to her family. I didn't realize she was stealing it. I mean, really, was she stealing it?"

"Yes, she was," Bill said. "But that may help you. I would say, if the police come to you, be up front with them. But talk to a lawyer first."

Craig ran a hand through his hair. "Man, I can't afford a lawyer."

"I'm sorry, but we know the police are questioning all four Nelson siblings. It's bound to come back to you. When that happens, tell them what you've just told us. At the time, you didn't know you were aiding a thief."

But that might not matter, Campbell thought. As soon as he learned it was stolen, he should have told someone, or at least taken it back to Diane. She pressed her lips together. Her father's advice was probably the best they could do for Craig.

He left soon after, and Campbell eyed her father. "What do we do now? He admits Diane gave it to him. Do we need to tell Keith?"

"I'm thinking on it. Is there any coffee?"

"I'll make you some." She scooped up his empty mug and headed for the kitchen.

When she came back with a steaming cup for him, he looked up at her and nodded. "I think we do need to report this. We now have knowledge of a crime, and it's in our client's best interest to tell the detectives what we've learned."

Keith tapped his cell phone to end his conversation with Bill. He left his desk and walked over to where Matt Jackson was scrolling through financial records.

"We just got a tip. Craig Smith says Diane Block gave him the painting twenty years ago, the same night it was stolen, and asked him to hang on to it for a while."

Matt blinked up at him. "Smith says it to who? He never told us that."

"Like I said, it's a tip. We need to bring him in."

"More important, we need to talk to Mrs. Block again. She swore she had nothing to do with stealing the painting."

"I'm hoping she'll tell us a different story now," Keith said. "She's certainly made several large payments to an anonymous party—"

"Smith?" Matt asked.

"I don't think so. Why would he admit she gave him the Banitier if he was extorting money from her because of it? And we know it wasn't in his possession for the last sixteen years. The blackmail only started ten years ago."

Matt sighed and shoved back his chair. "Let's go. Do you think she's at home, or at one of their three stores?"

Campbell spent Sunday afternoon with the Fullers, where she got to meet Keith's sister, Nicole, and her husband, Todd Webb. The cold wind made it too chilly to sit on the porch overlooking the lake, but they spent a cozy afternoon by the fireplace.

Not much business was discussed, although in a moment alone, Campbell asked Keith, "Have you arrested Diane Block yet?"

"No," he whispered back. "We contacted her yesterday, and she lawyered up first thing."

"So, what now?"

"Her lawyer's agreed to bring her in next week,

after the holidays. No promises, though. She may not admit a thing."

"Did you speak to Craig Smith?"

"We did, and he's sticking to what he told your father. But unless she cooperates, it's his word against hers."

Campbell scowled. "You still have no proof."

"Well, we're trying to put together enough to charge her, but right now there's no hard evidence. If we could nail the blackmailer, it would be another story."

Campbell heaved out a sigh. "Okay. You know what? I'm going to forget all about this painting mess and enjoy a few days off. I really like your sister, by the way."

Keith smiled. "Glad to hear it, since I'm partial to her myself. Come on. I'll bet we can get up a rousing game of Scrabble."

In addition to her hostess gift of tea towels, Campbell had brought a collector's tree ornament for Angela and a fishing fly her dad picked out for Nathan, but she waited for a moment alone to exchange gifts with Keith.

As they tidied up after a light supper, she sidled up to him and whispered, "I have a gift for you, but I didn't want to give it to you in front of everyone."

"I've got something special for you too. How about when I take you home after the carol service?"

Campbell was agreeable to that. The entire family was attending a special Christmas service at Keith's church that evening, and afterward he would drive her home. She was a little nervous about the exchange, but she'd heard Keith mention how much he wanted this particular item.

The service was uplifting, and she lingered afterward with Keith's family. As the last parishioners headed out the door, Keith said, "We'd better get going." Nicole and Todd got into Nathan and Angela's car, and Keith took Campbell to his SUV.

When he pulled in at the McBride house, all was dark except the front hall light.

"Dad's not home yet," Campbell noted.

"Where'd he go?" Keith asked.

"Our church had a cantata tonight, and he was meeting Jackie Fleming there. I expect there were refreshments afterward."

"Oh, and you missed it."

"It's okay," she said. "I had a great time."

"Hey, wait a sec." Keith put the SUV in park and switched off the engine. "I thought Bill decided not to see Jackie anymore."

Campbell sighed. "He did, but he still likes her as a person."

"So, was this a date?"

"I'm not sure. She may have invited him. But they were both going anyway, you know?"

"Yeah, they go to the same church."

She nodded. "And her daughter Lucy and her husband were going to come, so Jackie probably felt it was extra special."

"Oh, yeah, I've met Lucy and Garrett."

"Her son Michael was supposed to come for the weekend too. I don't know if he went to the cantata or not." She shivered. "Let's go in. I'm sure Dad will be home soon."

She picked up the colorful gift bag she'd taken to the Fullers' and back, and carried it inside with the presents Keith's parents had given her. The delay in presenting Keith's gift to him had played on her nerves, and it would be a relief to get it over with.

As they mounted the porch steps, she noticed that he was carrying a small bag. Inside, the old house felt chilly, and she tapped the thermostat up a couple of degrees.

"Want to start a fire?" she asked as they approached the fireplace.

"I can do it."

She accepted his offer and hung up their coats. Campbell sat down on the sofa, wishing she hadn't suggested they use the fireplace. It brought another delay, while Keith carefully arranged the kindling and ignited the tinder. It didn't really take long, but she wanted the gift-giving to be done before her dad walked in.

Finally the fire blazed to Keith's satisfaction,

and he came to sit beside her, snagging his gift bag from the end table on the way.

"So." He smiled at her and leaned in for a kiss. "Merry Christmas Eve. I love you."

"I love you too."

He eyed the bag she held on her lap. "You first?"

Relieved, she held it out to him.

"Oh. It's heavy."

She shrugged with a smile. "Maybe it's a big lump of coal."

"Somehow, I doubt it." He pulled a wrapped parcel from the bag and hefted it. *"Hmm."*

"I—" She stopped, not wanting to give any spoilers.

He began to peel off the tape, teasing her with each slow bit of progress. At last he pulled the paper away and gazed down at the box. "Oh, wow."

Watching his eyes carefully for his reaction, she touched his wrist. "You told me your dad lost your old set of binoculars overboard when he was fishing."

"That's true."

"You didn't go buy a new set, did you? My dad says these are the best, and I checked with your folks to make sure they hadn't bought you a new pair."

His eyes softened. "No, I haven't replaced them. I kind of wondered why Dad hadn't." Carefully, he opened the box, took out the binoculars, and walked over to the window. He lifted them to his eyes and looked outside. Although it was after dark, the lights from nearby homes and the street lamps showed him enough to focus on. "Yeah," he said softly, adjusting the focus. "These are great."

Campbell exhaled and walked over beside him. Keith held them out to her. "Want to look?"

"Sure." Campbell took the glasses and lifted them to her face. She adjusted them to her eyes and panned the driveway, the neighbors' yards, and the street. "Yeah, they're pretty good."

She froze as a vehicle pulled to the curb just beyond the Peeles' driveway. The headlights went off, but she could still see well enough to follow a figure that emerged from the car and cut across the lawn to the Peeles' porch.

Campbell quickly lowered the binoculars and ducked back behind the edge of the drapes.

"Keith, look at this." She thrust the binoculars at him.

"What am I looking at?"

"Our neighbors, the Peeles, aren't home. They left yesterday for Louisville, to spend the holidays with family. But someone just drove up and went up on their porch. There are no lights in the house, and no one's opening the door, but the person's still there."

Keith whipped the binoculars to his face and

adjusted the focus. "Do you think one of them might have come back early?"

"I don't know. That's not Allison's car, and her son drives a pickup."

Even without the binoculars, Campbell could see the stealthy figure leave the porch and blend in with the shadows at the end of the house.

"What . . . ?"

"I think he's going around to the back," Keith said. He shoved the binoculars into her hand. "Hold these. I need to make a call."

She lost sight of the figure after it slipped around into the Peeles' backyard. The corner of the McBrides' garage limited her view. While she watched, Keith quietly asked a dispatcher to send a patrol car to Willow Street. Then he shut off the overhead lights, and by the light of the blaze on the hearth, returned to stand beside her.

"Where'd he go?"

"Not sure, but—oh, look!"

She pointed toward the house, her extended finger colliding with the windowpane. "They're inside. See that light?"

"Yeah, someone's in there with a flashlight." A wavering light flicked toward the front windows and then away.

"Too bad their garage is on this end of the house," Campbell said.

"Yeah." Keith touched her arm. "The unit should be here soon. We'll sit tight until they arrive.

I'm going to step out to my car. You stay inside, please."

She nodded.

"Okay. I'll turn out your front porch light as I go." He gave her a quick kiss.

The fleeting thought of the Christmas gift he hadn't yet presented to her crossed her mind, but she didn't mention it. Keith needed to concentrate on the intruder right now.

He went out the front door quietly.

Chapter 22

Keith stopped at his vehicle only long enough to retrieve his flashlight and a pistol he carried in in the glove compartment as a backup weapon. How could he have imagined he'd have a real day off?

He circled quickly between the McBrides' garage and the Peeles', into the new neighbor's backyard. The door leading into the Peeles' kitchen yielded to his touch. He opened it a couple of inches and looked inside.

No one seemed to be in the kitchen, but a bobbing light moved about in the next room. He slipped inside and cautiously made his way toward the doorway. The intruder was shining a flashlight beam on several boxes in the living room. Belongings still not unpacked from the Peeles' move?

As the housebreaker bent over one of the cartons, long hair fluttered around the shadowy face. Keith was almost sure it was a woman. Maybe Mrs. Peele *had* come back. But if so, why didn't she turn on the lights?

In a split-second decision, he reached for the light switch just inside the doorway. As light flooded the room, the woman clad in dark sweats whipped around with her flashlight in one hand and a camera in the other.

"Police. Don't move."

She jerked her head toward him then looked helplessly down at the camera. "I can explain."

Keith stared at her. He'd seen her before, on his computer screen. "You're under arrest for breaking and entering, Ms. Chilton."

Campbell stayed behind the drapes, lifting the edge next to the woodwork carefully so she could peer out toward the Peeles' house without being seen. Keith was a dark shadow crossing the grass to the Peeles' driveway. He disappeared behind the garage, and she waited, scarcely daring to breathe.

A minute later, light spilled out from the Peeles' living room windows. At the same moment, a squad car arrived without lights or siren and parked on the street. Two officers got out and approached the house. The front door was flung open, and Keith went out onto the porch with them, pulling with him the black-clad intruder they'd seen earlier.

Campbell squinted at them as the officers held a brief confab. Definitely a woman, but she was almost certain it wasn't Allison. She raised the binoculars and, with the benefit of the porch light now, she was sure. Keith had caught someone inside the house, and that woman was now hand-cuffed.

Another car drew up at the curb, and Detective Matt Jackson got out. Campbell clenched her teeth as the two patrol officers led the prisoner away and the detectives entered the house.

About five minutes passed, and Campbell's curiosity tortured her. Another police car arrived and parked in the Peeles' driveway. Finally her father's blue Camry crept down Willow Street. He pulled into the McBride driveway, but Campbell kept her stance at the window.

As soon as he opened the front door, Bill yelled, "Campbell?"

"In the office, Dad."

He joined her by the window. "What's going on?"

"We saw someone sneaking into the Peeles' house, and Keith went over and took her into custody. It's a woman. Two patrol officers took her away, but now there's more police over there. Keith and Matt and at least two uniforms. For what it's worth, I was using the new binoculars I gave Keith when I saw the person." She held up the field glasses.

Her father smiled. "How'd he like them?"

"He thinks they're great."

They stood in silence for a moment, then Bill said, "You want coffee? It could be a while."

"Maybe some chamomile tea."

She fixed her tea and her dad's coffee then made herself sit quietly with him as they waited for something—she wasn't sure what.

"We were giving our gifts. I hadn't opened

mine yet." Campbell glanced at the small gift bag still sitting on the end table. "Keith opened the binoculars, and we were trying them out. That's how we saw the person sneaking around."

"Open yours now."

"No, I'll wait until he's here. But you should open yours from me."

"I can wait."

"Well, I can't." They'd always had their tree on Christmas Eve, and Campbell was determined to keep the tradition. She went over to the glittering fir tree and took a small box from beneath it.

Bill smiled when she handed it to him. "What's this, a new tie?"

"Open it and see."

He pulled the bow off and set it aside, then carefully peeled off the paper as she watched. When he lifted the lid and found an envelope inside, his eyebrows shot up, and he threw her a questioning look.

"Go on," she said.

He opened the envelope and took out a brochure and a sheet of paper. He glanced at the brochure then unfolded the paper and scanned it.

"What? You're sending me to a fishing resort?"

"You and Mart," she said with a grin. "You're booked for four nights in a cabin there the week bass season opens. And it's got plenty of room, so if you want to invite Nathan Fuller, too, that's not a problem."

"Aw, Soup, this is . . . too much. It's fantastic, but it's too much."

"No, it's not."

"Do I pay you too much?"

She laughed. "The fishing is supposed to be terrific there. I want you and Mart to have a nice vacation together."

"Well. How about that." He was smiling as he opened the brochure. "I'll tell Mart tomorrow. Or does he know about this?"

"No clue. I was going to tell Reagan, but I decided to keep it a secret."

"Thank you." He held her gaze for a moment then got up and approached the tree. He came back with two packages and held them out to her.

"Wow. If I'm getting two, you should open that other one for you." She pointed to her second gift for her father.

"There's more?" He stooped and retrieved it. Feeling the paper and the contours beneath it, he went back to his seat. "This feels like a book."

"Imagine that." She ripped the paper off her first present, the smaller of the two. "Aw, Dad." She held up a bracelet with green and amber stones.

"You like?" He wiggled his eyebrows.

"I love it."

"Good. I got some pointers from Angela on that. Well, I asked Jackie first, and she picked out a bangly thing that I knew you wouldn't like."

Campbell laughed. "This is perfect."

He nodded and freed his *History of Calloway County* from its wrapping. "Oh, good. I've been wanting to read this." He got up and moseyed to the window. "Looks like they're still busy over there."

"So, I should open this now?" She held up her second package.

"Yeah, go ahead."

She pulled off the holly-sprigged paper and found a small box. Inside was a folded sheet of paper. Had her father planned a vacation for her too?

Slowly, she opened it and read the message. The words blurred as tears filled her eyes.

"Really, Dad? A partnership?"

He came over and sat down next to her. "Yes. I'd love to have you as a full partner in the business, if you'll accept."

Her lips trembled. "I . . . I'm honored. But what about Nick?"

"I told him, and he's okay with it."

Campbell blinked. "Are you sure?"

Her father nodded. "I explained to him how important it's become to me to have the business in your name as well as mine. We don't know how long I'll be around, and I don't want you to be tied up in red tape if something happens to me."

One of her tears washed over her eyelid and

rolled down her cheek. "There's nothing you're not telling me, is there?"

"No, kiddo. It's just—well, you know how it is. Since you came home last summer, we've both had some incidents. I just want to make sure that if there's a bad outcome for one of us, the other McBride will still be in charge."

She sniffed. "It's kind of scary, but yes, I accept."

He nodded and put his arms around her. "I love you, Campbell."

"Love you too, Dad." She squeezed him and then drew back as the doorbell rang. "Did you lock the door when you came in?"

"I did."

They both rose and walked down the hall. Bill checked the peephole and swung the door open.

"Well, Keith. All done over there?"

"I have to go to the station." He threw Campbell a contrite look.

"You arrested an intruder?" Bill said.

"Yes. You'll never guess who."

"It wasn't Allison," Campbell said.

"No. It was Marissa Chilton, that new P.I."

"What?" Bill stared at him. "Why on earth was she poking around in their house?"

"Apparently young Peele's been pilfering from the university for a while—possibly businesses in town as well." Keith threw a look at Campbell. "I think I told you someone was stealing from MSU's theater department?"

"Yes. Cameras and things."

Keith nodded. "A lot of expensive equipment. We had narrowed it down to a group of a dozen or so students, and Greg Peele was on our list. I didn't want to tell you, because I didn't want you to suspect him if he was innocent. But I didn't think he was dangerous, or I certainly would have warned you. Anyway, the school decided we were too slow on the job and decided to hire a P.I. to look into it."

"And she found evidence to pin it on Greg Peele?" Bill grunted.

"I don't know why they picked her, Bill, but they did. Me, I'd have told them to hire you. But she did find the goods. Too bad she broke the law finding them."

"What are you going to do to her?"

Keith sighed. "We have to report her. She may lose her license."

Bill's face froze, and Campbell could read his dilemma. His unscrupulous rival was in trouble. Should he cheer the fact that she was getting her comeuppance, or be angry that the police would potentially ruin a private investigator's career? And maybe he was chagrined because Marissa had tracked down the thief before the police did.

Campbell thought it was time to change the subject. "So, you found loot in there?"

"Lots of stuff. Some of it matches things taken

from the university. There are some electronics and other things still in their boxes. We've got a team cataloging it all. Chilton admitted she lucked out. She expected to find a couple cameras and a microphone or two, but she hit the mother lode."

"Do you think Greg's mother knows about it?" Campbell asked.

"I don't see how she could help it, with all the stuff we found in his bedroom and the basement. There are even a few boxes in the living room. Who knows where he kept his stash before his mother moved here?"

"In his dorm room, maybe?"

Keith shook his head. "Not all of it."

Bill frowned. "Do you think Allison's in on it?"

"I don't know. I've alerted Louisville. They're tracking down her extended family. It sounds like they have some leads. If they locate the two of them, they'll take them both in for questioning. The son is definitely being charged. As for Mrs. Peele, well . . . I guess we'll see what forensics tells us."

"I wonder if Greg was glad she moved over here or not," Campbell mused. "It gave him more space, and private space at that, for his loot, but . . ."

"It does seem unusual," Keith said. "She may have been knowingly abetting him. Right now, I have an open mind."

"Oh!" Campbell looked over her shoulder toward the living room-turned-office. "The present you brought is still here."

"Right." Keith scrubbed his eyes with the back of his hand. "I was hoping we'd get to that tonight, but I won't be done until late."

"I can save it for when you're free. But, remember? We're going to Mart Brady's tomorrow."

Keith sighed. "I really want to be there when you open it."

"And I kind of hate to leave it in the empty house while we're gone."

"How long will it take?" Bill asked. "You can come in for a few minutes right now, can't you?"

Keith glanced over toward the Peeles' house, where a few officers were still at work.

"I'd better not. Why don't you give it back to me? I'll keep it until you're back."

"Okay. Hold on." Campbell hurried in and grabbed the small package. A little disappointed, she gave it to Keith at the front door with an exaggerated pout. "Here, Santa."

He laughed. "Sorry. But I promise you, it's not a lump of coal."

Bill opened his mouth and closed it.

"What?" Campbell asked.

"Nothing." Her father turned away with a wave. "Excuse me. I think I can still catch the late news."

She turned to Keith. "I think he's just giving us a moment alone."

"I'll accept that." He leaned down and kissed her. Then he was off down the steps with the gift in his hand.

Chapter 23

Monday morning, Campbell was up early. She made waffles and brewed coffee. When her father entered the kitchen yawning, she sang out, "Merry Christmas, Partner!"

Bill grinned. "Does that mean half the waffles are mine?"

"Yes, and half the sausage too. Actually, you can have most of the sausage. I only want one link."

"So, all packed?" He poured himself a cup of coffee.

"The gifts are ready to go. We're coming back tonight, though, right?"

"Yeah. Mart said we could stay over, but since we're hanging with the Fullers tomorrow, I think I'd rather come back tonight."

She nodded. "I'll just take an emergency shirt, then."

Her dad's eyebrows shot up.

"You know—in case I spill something on myself."

"Oh, right. Maybe I should do that too."

On their two-hour drive, they couldn't stay off the topic of the Abbott case.

"I wonder where the police stand on Diane Block," Bill said.

"I'm pretty sure they haven't arrested her. Keith mentioned last night that the financial records are taking time. You know, warrants and all that."

Her father sighed. "I'll be glad when this thing is settled."

"Me too, but now Keith and Matt have the Peele case to worry about."

"That kid's got to have accomplices on campus."

"I think so too, but Keith hasn't told me anything yet."

"Well, we'll have to leave that one all to them. I just hope it doesn't take them away from the Abbott case. Or should I say the Block case?"

Campbell smiled. "The Nelson-Block case?"

He nodded and signaled for his exit.

"I wonder what that New Year's Eve party's going to be like," Campbell said. "If Diane gets arrested, maybe they'll cancel it."

"It's at her brother's house. I'm not sure he'd do that. I gather David and his wife are thick-skinned when it comes to society."

"I wonder if I should buy a new dress."

"Maybe you should. On me. After all, giving you the partnership didn't cost me anything."

She laughed. "Don't give me that! You said you want to make it all official. That means having one of your lawyer friends draw up new papers."

"Well, that's true, and partners get a share of the profits, not wages."

"I never thought of that." She turned in her seat

to look at him clearly. "You didn't say anything about it. Are you sure?"

"I figure we'll have a partners' meeting every month and decide how much to pay ourselves and how much to reinvest in the business."

"Okay." She frowned. "Dad, have you been taking a salary?"

"Mostly I just take what I need."

"*Hmm.* I know we're not rich. I guess we'll have to see how our own financials look, for a change."

"My accounts are fully open to you. They're yours now too."

She wasn't sure she liked that. It would certainly mean more responsibility. But she was certain her dad had been responsible with his income over the years. Still, it was a little scary.

When they arrived at their destination, the Bradys greeted them en masse. Mart and Bill gave each other a bear hug and immediately began talking shop. Mart had retired from the local police department, and he and Bill had been colleagues there for several years.

"I'm thinking about following your advice and opening my own business as a P.I.," he told Bill.

"Fantastic," Bill said. "There's actually a new P.I. setting up shop in Murray."

"Really? I didn't suppose there was enough business over there for another agency."

"Neither did I." Bill and Mart moved toward the living room. "The hilarious thing is, Keith

Fuller arrested her last night for breaking and entering at our neighbor's house while the people were out of town for Christmas."

"You're kidding!"

The men's voices were muted as they moved away, and Campbell turned to her friend Reagan.

"How's it going at WKU?" Campbell asked.

Reagan, the youngest of Mart's three daughters, was now a junior at Western Kentucky University.

"Good, but as usual, I'm glad for a break."

Her older sisters, Jasmine and Heather, greeted Campbell. Each had come during the weekend with her husband and child. Jasmine's toddler, Marcus, sprinted to Campbell for a hug. Heather introduced her eight-month-old daughter, Ella.

The day flew, with dinner being the highlight. The Bradys had already exchanged their gifts within the family, but Bill and Campbell had brought small presents and received some as well. Reagan seemed delighted with her trinket box, and she presented Campbell with a leather-covered journal.

"I love it!" Campbell gave her a big hug.

When Mart heard about the fishing trip Campbell had set up for him and her father, he was flabbergasted. "Wow! That would be great, Bill!" He looked at Campbell. "Are you sure? Thanks very much!" He checked his schedule, and he and Bill were soon deep in plans for their odyssey.

Campbell chatted with the sisters as they

cleaned up the kitchen. For supper, they laid out the leftovers for open-face turkey sandwiches with salad and vegetables on the side.

Finally, about eight o'clock, Bill looked over at his daughter and raised his eyebrows. "Time to hit the road, Soup?"

She sighed. "I hate to, but we'd better." She looked apologetically at their host. "Sorry to leave so early, Uncle Mart, but we're planning to work tomorrow."

They began gathering their scattered belongings and expressing their hopes to see their friends again soon.

On the way home, Bill gave her more details about Mart's plans to open his agency in Bowling Green.

"He's done all the groundwork and the paperwork. He got his license last week."

"I'm proud of him," Campbell said.

"He followed my advice and touched base with all the lawyers and insurance agents he knows, and it sounds as if he'll pick up some work pretty quickly."

Darkness had fallen when they left Bowling Green, and the stars glittered above as they crossed the Land Between the Lakes. At last, they pulled into their driveway.

"We forgot to leave any lights on," Bill noted. He hit the button on the garage door opener and waited for the door to roll up.

"I love you, Dad." Campbell leaned over and kissed his cheek.

He smiled and drove slowly into the garage. Campbell hopped out and felt her way to the steps and found the light switch. As Bill shut the car off, she also tapped the button to make the door go down. Just as it started, a vehicle turned in at the end of the driveway. She paused the door a third of the way down.

The vehicle stopped close to the garage, and its lights went off. Only then did she recognize the SUV.

"Keith's here," she told her dad as he climbed out of the Camry.

"Somebody couldn't wait a day to see you." Bill strolled to the doorway and stooped a little to go through. "Well, young fella, are you here to see my daughter?"

Keith laughed. "Partly. But my message for you is my excuse."

"What message?" Bill asked.

"We think our team found some property of yours in the house next door."

"What?"

Campbell edged past the car toward the doorway so she could hear better.

"We found a package with your name on it," Keith told her father. "Did you order a security camera?"

"Well, yeah. I got an email saying it had been

delivered, but it hadn't. I called the company a few days ago to tell them I never got it and to send another one."

"I'd say it was delivered to the wrong house," Keith said. "Or maybe . . ."

"That bum," Campbell cried. "He stole it off our porch!"

"Might have," Keith agreed.

"They know who we are. If it came to their house, Allison would have brought it over here."

"Maybe." Keith looked skeptical. "It was opened, though."

"That little snake," Bill said. "Where is it now?"

"I wasn't sure you'd be home, so I left it at the station. You can drop in and get it anytime tomorrow."

"Thanks. I'll call the company in the morning, but they've probably already sent the replacement." Bill shook his head. "Next time, Nell Calhoun had better screen her clients a little better."

Campbell gave Keith a smile that she hoped wasn't too weary. "Coming in?"

"If you want me to."

"I do."

His smile spread across his face. "I've still got your present."

"I can't wait."

"Greg's at the county jail waiting for indictment," Keith said. "They brought him over from

Louisville this afternoon. We had his mother at the station for several hours, but we released her tonight. There's no proof she was involved in his activities, although I can't see how she could avoid knowing. There was a ton of stuff in that house."

"Well, kids, I'm going to bed," Bill said. "Keith, thanks for the update. I'll see you tomorrow at the station." He went into the garage and through the door to the kitchen.

"Come on in," Campbell said.

"Let me get your present." Keith retrieved the gift bag from his car and handed it to her. In it was a box about the size of one that a mug would come in, and Campbell wondered if she'd overspent on the binoculars.

After closing the garage door, they went inside. Campbell reset the alarm system.

"I'm glad you got the security system," Keith said.

"Me too. Would you like something to drink? I don't want caffeine right now, but I think I'll make myself some herbal tea."

"That little coffeemaker in the office makes cocoa, doesn't it?" he asked.

"It sure does. Help yourself." Campbell put a cup of water in the microwave and dug out the teabag she wanted. When she entered the main office a couple of minutes later, Keith was standing near the window gazing out at the Peeles' house while his drink brewed.

"I hope this doesn't leave us with neighbors who despise us." Campbell carried her tea and the package over near the fireplace and sat down on the sofa.

Keith soon joined her. "I doubt you'll see much of them for a while."

"Greg's going to jail?"

"That's pretty certain. We're still not sure if his mother will be charged."

Campbell frowned. "She just bought the house."

"With a whopping mortgage."

"Hmm." Campbell had no experience in buying real estate, except for watching her father wade through it when he bought the house they now lived in. "What a way to spend Christmas. I thought maybe Allison and I could be friends."

"Give it time. It may work out." Keith took a sip of his hot chocolate and set the mug down on the coffee table. "Ready for your present?"

She smiled. "I've been ready for a while."

"Oh?" His eyebrows shot up.

"I mean, in general. I have no idea what this is."

"So open it."

She hesitated, looking up into his rich brown eyes. "Okay." A little self-conscious, she removed the ribbon and paper and set them aside. Inside the box, cushioned by bubble wrap, was a smaller, velvet-covered box.

"Oh." Her throat constricted. "I—I thought it was a mug, but I guess it wasn't heavy enough."

He chuckled then sobered. "It's not too soon, is it?"

"I . . ." With butterflies swirling in her stomach, she opened the spring catch and caught her breath.

The diamond sparkled up at her, and she sat transfixed.

"You knew, right?" Keith said softly.

"No, really, I didn't."

He slipped to his knees and reached for her hand. "I love you so much, Campbell. I know we've had to grab a few minutes here and there lately, but I want to spend the rest of my life with you. Will you marry me?"

Questions crashed down on her. Did she want to be married to a police officer? Was she ready for marriage in general? She'd just regained a close relationship with her dad. Would she be giving that up if she accepted? *Do I love him enough?*

She knew the answer to that last one. She did love Keith with all her heart.

Over all her doubts, hung one huge question, the importance of which she couldn't ignore. Was this what God wanted for the two of them?

Keith was watching her closely. She met his gaze and realized she should have answered by now. He swallowed hard.

"Yes."

He rose to sit beside her and put his arms around her. As he kissed her, Campbell's doubts splintered and floated away.

Chapter 24

Bill went down to breakfast Tuesday morning smiling to himself. When he got to the kitchen, there was his daughter, making blueberry pancakes. A diamond glittered as she flipped them out onto a waiting plate.

"Morning, Dad."

"A very good morning to you, sweetheart." He went over and slipped an arm around her waist. "I see congratulations are in order."

She turned and held out her hand. "Yes, I guess they are." She looked up at him anxiously. "What do you think?"

"I think I'm very happy about it. How about you—what do *you* think?"

She smiled then, and she looked more contented than he'd seen her since her mother died. Even when she read his letter giving her partnership in the agency, she hadn't looked this satisfied.

"I think I'm ready, and it's going to be a wonderful thing."

He nodded and picked up one of the plates she'd left on the counter. "Any plans yet?"

She shook her head. "This summer, I suppose. Keith doesn't want to wait too long."

"And why should you?"

"Yeah," she said, holding the spatula up in the air. "Why should we?"

"I suppose you'll go live at his house then."

"We didn't really talk about that yet."

Bill nodded. "Take your time. Just keep me posted."

A line formed between her eyebrows as she looked around the room. "I suppose this big old house is . . . kinda big for you alone."

"Oh, not with the business headquarters here. Don't worry about me, kiddo. I'll be fine."

Her smile came back. "Yeah, you will." She set down the spatula and poured more batter into the big frying pan.

"You expecting company?" Bill asked. "That's a lot of hotcakes for two."

"Nick texted. He's coming in to work, and I told him breakfast would be waiting for him."

"I told him not to come back till tomorrow. I'm not sure we can do much more on the Abbott case. We'd better wrap up the background checks we were doing and start on the case Chris Powell gave us."

"What about Leila? Do we just drop it?"

"No, I've arranged to meet with her tomorrow. I'll tell her what we think happened with the painting. We're pretty sure now that Diane gave it to Craig, and after a while, he gave it to Jacob, who put it in her grandparents' attic."

Campbell nodded slowly. "I just wish we knew

who shot Brad Standish and if it's related to the case."

"You, me, and the world. Let's let it rest and see what Keith and his team come up with. Meanwhile, we've got that embezzlement case too. We need to start on that this week." He eyed his pancakes. "Is the syrup out?"

"It's in the dining room, with the orange juice. Oh, get your coffee."

Nick arrived a few minutes later and fixed himself a plate of pancakes.

"How was Florida?" Campbell asked.

"Great. The beach wasn't crowded at all."

She smiled. "How are your parents doing?"

"Fantastic. But they'll probably come up to visit this summer, when it's too muggy for them down there. So, what's happening here?"

"We're going to the theater with the Fullers tonight," Campbell said. "But the real news is what happened next door."

"Oh? What'd I miss?"

Bill filled him in on the break-in, the loot at the Peeles' house, and their cases. He doled out assignments as they finished breakfast.

"Hey," Nick said suddenly, his gaze riveted on Campbell's left hand.

Bill laughed. "You just noticed?"

"Well, yeah. Why didn't somebody tell me?"

Campbell blushed. "Sorry. It's official." She held out her hand so he could see the ring better.

"Wow. Congrats, Professor."

"Oh, she's not a professor anymore," Bill said drily. "She's now one of your bosses."

That evening, the Fullers met Campbell and her father at the Playhouse in the Park. Angela and Nicole were especially buoyant at welcoming her into the family. Nathan swept her into a hug after the customary inspection of her ring.

"If I could have chosen another daughter, I'd have picked you."

"Thank you." Tears filled Campbell's eyes as she squeezed Nathan.

He turned to Keith and clapped him on the shoulder. "Well done, son."

They all enjoyed the local actors' presentation of *A Christmas Carol*, but seeing it with her new family was the most fulfilling part for Campbell.

The rest of the week flew by in a blur of routine assignments. Rita came in on Thursday and cooked them some comfort food. After eating out for most meals on Tuesday and Wednesday, Campbell felt they were somewhat back to normal. Hearing the vacuum cleaner running upstairs was almost like background music for her online searches and typing up reports.

Nick was slightly outraged when he heard that Campbell was going to attend the Nelson party with Christopher Powell.

"What? Does Keith know about this?"

"He does. He and Chris both know it's more or less a business outing for me. It is for Chris, too—he's going there to rub elbows with clients and potential clients."

Her father gave her Saturday off. She almost wished he hadn't. Work might help distract her from thoughts of the party. New Year's Eve fell on Sunday this year, which she didn't appreciate. It would have been much better for her on Friday or Saturday, so she wouldn't have to fret all weekend in anticipation.

Of course, her dad said there was no sense in fretting, and she knew he was right.

Finally, about ten on Saturday morning, she went to him and begged for an assignment.

"Well, I've gone over the month's books, and now I'm working on end-of-the-year stuff."

"Tax forms?" she asked.

"Not yet. Would you like to work on the annual report?"

"Sure. What's involved?"

He gave her a copy of the three quarterly reports he'd already done that year and the previous year's annual report.

Soon Campbell was typing away, listing cases they'd solved in the final quarter and consolidating each quarter's events into one final document. She didn't finish until after noon. She was about to go scrounge up lunch in the kitchen when Bill came to the doorway.

"Hey. Want to go to lunch?"

"Go out, you mean?"

"Yeah. How about that Fruity Bowls place Angela and Nicole were talking about?"

Campbell laughed. "It's Frutta Bowls, Dad. I didn't know you liked salad that much."

"Eh, they said you can get them with meat and just about whatever you want in them, and the fruit stuff sounds like a nice dessert."

"Okay, I'll give it a try."

She had to admit their meal was delicious, but their lunch took barely an hour, including the short drive.

"What have you got for me now?" she asked him when they got home.

Bill frowned. "I dunno. I'm running out of stuff. New Year's resolutions?"

"No, thanks. I already know what I'll do this year. It's just today and tomorrow that are weighing on me."

"The party?"

She nodded.

"Did you buy a new dress?"

"No."

"That's it. Go shopping this afternoon."

She suspected he was just trying to get her out of his hair, but she went.

Knowing the other guests would be well dressed, she drove to Paducah and visited several shops there before finding a dress she loved that

302

cast the right tone. The price was more than she really wanted to spend, especially since she didn't know how much her income would be now, but she decided to go for it. She could wear the shimmery blue dress to the engagement party Angela was talking about throwing for her and Keith.

As she left the store and headed for her car, her cell rang. She smiled. Her fiancé was calling her.

"Hi," she said.

"Hello, beautiful. I get off at six. Can we spend the evening together? I know it's last minute."

"I'd love to." They talked for another minute or two, then signed off. Campbell realized she had an hour-long drive ahead of her, and just about time after returning home to get ready for the date.

Sunday evening finally arrived. The morning church service calmed Campbell, but her nerves kicked up again as Chris's arrival and the party drew closer.

She did her makeup with more care than usual and slipped on the perfect dress. It didn't look so wonderful now. Gazing into the mirror, she knew she'd feel differently if it was Keith picking her up in thirty minutes, not Chris.

When she went out into the hallway, Bill came from their sitting room, where he'd been watching the news. He gave a soft wolf whistle.

Campbell laughed. "Thanks, I think."

"You're wearing your ring tonight?" he asked.

"Well, yeah. Should I not?" She looked down at the diamond in confusion.

"I just thought, if you show up with Chris Powell and a diamond on your finger, people might assume he's your fiancé."

"Oh." She hadn't thought of that. Her first impulse was to say, "Let them think that." She didn't want to leave the ring at home. However, her dad was right. She and Chris might end up having to answer some questions they didn't want to deal with. "You're right," she said. "I'll put it in my jewelry box. You'll be here all evening, right?"

"Sure. I was going to pop over to Arby's, but . . ."

"Okay."

Bill shook his head. "Forget it. We've got plenty of food here. I won't go off and leave your engagement ring unprotected."

She laughed. "I guess I'm pretty silly, huh? With the security system and all that . . ."

"And the thieves next door," he said.

Campbell winced. "Yeah. Thanks, Dad. I really appreciate it."

"I saw Allison over there this afternoon," he said.

"Really? I've only seen her once since they arrested Greg and hauled her in for questioning."

"I think she's been lying low. Did Keith say anything last night?"

"About the Peeles? Only that the D.A. said they didn't have enough to charge Allison. Greg's still under the gun, though. Big time. Keith said there was enough loot in his bedroom and the basement alone to support a grand larceny charge."

"Wow."

"It's kind of weird," Campbell said. "I feel as if I should reach out to Allison again. But I'm not sure she'd welcome me, since my fiancé is the one who had her son arrested."

"Maybe not. But does she know he's your fiancé?"

"I'm not sure."

"Well, technically he wasn't your fiancé yet when it happened, right?"

"That's right. Keith didn't propose until Monday night."

"Give it some thought. Maybe we'll go over together tomorrow and take her some cookies or something."

"We're all out of cookies."

He shrugged. "Rita's working tomorrow, isn't she?"

"No, Dad, it's New Year's Day. It's a holiday."

"Oh. Why did we start having her come Mondays right before a raft of Monday holidays?"

Campbell laughed. The doorbell rang.

"Oops, that must be Chris. I'll see you later."

She kissed her father on the cheek and dashed to her room, where she took off her ring. With a rueful smile, she placed it gently in her jewelry box and went down the stairs.

Chapter 25

The drive to the Nelsons' estate was a bit awkward. Campbell cautiously fingered the orchid corsage Chris had brought her. He hadn't needed to bring her so much as a carnation, yet he'd sprung for an orchid. She flicked a glance at him in the half-light of the car's interior. Her father had made it clear she was seeing someone else, right?

Chris followed his phone's GPS into a swanky neighborhood. Campbell hadn't realized there was a neighborhood down here, nearly to the city limits, that boasted such fine houses. They pulled in at a horseshoe drive before a three-story mansion—she couldn't think of it as anything else.

A young man in a suit came and opened her door. Campbell got out and watched as Chris emerged from the driver's seat and handed his keys to him. Valet parking—when was the last time she'd seen that? Probably several years ago, at a dinner for new faculty thrown by Feldman College. Never, at a private party.

"How the other half lives," Chris said with a grin as he joined her.

"Right." But then, Chris was a lawyer. He'd probably been to plenty of posh parties.

In the entry, a uniformed maid took their coats. Campbell kept her clutch purse, which contained her phone, driver's license, a twenty-dollar bill, and lipstick. She'd managed to cram in a tissue and decided that was her limit.

They were directed to a large room, and David Nelson, Jr. and his wife, Hillary, stood just inside. A man in a tuxedo took the invitation Chris handed him.

"And your guest is . . . ?"

"Miss Campbell McBride."

The man turned to the Nelsons.

"Mr. Christopher Powell and guest, Ms. McBride."

"Welcome, Mr. Powell." Nelson shook Chris's hand. "Thank you for coming."

Chris presented Campbell, and she shook hands with both David and Hillary Nelson. Mrs. Nelson gave her a swift appraisal and smiled graciously. Although she must be close to sixty years old, Hillary's skin was smooth and obviously well looked after. Maybe she was much younger than her husband. Her silver gown was stunning, and her understated makeup set off her pale blonde hair and blue eyes.

"Welcome, Ms. McBride. I hope you'll enjoy the evening."

"I'm sure I will. I was thrilled when Chris extended the invitation to me." Not exactly the truth, she admonished herself inwardly. *Oh, dear,*

I don't want to end up being a liar, even in the interest of doing my job.

As she walked with Chris into the midst of the gathering, she found herself shooting up a silent prayer of confession. She wanted to be a good detective, but more than that, she wanted to please God.

She recognized all of the Nelson siblings from online photos True Blue had added to its case file. Diane Block and her husband, Travis, were easy to spot. They both had cocktail glasses in hand and were conversing loudly with a circle of people. Most of the men wore tuxedos, though some were in their best suits, and the women were elaborately gowned.

Campbell gave Chris a sidelong glance. He measured up. She wondered if he'd rented the tuxedo or owned it. Probably owned, she decided. His profession would present many formal occasions.

The vast room seemed to be three smaller chambers with pocket doors pulled back, making a room large enough to hold a hundred guests easily. A glittering chandelier lit the space they were in, and the carpet underfoot felt deep and luxurious. Several seating areas were set up around the edges of the open space, and the art hanging on the walls looked interesting. She wondered if any Banitiers were among the paintings.

How could she hope to have a conversation with Diane? Mrs. Block seemed the center of attention right now, with half a dozen guests surrounding her. Maybe it would be easier to initiate an acquaintance with her sister Charlotte, who'd moved to Tennessee years ago, or unpresuming younger brother Eddie.

"See someone you know?" Chris asked softly.

"Someone I'd like to know."

"Ah. Well, I've spotted a doctor and a judge I'm acquainted with. Do you want to come along, or is it time to go our own ways?"

"Thanks. I think I'll see if Eddie Nelson will talk to me."

Chris smiled and nodded. With a brief touch on her arm, he moved away toward a cluster of guests.

Eddie somewhat resembled his older brother, whom she'd met at the door. David, Jr. looked more like their father, however. Eddie was a couple of inches shorter than David, a little rounder, and appeared to be more jovial. As Campbell approached his group, he was apparently telling a joke. The woman beside him wore a nice burgundy gown, but she couldn't carry it off with the same flair her sisters-in-law did. This must be Sally, Eddie's wife and baking partner.

Campbell made her way toward them and was stopped by a waiter carrying a tray of full glasses.

"Cocktail, ma'am?"

"Oh, uh, do you have any soft drinks?"

"Not with me, but you can get them at the bar, over there." He nodded toward a counter set up in a corner of the vast room.

"Thanks." Not enticed by diet soda, Campbell continued toward her target.

She edged into the small group near Eddie just as they all laughed at his punchline. A couple of the listeners moved away, and Campbell sidled up to Sally.

"Hello," Sally said, eyeing her critically. "That's a fabulous dress."

"Oh, thank you. I was admiring yours as well."

"Thanks. I'm Sally Nelson."

"I thought so." Campbell turned up the wattage on her smile. "I've had your doughnuts, and they are out of this world."

"Oh, thanks." Sally waved a hand as if it wasn't important.

Eddie, however, had caught her remark and turned to her with his hand extended. "Always glad to meet a doughnut aficionado. I'm Eddie."

"I'm Campbell." She shook his hand.

"So, you've been to our store?"

"Not personally, but a friend brought a box to my dad and me the other day. I will definitely be in soon to get some more."

"What's your favorite kind?"

The other guests seemed to be uninterested in

discussing doughnuts and drifted away. Sally's smile looked a little strained.

"Oh, uh, I tasted the glazed and the chocolate frosted, and they were both great. I think my lifetime fave is lemon filled, though."

"We make them fresh every morning." Eddie grinned.

"I'll keep it in mind."

Sally said, "So, we haven't met before. Did one of Eddie's sisters invite you?"

"Oh, I'm here with Chris Powell." At their blank expressions, she added, "He's a lawyer."

"Oh, probably one of David's legal eagles," Eddie said. "Or Diane's. They have a ton of legal and financial advisors for their businesses. Sally and me, we have a small operation. Uncomplicated. Just doughnuts, crullers, and more doughnuts." He pulled his hand through the air as though he was drawing an extended line, and she pictured an endless parade of doughnuts.

"Right. I'm in a small family business, too, so I know what you mean." Immediately, she wished she hadn't mentioned it.

Sally pounced. "Oh? What's your specialty?"

"Uh, my father's an investigator, and I help him."

"An investigator?" Sally frowned.

"Like a private eye?" Eddie asked.

"Well, yes."

Change of subject needed. Campbell glanced around the room and spotted Chris talking to an older man. "That's my date, over there."

"He's good-looking," Sally said.

Campbell smiled but offered no comment. She barely knew Chris, so he wasn't really a safe topic either.

"Been dating long?" Sally persisted.

"Uh, no, actually this is our first date." She looked around, almost frantic now. At last! A familiar face. She recognized a woman in her late sixties from a case she'd worked on earlier in the year with her father. "Isn't that Mary Willingham in the pale blue dress?"

"Yes," Sally said. "We invited her. Do you know her?"

"I do, but only slightly."

"Her husband Leon was a friend of Eddie's, but he's gone now."

Campbell nodded. "Yes, I met Mary and her daughter. They seem like nice people."

"Oh, there's Roland," Eddie said. "Excuse me."

Sally smiled. "And I should check on the caterers. David and Hillary are still greeting newcomers, and they asked me to make sure things went smoothly in the kitchen."

"Of course."

Campbell stood for a moment, feeling awkward. She walked slowly to the bar and asked for a ginger ale then ambled among the groups, sipping sparingly from her glass. Mary Willingham caught her eye and strode toward her.

"Ms. McBride! Nice to see you again."

Campbell smiled. "You too, Mrs. Willingham. How are you doing?"

"Quite well, thank you. I've decided to move in with my daughter next month."

"Nicole?" Campbell had met Mrs. Paxton. She doubted Mary and her daughter would get along well, especially living in the same house.

"No, my other daughter, Stacie. She lives in Virginia."

"I see. You're selling the house, then?"

"We already have a buyer."

"Good. I hope it goes well for you." But would Mary regret selling the dream house she and her late husband had built?

"I think it will. Stacie's husband is very agreeable, and let's face it—that house is too big for me alone."

"I'm glad you've found a good solution."

"Thank you." Mary's brow clouded. "You know the Nelsons?"

"Not really," Campbell said. "I came with a friend."

Mary nodded. "Well, I'm tickled I got to see you before I move. You were a real help to me."

"I'm glad."

Campbell watched her move away and enthusiastically join a cluster of women she obviously knew. Chris Powell was deep in conversation with David Nelson and a man who could pass as another lawyer. She didn't see Hillary Nelson, but apparently the hosts had stopped standing near the entrance. Most of the guests must have arrived.

Another survey of the room turned up only a couple more faces she recognized—Dr. Aiken, who was Bill's ophthalmologist, and Mitchell Vaughn, the prosecuting attorney in Leila Abbott's case. She hoped she wouldn't draw Vaughn's attention. It might not be good if he spotted her and alerted the Nelsons that she had been involved in the case of their stolen painting.

She set her glass down on the nearest tray table and edged out into the hall. A uniformed teen girl came toward her carrying a tray of finger sandwiches.

"Excuse me," Campbell said. "Could you direct me to the restroom?"

The girl nodded toward a door a few yards back along the corridor. "Just down there, ma'am."

"Thanks." Campbell hurried past her and was surprised to find two doors with Ladies and Gentlemen plaques on them. The Nelsons must hold a lot of large gatherings here. Maybe Hillary hosted charitable events open to the public. It did seem odd, in a private home, even a large and ostentatious one.

The décor inside the ladies' room also surprised

her. She lingered in the outer part, which included a vanity counter with two sinks, a huge mirror, and a pair of wicker chairs with bright cushions. As she brushed a few stray hairs back into place, the door swung open and Diane Block entered.

"Hello, Diane," Campbell said with a smile.

Diane paused and eyed her keenly. "Have we met?"

"Oh, maybe not." Blunder, big time. Campbell sucked in a breath. "I'm Campbell McBride. I . . . I'm here with Chris Powell."

"McBride . . . McBride. I've heard that name recently." Diane shook her head. "Well, I hope you're enjoying the party."

"It's great."

"Good." Diane walked past her into the inner room, where the toilets were.

Campbell swallowed hard then took a deep breath. Diane would be someone to avoid for the rest of the evening.

Chapter 26

As she walked down the hall toward the big party room, Campbell berated herself. Didn't she come here hoping to talk to the Nelson siblings? Why did she feel so inept? Maybe she ought to have stayed and tried to have a real conversation with Diane.

She entered the room, which seemed packed with even more people now, feeling she was botching her first undercover assignment. She looked around and spotted Chris. He lifted his glass a few inches and nodded. She returned the nod and walked along the wall into the middle section of the combined chambers. A string quartet was playing classics quietly, and half a dozen couples were dancing in their vicinity.

Lingering to hear the music, she was aware of someone hovering beside her and turned to find herself face-to-face with Chris.

"Dance?" he asked.

"Oh . . ." She glanced at the couples maneuvering around the limited space cleared by other guests. They were being watched by a dozen or two other people. "I don't want to draw attention to myself, but thanks."

He nodded. "Any success on your mission yet?"

"Well, I've spoken to Eddie and his wife, and

317

I just ran into Diane in the ladies' room. She thought she recognized the McBride name. I'm afraid I bolted."

"Are you scared of her?" Chris asked.

"Not exactly. I just panicked. I guess I was afraid she'd realize I'm an investigator, and that my dad and I are looking into the theft of the painting."

"Would that be so terrible?"

"I guess not. I mean, it would be hard to find out more about a twenty-year-old crime if I don't talk to the people who were close to it."

Chris nodded in approval. "Tell you what, let me put my number in your cell, and if you feel you need to leave or just want someone to come support you, hit that and I'll come find you."

She hesitated, and he chuckled.

"Well, not in the ladies' room, of course."

It made sense, and she opened her contacts and handed him her phone. He tapped away quickly and handed it back.

"Do you like the Nelsons?" she whispered.

"*Hmm,* I wouldn't say I *like* them exactly. David Nelson is a client. He and Hillary seem all right. I take it this is their annual way of saying thanks to a lot of their business contacts, as well as getting together with their sisters and brother."

"So, it might free them from other obligations throughout the year?" Campbell asked.

"I didn't say that." He smiled. "Could be, though."

"Thanks, Chris. Is there anything I can do for you?"

"I can't think of anything. I'm just mingling and mentioning the firm's name here and there."

"Hoping to drum up new business?"

"Something like that."

"How long do you want to stay?"

The string quartet stopped playing and moved aside to put away their instruments. In their place, a well-known country singer and two backup musicians stepped onto the dais.

"Oh, wow," Campbell said.

"Yeah, even I know who he is," Chris replied. "Maybe we could stick around for another hour or so? I don't mind hearing this guy sing."

"Me either. Okay, if I haven't heard from you in an hour, I'll come looking for you."

He seemed amenable to that. The artist strummed his guitar, and Chris's attention was already glued to him. Campbell got the impression that he was a bigger country music fan than he'd let on.

She meandered on, to the farther reaches of the party area. There was the ophthalmologist again. She nodded at him, and he responded with a puzzled look. He knew Bill, but Campbell wasn't a patient, and apparently he didn't remember her from the one time she'd accompanied her father to his office.

She edged into a small group and was soon talking to three couples. They didn't seem to mind her horning in on them, and she soon learned one of the couples owned a car dealership on the edge of town. Another of the men was a park employee at Land Between the Lakes, and his wife was an elementary school teacher in Murray. Campbell was about to enquire about the third couple's occupations when a man tapped her on the shoulder.

"Excuse me. Are you Ms. McBride?"

Travis Block. Her mouth went dry.

"Uh, yes. Mr. Block, isn't it?"

He smiled. "Yes. How do you do?"

She nodded. "Fine. Lovely party."

"My wife would like to speak with you."

"With me?"

"That's right. She asked me to show you to the breakfast room." He turned away.

Campbell hesitated then followed him. He led her to the far end of the room, to a door she hadn't noticed earlier. It opened off the end of the three-room party area.

This house is huge! She turned sideways to ease between other guests. *What on earth could Diane want me for?*

The room they entered was small and almost cozy. The warm walnut table and four chairs looked like the ideal spot for a family breakfast. The walls were a pale yellow, with a lovely

Impressionist print hanging across from the table. The long green drapes completed the springtime atmosphere.

Diane Block stood in the center of the room. Her gold, off-the-shoulder gown swept gracefully to her ankles. An empty highball glass sat on the table, on one of the bright yellow placemats.

"Mrs. Block," Campbell said.

Diane's chin lifted a fraction of an inch, and Campbell could almost read her thoughts through her steely eyes. She'd called her by her first name when they crossed paths in the restroom.

"Ms. McBride. I believe you're associated with True Blue Investigations."

Campbell's pulse rocketed. Someone had been checking up on her, probably online.

"That's right," she managed. "My father owns the agency." Uneasily, she noted that Travis hadn't left the room. "Is there some way I can help you this evening?"

"Now that's amusing. You think you can help us."

As Diane spoke, another door, which must give on the hallway, opened. Eddie Nelson walked in, and he wasn't smiling. Campbell wanted to ask what was going on, but she couldn't get a word out.

Diane's hard gaze turned on her brother. "Eddie, I think you can take care of this."

"Me?" His eyebrows shot up. "Why can't Travis handle it?"

"We need to get back to the party. If we're not seen, people will miss us."

"Oh, and they won't miss me?"

Diane gave him a dismissive glare. "Just be discreet." She went past Eddie and out into the throng of guests, and her husband followed.

In the doorway, Travis turned to Eddie. "Be quick. We'll cover for you."

Campbell barely heard his words, but her heart pounded as he closed the door behind him.

"Eddie," she choked out. "Mr. Nelson. What's going on?"

His face skewed in an almost comical frown. "It seems you've made things awkward for my sister."

"Wh-what did I do? You mean, just by being here?"

"Apparently she thinks you know too much."

"That's ridiculous. Look, I came as Christopher Powell's guest. Do you know Chris?"

Eddie pursed his lips. "He's a lawyer, right?"

"Yes."

"Did he have anything to do with the Abbott woman's arrest?"

"No, not at all. He wasn't involved in the case."

"How do you know him?"

Campbell pulled in a shaky breath. "He knows my father. He came to the house to see Dad last week, and he . . . he mentioned he was going to this party. He asked if I'd like to go with him."

Eddie's eyes narrowed. "So, just a date?"

"Yes. Our first date." She almost choked on the words.

"You like him?"

"Sure. He's nice."

"Why aren't you out there with him? You've been drifting around by yourself all evening."

Another blunder. Campbell tried to swallow the lump in her throat.

"I . . . I saw a few people I knew, and I wanted to talk to them."

"You came and talked to me and Sally, and you don't know us."

"Right. I wanted to meet you."

Eddie sighed and reached inside his tuxedo jacket. Why hadn't she noticed the slight bulge before? By the time he had the pistol out and pointed at her, she was no longer surprised.

Chapter 27

Campbell tried to swallow, but her mouth was too dry.

"Wh-what's going on?"

"We're going for a little walk."

She stared at the gun and focused on trying to breathe.

"Come on. We're going out this way." He waved it a little toward the hall door.

"Mr. Nelson—"

"Now." His eyes hardened.

Campbell believed he was as unfeeling as his sister, not the jolly doughnut maker she'd pegged him for earlier.

"I don't understand," she croaked out.

"You're too nosey, Ms. McBride. My sister told me to handle it, and I will. Let's go."

"No." She focused on the pistol and was reasonably sure it wasn't carrying a silencer. "I'm not going anywhere with you."

"Oh, really?" His tone was sarcastic.

She shivered. "No. What are you going to do if I won't? Shoot me right here? In David's house? Where a hundred people will hear the shot?"

"I doubt that many will hear it," he said easily. "There's the music and all that."

Campbell sucked in a breath. "Yeah? Well, what

about the blood spatter? You're statistically likely to get some on that fancy tuxedo."

Eddie glanced down involuntarily then met her eyes once more. "I think I'm far enough away from you."

"What about the cleanup? Will David pay his maid extra to get rid of the mess?" To her surprise, when she elevated her voice a little, her inner quaking didn't transfer to the sound.

Beads of sweat stood on Eddie's brow. He glanced toward the doorway through which Diane and Travis had disappeared. Campbell watched him closely. Could she make a run for it through the other door? Would he really shoot? Was it worth the risk?

Eddie edged over to the table and glanced down then bent over for a second. He stood and leveled the gun at her again.

"Don't move." Watching her intently, he sidestepped and bent again. He straightened with one of the yellow chair seat pads in his left hand, the bias ties that had held it to the chair fluttering.

Horror gripped Campbell. He was going to shoot through the pillow to muffle the sound.

Chris Powell leaned against the wall for a few minutes, listening to the music. A man he knew slightly spoke to him as he walked past, and Chris nodded in return. A waiter came by offering a tray of drinks, but he declined. Just listening.

When the second number ended, he checked his watch and gazed into the farthest part of the party area. Way over near the wall, he caught a glimpse of Campbell in her eye-catching dress. She was quite a woman. Too bad she already had a special man in her life.

As his gazed lingered, an older man stepped up behind her and spoke. Campbell turned around. Chris frowned. Travis Block. Why did he seek her out? Oh, well, probably something to do with Bill McBride's case. The singer opened another number, and Chris turned back toward the dais.

When the song ended, he clapped with the rest of those who'd paused their networking and chitchatting to actually listen. He looked over to where he'd seen Campbell. She was gone.

Quickly, he scanned all the people on that end of the room. A dozen women were there, chatting, drinking, flirting—but no Campbell. Had she stepped out to the ladies' room?

A door at the far end of the room opened. Diane Block and her husband came through it. But no Campbell. Had she gone into another room with them? If so, why didn't she come out when they did? Maybe she'd left Travis after Chris saw them together and moved to another spot, but he couldn't locate her, try as he might.

He waited until the Blocks had separated and Diane was engaged with other guests. Travis ambled across the middle room, not stopping to talk to anybody. Chris's assessment—probably heading for the bar.

When Travis was well past him without so much as a glance in his direction, Chris slipped between other guests toward the farthest part of the gathering. If that door the Blocks emerged from wasn't locked, would opening it cause a calamity?

He eased up to the door and turned his back to it. Looking around the room, he assessed the nearby partygoers. None of them knew him well. He'd been introduced to a few that evening, and he recognized a man who'd been a client at his firm, but one of the other attorneys had handled the account. Good.

Deliberately, he didn't make eye contact with anyone as he reached behind his back and felt for the doorknob. His hand touched it. Chris adjusted his position until he was able to turn the knob cautiously without turning to face the door. It wasn't locked.

Was he nuts? Campbell could take care of herself. But he couldn't get rid of the nagging doubt.

Be casual. Just turn around and do it.

He swallowed hard and opened the door.

Campbell's pulse sprinted then caught and seemed to skip several beats. Would Eddie shoot her right here in David and Hillary's breakfast room? And Eddie had seemed like such a nice guy.

"We're going out the door into the hallway." He enunciated each word precisely. "Don't even think of trying anything."

His sidled around until he was between her and the door she'd come in, with his back to it, and nodded toward the hall door.

Campbell flicked a glance past him toward the door that would mean possible safety, if she could only get through it and into the crowd. No chance now, with Eddie and his handgun between them.

She froze. Were her eyes playing tricks? She thought the doorknob moved. Was she dizzy? She did feel a little lightheaded. This wasn't real. Or was it?

Maybe she just wanted a rescue so badly, she'd imagined that little twist.

There! It happened again. The door opened about a foot, but Eddie seemed totally unaware.

"Move." He gestured with the gun and pillow toward the other door, at the side of the room. "If you try to run, I'll shoot. Don't think I won't."

As he spoke, Campbell forced herself to remain still. She mustn't let her face reveal what she saw behind him. Chris took a step forward, his mouth hanging open, staring at her and at Eddie Nelson's back.

The music and chatter swelled suddenly, and Eddie whipped around.

"Run," Campbell screamed.

But Chris advanced. "What's going on?"

Eddie dropped the pillow and pointed the gun at Chris's chest. "Shut the door. Now."

Time to make her move.

Chapter 28

Campbell glanced around frantically for something close by that she could use as a weapon.

Tall ceramic salt and peppers on the breakfast table were the closest and most maneuverable. She grabbed the pepper mill and launched herself at Eddie, bringing the sleek cylinder down on the back of his crown, where a bald spot was forming.

He let out a grunt and staggered around to face her.

Campbell's heart lurched. She'd meant to take him down.

It was enough for Chris. Before Eddie could regroup and focus the gun on her again, Chris dove at him. All his weight landed on Eddie's arm, forcing his hand down.

They struggled, and a shot exploded in the room.

Campbell and Chris stared at each other over Eddie's bent form. Campbell jumped on Eddie's back, hearing nothing but pounding sea waves and church bells assaulting her ears in the wake of the shot. She carried Eddie to the floor and sat on him.

The pistol flew from Eddie's hand and skittered across the tile. Chris chased it and stood with it in his hand as the door to the party area flew open.

David Nelson, Jr. and two other men rushed into the breakfast room. David appeared to be screaming, though to Campbell it sounded as if he was in a bubble. She squinted at him and read his lips.

"What is going on?" His face was twisted in fury. "You!" He glared at Chris and said something Campbell couldn't make out.

Another man pulled her off Eddie's back. "What happened here, ma'am?"

So polite. Campbell realized her hearing was returning.

"He tried to kill me. Eddie Nelson was going to shoot me. Then Chris Powell came in, and Eddie was going to shoot him, so I brained him with—" She looked around, spotted the pepper mill under the table, and pointed. "With that. And Chris jumped him to get the gun away."

At least a dozen people were in the room now.

"Put the gun down," David Nelson shouted.

Chris shook his head. "I'm not doing that until the cops get here. Your brother was threatening Miss McBride. Your sister Diane had something to do with it, too, and I'm not giving you this gun until I'm sure she's safe."

Aw! That's some streak of bravery.

Campbell's clutch bag lay on the floor where she'd dropped it, almost under the foot of the large man who'd pulled her off Eddie. She stooped to retrieve it. Eddie was starting to rise, and his brother reached out a hand to help him.

"Did anyone call the police?" she asked in her classroom lecture voice.

Everyone stared at her.

"I will."

Campbell whirled toward the hall door. The waitress from the Barn Owl stood in the open doorway, wearing a catering uniform and with a cell phone in her hand. She snapped a picture then started swiping and tapping.

"Lily?" Campbell said.

"Yeah, Miss Campbell. I got it." Lily put the phone to her ear. "Yeah, this is Lily Tuft. We need some policemen fast, here at the Nelsons' house." She rattled off the address. "Oh, they are?" She smiled at Campbell. "They're already on the way. Somebody called and told them there was a rowdy party here, and they thought they heard a gun go off. Or fireworks."

"Thank you," Campbell mouthed.

Lily listened for a few more seconds. "Right. I'll tell 'em." She turned to the crowd, which now numbered at least twenty in the breakfast room. "Hey, y'all, the cops will be here in five minutes."

David said something quietly into his brother's ear.

"You're not going anywhere," Chris said, keeping the gun leveled at Eddie. "The rest of y'all can just clear on out of this room, and we'll wait in here for the officers."

A few squeezed out into the party area, and Diane Block managed to get in. She stared at Eddie, her mouth open, then at David, and swore. She whirled on Chris.

"You shot the Mary Cassatt?"

They all turned their heads to stare at the painting on the opposite wall. The woman portrayed in the exquisite Impressionist portrait had a bullet hole almost exactly in the middle of her chest.

That can't be a real Cassatt! Can it? Campbell itched to go closer, but prudence told her to stay put. But if it was . . . *No wonder Diane never asked Craig to give back the Banitier. Small potatoes!* No, it belonged to David and Hillary, not Diane. But it *had* to be a reproduction. Didn't it?

"Not me," Chris said quickly. "Mr. Eddie did it. I just picked up the gun afterward."

David grabbed his brother by the lapels. "Eddie, you moron! Hillary's going to kill you."

When she reached Keith on her phone, Campbell accepted that she would probably spend half the night waiting and the rest of it being grilled by the police. Keith didn't say "grilled," but she knew things looked bad for her and Chris, and the officers always had a million questions.

"I'm coming down there," Keith said. "We just

got the call from the first responders. But Matt will have to question you, since you and I are so close."

"Understood," she managed. Dread knotted her stomach, or maybe it was the shock of almost being killed. And Matt Jackson wasn't so bad. She'd met him several times. He was a good detective, and he got along well with Keith.

"We'll be there in fifteen minutes."

Enormous relief swept over Campbell. "Thank you. Could you tell my dad what happened too? I sorta don't want to talk to him right now. He'll want all the details, and I'm still not clear on why they wanted me dead."

"I'll tell him. Thank God, Chris Powell was curious."

"Amen to that."

"I've got to go, but I'll call Bill."

Keith signed off, and Campbell turned to Chris, who now stood beside her in the huge, combined room of the party area. The patrol officers who'd responded had instructed all of the guests to stay out there until someone had taken down their statements and contact information. They'd been cautioned to keep away from all the doors. Meanwhile, one of them remained with Eddie Nelson in the breakfast room.

The other three Nelson siblings and their spouses, along with Eddie's wife Sally, were sequestered in David's den, somewhere in a remote part of the house. Campbell wondered if they were all on their phones, putting damage control into high gear.

As more officers arrived, the first responder in charge of the party room briefed them, and they separated to various assignments. Campbell was sure at least one was posted outside for traffic control.

"I hope they're putting one of those officers with the Nelson family," she said to Chris. "They could be conspiring right now, or even destroying evidence."

"Well, I saw a senior partner from our firm here earlier, but he's not in the room now," Chris replied, leaning close. "David's probably getting some legal advice."

"What about you? Didn't you do some legal work for him?"

"Just a small job. I was assisting the partner."

"Wait, one of your bosses represents David? I guess I knew that, but it didn't seem significant at the time."

"Yeah. It will be plenty significant now," Chris said grimly.

"Does he know you're here?"

"Yes, I spoke to him about an hour ago. I guess if he thinks he needs me, he'll get word to me."

Two uniformed officers, one male and one female, roamed the party space, a constant reminder to the guests that they couldn't leave.

After a few minutes, they'd allowed the bartender to serve drinks, but only one per person.

"Keith is on his way down here," Campbell whispered to Chris. "And he'll tell my dad what's going on." She would be surprised if Bill didn't show up, too, though they probably wouldn't let him in.

"Your fiancé?"

She nodded.

"I've heard he's a good detective." Chris put his mouth closer to her ear. "I'm surprised they haven't confiscated our phones yet."

"That's probably next, although . . ." She swept a gaze around the room. "It would be a nightmare. How many people do you think are in here?"

"At least a hundred." He frowned. "Maybe a hundred and fifty. Oh, great, more chairs."

Two people in black catering uniforms carried in a stack of plastic chairs and half a dozen folding deck chairs. Since there'd been only about twenty seats scattered throughout the room to begin with, this new offering was welcome.

"Ladies first," called out an older man, for which Campbell was grateful. Two more staffers carried in assorted straight chairs that she assumed they'd collected from various parts of the house. Soon about half the guests had seats. She turned down the first offer, since she was younger than many of the other guests.

"You should take one," Chris said. "We could be here a long time."

She relented, and just as she accepted a pressed-back oak chair, Keith and Matt entered through the main door.

"Save my chair," Campbell told Chris. She quickly closed the distance between herself and Keith. Another officer was already briefing them, and she paused a yard away, waiting for him to be free to give her his attention.

"Hey." Keith turned to her with a noncommittal smile as Matt walked away with the other officer. Campbell understood that he didn't want all the guests to know about their special relationship. "Your dad was ready to jump in his car, but I think I talked him out of it. He knows we wouldn't be able to let him in here, and he wouldn't be allowed to speak to you yet."

She nodded. "Thanks for telling him. Chris and I are over there." She pointed to where Chris was sitting on the chair she'd claimed.

"As I understand the situation, you'll probably be called in soon," Keith said. "You two were the only ones in the room with Eddie Nelson when the incident took place?"

"Yes. Travis Block took me in there to see his wife. Then Eddie came in, and the two of them left him—to 'take care of me.' He was trying to force me to go out another door when, thank God, Chris came in."

Keith nodded. "Okay. Matt's in with Eddie now. I'll go in there, but I'm sure we'll have Eddie transported soon. Then we'll want to talk to you two."

"We'll be ready. What about all these other people?" She waved a hand at the restless crowd.

"We've got a couple of uniforms going around and getting contact details. If they weren't anywhere near the room where it happened, we'll let them go for now. If someone has information to contribute, we'll put them on our short list and either talk to them later or ask them to come to the station tomorrow and give a detailed statement."

Shouted chants arose from a group halfway down the long room, and Campbell jerked her head around.

"The midnight countdown," Keith said evenly. "Happy New Year."

"Oh." She let her shoulders slump. "That's a little crass, don't you think? I mean them." She nodded toward the guests, who were shouting and laughing, toasting each other.

"Yeah, I think we'll shut down the bar."

"Again," she said.

Keith arched his eyebrows.

"Yeah, they reopened it a while ago." She shrugged.

"Well, I'll go see if Matt needs me in there. I expect I'll be his dogsbody, bringing in the people he wants to question next."

Chapter 29

Campbell only had to wait another half hour before Keith was back to get her. She relinquished her chair to Chris again. More than half the party guests had been allowed to leave by then. The caterers had laid out what food was left in the kitchen and left.

Following Keith to the breakfast room, she tried to breathe slowly and evenly. She hadn't done anything wrong, but she was still apprehensive.

"Hello, Campbell," Matt said, standing as she entered the room.

She exhaled. He'd used her first name, not 'Ms. McBride,' which at that point would have put her more on edge.

"Have a seat," Matt said. "I'm sorry you got caught up in all this."

Campbell sat down at the table and was relieved when Keith took a seat beside her.

"We'll be recording this." Matt turned on his recorder and stated her name, the time and date, which was now in another year.

She flicked a glance at Keith, and he nodded with just a ghost of a smile.

Why, oh why didn't I make a New Year's Eve date with Keith instead of coming to this nightmare party?

"If you can tell us what occurred this evening, from the time you encountered Mr. Block—I understand it was he who brought you into this room."

"Yes."

"And then we'll let you go and ask you to come to the station tomorrow—that is, later today—and sign your statement. We'll have it transcribed for you at that time, and you can make any additions you think are pertinent."

"We'll bring Chris Powell in next," Keith said. "That way, you won't have to wait around long for your ride."

"Okay." Campbell had thought of asking him to call her father to come pick her up, but Keith was right. This way would be better. She didn't want her dad to drive down here for her, after he'd already been told to stay away.

"Travis came up to me and said Diane wanted to speak with me." She frowned. "I thought that was odd at the time. For one thing, I didn't know him, and for another, Diane acted upset when I saw her earlier in the restroom. So I had a bad feeling about the meeting." She looked at Keith. "Do you think Travis was in on all this—the painting, paying the blackmail—all of it?"

The two detectives exchanged glances. Matt cleared his throat. "We can't say too much, Campbell, but I will tell you this—Travis Block claims he knew nothing about it and was just doing what his wife asked him to do tonight. Diane backs him up. She says her husband was completely out of it and that she did some fancy footwork to keep him from finding out about the blackmail payments."

"So we were right all along about the blackmail." Campbell caught her breath. "We thought at first it was Craig, but now . . ."

"Diane thought that too," Keith said.

Matt frowned at him. "Let's just get your story down tonight, Campbell. We haven't sorted everything out yet."

For the next fifteen minutes, she went over what had happened. She tried to remember every detail, including how much Travis had witnessed before he left the room with Diane.

"He didn't make any objections at all," she said. "And you can't tell me he didn't know what she meant when she told Eddie to handle the situation." Another memory smacked her. "Eddie asked her why Travis couldn't handle it. And Travis told Eddie they would 'cover for him,' and to be discreet. Those were his exact words. Travis *must* have known what they were talking about!"

Matt remained impassive. "What *were* they talking about?"

"I . . . I don't really know for sure. I asked Eddie, and he said I'd made things awkward for his sister, and that I knew too much."

"Too much about what?"

"He didn't say, but he asked me how I knew Chris Powell and if he was connected to the Abbott case. That ties it to the stolen painting, right? Of course, I told him Chris had nothing to do with that, and that he came to see my father on business and wound up inviting me to the party."

Keith said nothing.

"So, you don't know Mr. Powell well?" Matt asked.

"No. This is only the second time in my life I've seen him. He seems nice, and I think he invited me to humor my dad—well, I'm pretty sure of it. Dad probably hinted that it might help us learn more about the Nelson family, in regard to the Abbott case, if we had an agency member at the party. We'd talked to Craig Smith about the painting, and we knew Diane was involved."

"Smith told you that?"

She nodded. "I think he was scared when we suggested he had been blackmailing Diane. He insisted he hadn't."

Matt nodded. This was probably old news to him. They'd told Keith, and surely he'd let Matt in on it.

"Are you arresting anyone tonight?" she asked.

Matt leaned back in his chair, and at first she thought he'd clam up, but with an oblique look at Keith, he said, "We've already sent Eddie Nelson to the station in a patrol car, because of what he did to you."

"Good. Chris won't get it trouble for holding the gun on Eddie and David Nelson, will he? I mean, he was only defending me. Both of us, really. Eddie pointed the gun at him too."

"We want to hear his full story, but we expect to release him," Matt said. "As to the rest of the Nelson family, that remains to be seen."

"But you know Diane ordered Eddie to—"

"To what? Did she tell him to kill you?"

"Not in so many words."

Matt nodded. "We'll talk to her a lot more, but she did ask for a lawyer when we attempted to question her. I expect we'll spend some time with her and the attorney tomorrow."

Campbell felt that was less than satisfactory, but what could she do? She looked at Keith and back to Matt. "So, what do I do now? Just go home and twiddle my thumbs?"

"Pretty much," Matt said, and she was sure Keith held back a smile. He knew how hard it was for her to do nothing.

"This pertains to our case. I'll have to talk it over with my dad. He's my boss."

The detective laid down his pen with a sigh. "I suppose you will. But please, nobody else. We don't want any details leaking to the press, and you'd be surprised how easily that happens."

"Okay."

Matt stood. "You can go. Keith, please bring in Mr. Powell."

Campbell waited, yawning, for Chris to finish his interview.

Most of the other guests were gone, and so was most of the food. She found an upholstered chair that looked more comfortable than her previous seat and settled in it. After five minutes or so, she leaned her head back and closed her eyes. Would they ever be done?

"Hey. Ready to go?"

Her eyes flew open, and she looked up at Chris. "Oh. Sure. Sorry, I must have drifted off." She pulled her purse out from where she'd tucked it beside her. "What time is it?"

"Almost one thirty."

Keith crossed the nearly empty room. "I guess you two are leaving?"

"Yeah, we need to go get some sleep," Chris said.

"We're almost done here. Matt wants to have one more chat with the Nelson sibs, but then we'll head out too." Keith gazed mournfully at Campbell, as though not being able to offer her a ride home was the saddest thing in his life.

"I'll come by the station tomorrow," she said. "When will you be there?"

Keith sighed. "After this night, we probably won't go in until noon."

"Can I wait until then?"

"Sure. If you get there and I'm not in, ask for the detective sergeant."

The drive home took only about fifteen minutes. Chris commented on the questions Detective Jackson had asked him, but both of them were exhausted. When he pulled in at the McBride house, the porch light was on and Bill barreled out the front door to meet them on the driveway.

"Dad. You shouldn't have waited up." Campbell gave him a hug.

"How could I not?" he said gruffly. "Are you okay?"

She drew back. "I'm fine. Between Chris and Keith, I was well looked after."

Her father looked over at Chris, who stood just outside his car door. "Thank you. I hope my daughter didn't drag you into too much of a mess."

Chris smiled. "It wasn't what either of us expected, but it seems to have turned out all right, sir."

"Thank you again, Chris," Campbell said.

He shrugged. "I didn't do much."

"That's a fib." She squeezed her father's arm. "Come on inside, Dad. I'll tell you exactly how much he did for me. I can tell you aren't going to unwind until I tell you every little detail." She smiled at Chris. "Good night."

"Good night." He got in the car and backed out the driveway.

Campbell turned her dad toward the steps and tugged him forward. "Come on. It's cold out here, and you don't have a coat."

Chapter 30

Bill slept late the next morning, having stayed up another hour after Campbell's return in order to satisfy his curiosity and concerns. Even so, he beat Campbell downstairs and made a pot of coffee.

He'd come up with a few more things to ask Campbell about, but he didn't want to disturb her. She'd had a rough time last night, and Chris Powell too. The young lawyer may have saved Campbell's life.

Glancing at the clock while his toast cooked, he saw that it was after ten thirty. But that was all right. The holiday, like Christmas Day, fell on a Monday. He'd given Nick the day off and told his daughter to sleep in. She was doing just that, so why was he so antsy?

A few minutes later, Campbell straggled into the kitchen. Since there was no newspaper on New Year's Day, Bill was sitting at the pine table drinking his coffee, with his laptop open before him and a dirty plate and fork shoved off to the side.

"Morning, Dad." She gave him a bright smile as she approached the refrigerator.

"Happy New Year," he said.

"Same to you. So, do we just take the day off?"

346

"If you want. I thought I'd do some online work."

"Keith told me to go by the station later and sign my statement."

"Okay."

She fixed herself a glass of juice and a bacon-and-egg toaster pastry. While it heated, she peeled a banana and took a bite. "I don't suppose any stores are open today."

"Oh, the grocery stores will be open, at least. After the tornado last fall and Christmas, they won't want to lose any more days than they have to."

She eyed the grocery list hanging on the refrigerator door. "Maybe I'll go pick up a few things after I'm finished at the police station. Is there anything you want me to do this morning—what's left of it?"

He sighed and set down his mug. "I wish we could talk to David Nelson and Diane Block, but I don't suppose they'd want to talk to me."

"Maybe I'll get some info from Keith when I go in. But he's not reporting until noon at least."

"Mm. Tell me again what Travis Block said to you last night."

While she ate her breakfast, they hashed over the events at the party once more. Then they turned to routine work. Bill gave her an assignment on one of the new jobs that had come in over the past week, while he did some searching and fact-finding to wrap up the case Chris Powell had brought him.

At quarter to twelve, Campbell came and leaned on the jamb in his office doorway. "I guess I'll head over to the station."

"Did you eat lunch?"

She made a face. "Dad, I just ate breakfast. I'll fix something when I get home."

Bill knew he'd want a sandwich before that happened, especially if she was going to shop. When he went to the store, he went directly after each item on the list. Campbell, on the other hand, had to go down every row, even if nothing there was listed. True, she often found bargains or special treats they hadn't written down, but it took her twice as long as it did him.

A few minutes later, he heard her car pull out. He was on the home stretch of the case he was working on, and he didn't even look up.

He was just saving his finished report when the doorbell rang. They left the front door unlocked on weekdays for clients, but he hadn't unlocked it this morning, and Campbell would have gone out through the garage. With a sigh, Bill pushed back his chair and made his way down the hall. Somebody—Campbell—had told him to get up and walk around every hour, anyway, to help his circulation.

He opened the door to find his neighbor, Frank Hill, on the porch.

"Frank, hi. What's up?"

Frank looked over his shoulder toward the street. "It may be nothing, but . . . Can I step in for a sec?"

"Sure." Bill swung the door wide. "Cup of coffee?"

"Nah, I'm not stayin'. Vera wants me to drive her up to Paducah. But I saw something a little odd this morning, and I thought you ought to know."

"What's that?" While Frank's wife was apt to gossip a little now and then, Frank wasn't usually one to bear tales, and Bill figured he should take him seriously.

"Well, see, there was this car this morning, along about nine or so. It parked down the street a little from us, just beyond your place. Nothing unusual in that, but I was outside poking around the gutter over the porch, and I saw it park there. But the driver didn't get out."

"I'm hooked," Bill said. "Is it still out there?"

"No. That's the worst part. After I went inside, I kept looking out now and then. It was there at least an hour and a half. But then I saw Campbell's white car come out of your garage, and whaddya know? The other car starts up and leaves."

"Just left? Or followed my daughter?"

Frank shrugged. "Like I say, could be nothing, Bill, but it looked to me like they were tailing her."

"You didn't recognize the car or the driver?"

He shook his head. "But when they left, the

strange car went past our house, and I'm pretty sure it was a woman driving."

Bill frowned. "What sort of car was it?"

"I'm not sure what model, but I saw the Chevy design on the back. It was a dark blue sedan, four-door." Frank's face squeezed up in chagrin. "Didn't get the whole plate number, but it ended in 677."

"Now, that is very helpful, Frank. Thank you very much."

"Can you trace it? Or get Campbell's sweetie to trace it?"

"Ask me again tomorrow." Bill edged over to open the door. "I really appreciate the intel, Frank."

Campbell was a little disappointed that Keith wasn't at the police station yet. Matt Jackson came out to greet her and took her into the detectives' office.

"Here's the transcript of what you gave me last night. Please read through it and make any corrections needed. And if you think of anything else, you can add it at the bottom."

He handed her a file, and Campbell sat down at a chair next to his desk to browse the printout. She corrected a couple of typos and added a short note at the bottom about her brief encounter with Diane in the ladies' room.

"There's your fella," Matt said.

She looked up. Keith was walking in with his phone to his ear, his face serious.

"Yeah, we're on it. Thanks, Bill." He closed the connection.

"Was that my father?" Campbell stood and stepped toward Keith.

"It was. He told me your neighbor, Mr. Hill, saw a car sitting on the street near your house this morning, and when you left to come here, it followed you. At least, that was his impression."

"Someone's following me?" Campbell's chest squeezed. "Who? Why?"

Matt came over and eyed Keith. "What's going on? Is this related to the party last night?"

"I don't know. Bill called me just before I got here, and I got out of my vehicle and looked around. I didn't see a car like the one he described."

"What did he give you?" Matt asked.

"Dark blue four-door sedan, possibly a female driver, and a partial plate number, ending in 677."

"I'll get right on it." Matt hurried to his desk."

"So," Keith said, "have you done your statement yet?"

"Yeah, I just finished it." Campbell waved toward Matt's desk. "Do you think it's safe for me to leave?"

"Where were you going? Home?"

"No, I planned on doing some grocery shopping."

"I don't see any reason why you shouldn't. Just stay aware of who's around you, and when you leave the store, look around the parking lot. If you see a car like the one Mr. Hill described, call me right away and go back into the store."

"I guess that makes sense." She didn't really want to leave, and she didn't like the feeling that she might be in danger, or that she'd feel safer if she had Keith or her father—any man, really—at her side.

Keith's expression softened. "I wish I could go with you."

"What, you're reading my mind now?" She sighed. "You're just starting your workday. I'll be all right."

Keith's cell rang, and he answered it. "Hi, Bill. Okay, thanks." He lowered his phone. "You dad went out and drove around your neighborhood to see if he could spot the car, but he didn't."

"It's probably nothing," Campbell said.

"We can hope." He leaned down and kissed her cheek. "I'll call you this evening."

"Okay." She walked out into the lobby and through the front door, glancing warily around. Police vehicles and a few civilian cars sat in the parking area. No dark blue sedans. She got in her car and headed toward Twelfth Street.

Stopped at a traffic light, she looked back and studied the vehicles behind hers. The first was a white SUV, but behind it was a dark car. It sat lower than the SUV, so she couldn't see it well. The light changed, and she turned onto four-lane Twelfth Street, snapping glances at her mirror.

Yes, the second vehicle was a dark sedan, and it took the same lane she did. She tried to push down the surge of adrenaline that hit her. Probably not the same car Frank saw—but she'd stay vigilant.

She hit most of the traffic lights right on her way down the street to the local Kroger store. When she turned in at the parking lot, the white SUV went past. She slowed, waiting for the dark sedan. There it was—and dark blue for sure. But it rolled on past, northward on Route 641.

Campbell exhaled heavily. False alarm. She found a parking spot and entered the store. Twenty minutes later, she pushed her cart to one side and called her father.

"What's up?" he asked. "Everything okay?"

"Yeah, it's fine. I did my statement, and I'm at Kroger. I can't find your coffee, though. They seem to be low on it today. Do you think I can find it if I zip across to Walmart?"

"Oh." He sounded a little disoriented. Maybe he'd expected her to tell him she was still being followed. "Uh, you might, but you may have to go down to the Food Giant."

Campbell gritted her teeth. She didn't want to drive all the way down there, going the opposite way on busy Twelfth Street.

"I think I'll try Walmart first."

"Suit yourself."

"Okay. Anything else you want that's not on the list?"

"Uh . . . maybe, since Rita's not coming in until Thursday, some cookies?"

She smiled. "Will do." She found a package of his favorite Pepperidge Farm cookies and pushed the cart to one of the self-checkout counters.

Five minutes later, she entered the Walmart store on the other side of the street. She found her dad's favorite brand in the coffee aisle and headed for the front. Emerging from the store, she walked straight to her car but shot glances around her at the other cars in the huge lot. She couldn't see the suspicious vehicle in her row, but one lane over, a dark blue sedan was parked a couple of spaces down from hers.

Campbell frowned and started her car. She backed out of her slot and crept to the end of the row. Passing the adjacent lane, she looked up it and saw that the dark sedan was backing out of its space, heading her way. When she reached the exit, she had to sit at a red light before pulling out on Twelfth Street. She took advantage of the delay to pull out her phone and hit her father's contact.

"Dad? I'm just leaving the Walmart parking lot, and a dark car is following me."

"Can you go back in the store?"

"No. I'm already out to the traffic light."

"Okay. Is it right behind you?" She checked her rear and sideview mirrors. "Two cars back."

"Listen to me. Don't come home. Instead, go down Main Street like you normally would, but don't turn on Eighth. Go right past and on down to Fifth. I want you to head for the police station, and I'll put Keith on the alert."

The light changed. She said quickly, "Okay. Gotta go."

She drove up Twelfth, and when she came to the light at Chestnut Street, she had to stop again. The dark car pulled up close behind her back bumper. Campbell bobbed her head back and forth, trying to see the driver clearly in her mirror, but the sun glared off the car's windshield.

Her phone rang, and she dove for it. Keith's name showed on the screen.

"Keith? They're right behind me now, almost in my trunk."

"Where are you?"

"Twelfth and Chestnut."

"Can you change lanes and turn there?"

She glanced at the turn lane. "No. Too many cars to get over. I planned to turn at Main Street."

"Okay. Your dad's in position to roll out of Eighth after you go by. He'll wait to see if the other car stays with you. Just come over here to me."

"Right."

The light changed, and she drove on southward, her heart pounding. As they approached the intersection where Main Street crossed Twelfth, she hesitated to put on her signal. If she waited, could she dive over at the last second and keep the other car from joining her? A couple of cars were already positioning in the turn lane, and she decided that would be too risky. After checking her mirrors and over her shoulder, she quickly changed lanes without signaling.

The car behind her followed. When the light changed, Campbell rounded the corner as quickly as she could, hoping to put some distance between them. The vehicles in front of her, however, kept her from laying on much speed.

Behind her, the dark car crept closer until it seemed as near as if she were towing it. Campbell swallowed hard. Would it do any good to try to phone Keith or Bill? Better keep both hands on the wheel and concentrate.

She passed the elementary school, approaching Eighth Street. Throwing a glance down the street, she saw her dad's car rolling slowly toward the intersection on Eighth, as if he was minding his own business.

They were getting closer to downtown, and she watched the street signs carefully. She was about to signal to turn on Fifth when the car behind her tapped her bumper, throwing her back against the seat and the headrest. Her impulse was to hit the brake, but she held off, her heart pounding.

The way was clear, so she wheeled around the corner and stepped on the gas. It wasn't far to the police station, and she found orange cones blocking the street before it reached her destination, and two uniformed officers stood in the roadway. One waved traffic coming the other way to detour, and the other stood in front of her, holding up a hand indicating she should stop.

Campbell slowed cautiously, planning to stop well shy of the officer. A hard thump on the back of her Fusion pushed her forward. As the airbag inflated, she glimpsed the policeman diving to the side.

She sat for a moment, stunned. Engine sounds and squealing brakes drew her attention to the mirrors. The car behind her backed up a few feet and peeled off to the side, but Bill was now close behind in his Taurus. He effectively blocked the sedan from turning around in the street.

An official SUV pulled out from the police station, its light bar flashing and the siren giving a few swoops. The traffic officers quickly moved two cones, and Keith drove between those remaining and pulled up directly behind the suspicious sedan.

Campbell's pulse rioted, but she was able to pull over to the curb. She threw the transmission into Park and jumped out of the car. Oncoming traffic was being diverted at the corner she'd recently navigated, and she dashed across the street to join her father.

He pulled her in close. "You okay?"

"Yeah."

Keith had the driver out of the blue car and was reciting the Miranda rights to Sally Nelson.

Chapter 31

"You! You caused all of this!" Sally had spotted Campbell, and she shrieked at her with her face distorted and turning a deep red.

"Let's just calm down, ma'am," Keith said. He turned her around and efficiently handcuffed her wrists.

Sally spun back toward Campbell and Bill. "Why couldn't you just stay out of it? But no, you had to go after Diane."

"Are you talking about your sister-in-law, Diane Block?" Keith asked.

Sally glared at him. "Who else would I mean? She gave that foolish painting to Craig Smith to hide for her, and then he started blackmailing her, or so she thought. My Eddie saw her getting the money ready for one of the payments, and she dragged him into it."

"How do you mean?" Keith asked.

"She got him to help her drop the money. She paid, but Eddie did all the dangerous stuff. They were going to put a stop to it, and then they found out it wasn't Craig Smith at all."

"What do you mean, 'put a stop to it'?" Keith asked as other uniformed officers surged out into the street to help him.

Sally scowled at him for a moment then screamed, "I want a lawyer!"

"Okay, ma'am, we'll get you one." Keith handed her off to Sgt. Andrews and another officer, who led her toward the police station. He issued brisk orders for the other on-scene officers to move Sally's car and clear the street.

Bill stepped up to him, and Campbell followed. "You think she knows who Diane was really paying?"

"I think so. If Eddie knows, she knows."

"Too bad she lawyered up," Campbell said.

Keith nodded. "What about you? You all right?"

"I think so."

"Sally rear-ended her up on Main Street and then again right here," Bill glowered at Sally's car.

"I saw that." Keith looked toward Campbell's vehicle, and she followed his gaze. The rear of her Fusion had crumpled under the impact. "You sure you're okay?"

Bill put a hand on Campbell's arm. "What do you say, Soup? Shall we go over to the hospital and get you checked out?"

"It wasn't that hard. It just startled me."

"You sure?" Keith asked. "You don't want to shrug it off now and find out a month from now you're still sore."

She rubbed the back of her neck. "I think I'm okay."

"You should make sure."

"Yeah." Her father tugged at her sleeve. "Let's get over to the ER. It's only a few blocks."

"I think that's a good idea," Keith said. "And call your insurance company."

"Don't we need to fill out some forms or something for your records?" Campbell asked.

"Give me your registration. Matt and I will take care of it." Keith glanced at her father. "Bill, we'll put her car in the parking area, and y'all can pick it up later. Now go on over to the hospital."

The two men she loved weren't going to let her weasel out of it. "All right, all right. I'll go." Campbell flung up her hands in surrender and couldn't help a slight wince as a mild pain caught her between the shoulder blades.

"Good," Bill said. "You do what Papa tells you today."

Keith looked at her soberly. "Guess I need to go do my duty. Keep me posted."

"Drop by tonight," she said softly.

"I will. Oh, by the way, we've got some officers picking up Diane as we speak."

"For more questioning?" Campbell asked.

"No, we're arresting her. Between what she said last night and what we're getting from Brother Eddie, we think we've got enough to make it stick."

"Make what stick?" Bill asked. "Threatening my daughter?"

Keith shook his head. "Murder."

• • •

When Keith rang the McBrides' doorbell, it was nearly nine o'clock. Campbell swung the door open and pulled him inside. Keith swept her into his arms.

"You've had a long day," she murmured.

"Yeah, but I think we've finally got this thing figured out." He looked down at her. "They let you walk out without a neck brace, so I guess that's good news."

"I'll be fine. What did you mean, you figured it out?"

"When I told Eddie what Sally said about him helping his sister, he crumbled."

"Did he confess to murder?"

"No, but he's agreed to implicate Diane. According to Eddie, she pulled the trigger on Brad Standish."

"You're kidding." Campbell pulled back and stared at him. "After she told Eddie to 'take care of' me, I was sure he'd killed Standish."

"Well, she hasn't admitted it yet in so many words, but I'm pretty sure she's the one who did it."

"What if they blame each other? What will the jury do?"

Keith sighed. "I've seen that happen before. Pray that they'll tell the truth."

"How is Travis involved in this?"

"He may not be in it at all. We'll see what Diane

said. And I don't think their other siblings knew a thing about it."

Campbell considered that. "I can understand Charlotte being out of the loop, living over in Tennessee, but David? How could all of this go on right under his nose and he didn't know about it?"

"We'll be talking to him and Hillary again too."

On Thursday morning, things seemed back to normal at the McBride house. Rita was in the kitchen preparing lunch, Nick was at his desk working on a skip trace, and Bill and Campbell were collaborating on the embezzlement case.

When Keith arrived at ten o'clock, Campbell knew he had news. Otherwise, he wouldn't stop by until his shift ended.

Bill called Nick in to join them all around the dining table. Rita served them coffee and cranberry scones, hot from the oven, then disappeared upstairs to do some cleaning.

"I know I've been pretty tight-lipped this week," Keith told them, "but we have to be that way while we're still investigating."

Campbell nodded. They all understood that, though the waiting had been excruciating.

"As of this morning, the district attorney is filing some serious charges, headed by first-degree murder for Diane Block."

"Hooray," Nick said.

Campbell smiled. "That's one jury I'd love to be on."

"Well, you can't," Keith said. "You'll be one of the main witnesses for the prosecution. Bill, you'll be subpoenaed too, I imagine, since you were there when the body was discovered."

"Can't wait." Bill took a draught from his coffee mug.

"Did she confess?" Campbell asked.

"Well, she's pleading not guilty, but Eddie and Sally both say she admitted it to them, and—wait for it—the ballistics people have matched the bullet that killed Brad Standish to a handgun Travis Block bought for his wife two years ago for self-defense when she makes bank runs for the business."

"Are you sure Travis didn't do it for her?" Keith asked.

"Pretty sure. He was distraught when it all came out, and I don't think he was faking it. He knew something was going on, but according to him and his wife, he never knew that she was the one who stole the painting in the first place—she admits that—or that she was paying blackmail over it for years. Apparently she was pretty good at hiding those payments from him."

"Why did she kill Brad?" Campbell asked. "Did she just get tired of paying up?"

"Partly. When Leila Abbott was arrested, that's when Diane learned the painting had been stashed in Teresa Abbott's attic for years. All this time, she thought Craig had it. She was furious, and at first she thought one of the Abbotts was blackmailing her, likely Leila or her Uncle Jacob."

"How did she find out it was Standish?" Bill asked.

"By that time, her brother Eddie had learned she was paying someone off, and he'd helped her with the last couple of drops. He hid near where she was leaving the money, in hopes of catching the blackmailer. At the time when Leila was arrested, he hadn't caught him. But then Standish got greedy. He made another payment demand while Leila was at the police station being questioned."

"So clearly, Leila wasn't behind it," Campbell said.

"Right. Eddie again hid and watched, this time for hours. And this time he saw the pickup—done by Brad Standish."

Campbell slumped back in her chair. "But he didn't kill him."

"No. He stayed hidden," Keith said. "But he told his sister. And his wife. Apparently, he tells Sally everything."

"Which is good," Campbell said.

Nick scowled at her. "Oh, yeah? Why didn't Sally speak up? If she'd said something, this whole thing could have been avoided."

"Sally is very loyal to her husband." Keith

shrugged. "And normally, that's a good thing, too, but when he's conspiring to commit murder . . ."

"Is that what they're charging Eddie with?" Bill asked.

"Among other things, yes." Keith gave Campbell a sad smile. "Don't worry, we're going to get him for attempted murder in your case too."

"Really? I wasn't sure there was enough evidence for that. Threatening, yes, but . . ."

"He had a gun on you," Keith said, "and he was trying to get you to leave the house."

She nodded. "Travis knew something. He took me in there."

"He claims Diane only sketched in the bare bones for him that night, and that he didn't really understand why she was mad at you or what she wanted Eddie to do."

"Well, Eddie understood exactly what she was asking." Campbell shivered.

"Right." Keith reached for a scone. "So anyway, back to Brad Standish. Diane thought he'd stolen the painting from Craig and put it in the attic at the rental house. It was perfect, really. If the Abbotts discovered it, they'd think the landlord owned it and forgotten about it. When someone started blackmailing Diane ten years after she gave it to Craig, she assumed it was him."

"But Jacob Abbott took the painting from Craig and stuck it in the attic, not Standish," Nick said, frowning.

"Right, but when Leila's case went to court, and Diane learned it had been in the attic of a house owned by Standish, she started putting two and two together. She was pretty sure Brad had been blackmailing her, no matter who stashed the painting. By then, he'd touched her for over sixty grand."

Campbell shook her head.

"She confronted Standish at his house, madder than a hornet," Keith went on. "She shot him right there in his study. She realized too late that she was in big trouble, and she fled the scene, probably not long before you and your dad arrived to interview Standish."

"What did Brad do with all that money?" Nick asked.

"Invested it in more property. His wife took no interest in the business, just in what it could buy for them. I believe her when she says she had no inkling Brad was involved in blackmail."

"Wow." Nick took a second scone. "So, what I wanna know is, why didn't Diane ever ask Craig for the painting back?"

Keith smiled. "She admitted she took it so her father wouldn't give it to the museum, but she said she intended to give it back later and tell her father it meant more to the family than he realized. But when he died, she realized Dad had left the four siblings a lot anyway, far more than the painting would add to the estate. She decided to forget it and not say anything to anyone, so she'd never get in trouble for it."

Campbell nodded grimly. "But she couldn't forget it, because of the blackmailer."

"Right. When that started, she was afraid to try to retrieve the painting. She thought Craig would turn her in, and she was afraid she'd go to prison. So she shut up and paid, not realizing Craig didn't have a clue about the blackmail."

Rita came to the doorway with a coffee carafe in her hand. "Anybody for a refill? It's fresh."

"Rita, you're an angel." Bill held out his cup. "I've asked Leila to come in this afternoon so we can share the news with her. We won't give her any details of the investigation, Keith, but after what she's been through, she deserves to know that her family wasn't at fault."

Keith nodded. "I think you're right. We don't want her to go on wondering if her uncle killed Standish, and if her grandpa was a thief."

"How do you think Brad found the painting?" Nick asked.

"Probably while he was doing repairs or inspecting the attic for damage," Keith guessed.

"Don't forget, Brad knew the Nelsons," Bill said. "He would have heard about the theft back when the painting went missing. We've seen old newspaper stories with pictures of the Banitier. I'll bet Brad recognized it the minute he saw it."

"He must have been shocked to find it in his house," Campbell said.

"Maybe. He could have gone and told the Nelsons, but if he realized David, Sr., had no idea where the painting was, he probably saw it as a windfall—a way to get something himself."

Campbell pulled in a breath. "And if it was after Stanley Abbott died, he could have assumed Stanley put it there. He didn't have to say anything to Teresa or ask how it got there. He just started blackmailing."

"He found the note," Bill said with certainty. "He knew Diane took it because of the note, and he started putting the screws to her. That worked fine until Teresa died. I wonder if he hoped to retrieve the painting, but Leila found it before he had a chance."

"That must be it," Campbell said. "And then Diane showed up at his house and confronted him. Eddie had learned who was really demanding payment, and she wanted revenge."

Keith was scribbling frantic notes. "That's definitely a theory I will pursue. It fits all the facts."

Bill smiled and sipped his coffee. "Anything else we should know?"

"Not at this time." Keith tucked his notebook away. "I mostly wanted you to know that Eddie and Diane are both being charged. Travis may be—I'm not sure about him. And Sally." He glanced at Campbell. "Sally will mostly be looking at charges for what she did to you Monday, but we might also be able to tie her in with aiding and abetting Eddie. I don't think Dylan Standish or his mother knew anything about the blackmail."

"Wow." Campbell's appetite had fled, and she set down her half-finished scone. So many people's lives she'd upturned.

"Well, I'm getting back to work." Bill pushed back his chair. "How about it, Nick?"

"Yeah, me too." Nick grabbed the last scone as he stood and headed out into the hall. "See ya, Keith."

When they were alone, Keith reached for Campbell's hand. "Are you all right?"

"In what way?"

"In every way. I know this has been a crazy week."

"I think I'm okay. My neck isn't sore anymore, and Dad's been keeping me busy. I think he knew I wasn't ready to do a complicated case on my own, so he's kept me pretty close, helping him. I'm being useful but not straining my brain too hard."

"Right. Come here." Keith rose and pulled her up and into his embrace. "Have I told you how much I love you?"

She smiled and cuddled in against his shoulder. "You have, but I don't mind hearing it again."

"I intend to tell you every day for the rest of my life."

She sighed in contentment. "I love you too." After a minute, she looked up at him. "People keep asking me if we've set the date."

"Do you have thoughts on that?"

"Some. This year. I don't want to go through another New Year's without you beside me."

He chuckled. "What about Fourth of July? Do you want to be Mrs. Fuller before the fireworks go off?"

"Well, yeah. Maybe even before Father's Day."

"Do I hear Memorial Day?"

Campbell squeezed him. "I'm not hard to please. I could even be happy with April Fool's Day. Or Saint Patrick's. Or some non-holiday."

He kissed her, and she knew the day didn't matter, so long as it was soon.

About the Author

Susan Page Davis is the author of more than one hundred books. Her books include Christian novels and novellas in the historical romance, mystery, and romantic suspense genres. Her work has won several awards, including the Carol Award, three Will Rogers Medallions, and two Faith, Hope, & Love Reader's Choice Awards. She has also been a finalist in the WILLA Literary Awards and Selah Awards, and a multi-time finalist in the Carol Awards. A Maine native, Susan has lived in Oregon and now resides in western Kentucky with her husband Jim, a retired news editor. They are the parents of six and grandparents of eleven.

Visit her website at: https://susanpagedavis.com.

Center Point Large Print
600 Brooks Road / PO Box 1
Thorndike, ME 04986-0001 USA

(207) 568-3717

US & Canada:
1 800 929-9108
www.centerpointlargeprint.com